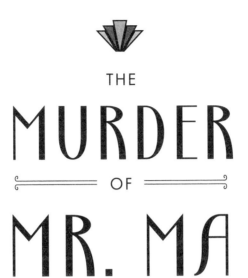

# THE
# MURDER
## OF
# MR. MA

# THE
# MURDER
## OF
# MR. MA

John Shen Yen Nee

SJ Rozan

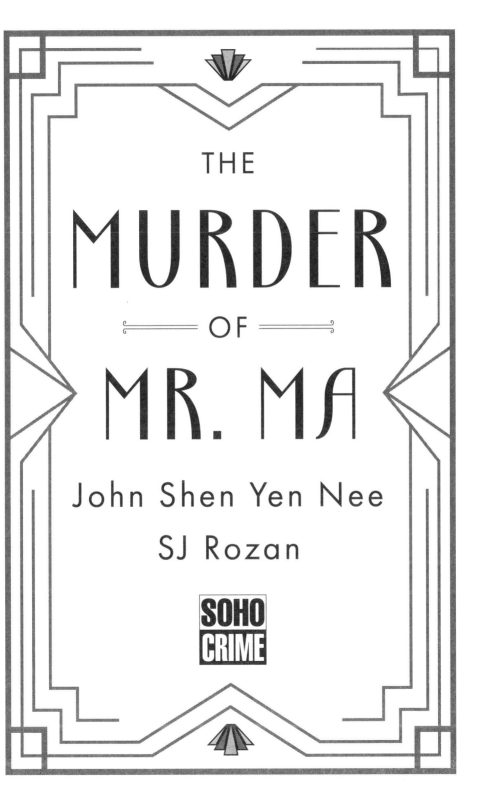

SOHO
CRIME

Published by
Soho Press, Inc.
227 W 17th Street
New York, NY 10011

Library of Congress Cataloging-in-Publication Data is available
upon request.

ISBN 978-1-64129-549-9
eISBN 978-1-64129-550-5

Interior design by Janine Agro

Printed in the United States of America

10 9 8 7 6 5 4 3 2 1

*There are many people without whom this book wouldn't have happened, but*

*Alex Segura*

*is the without whomest. We dedicate this book to him.*

# THE
# MURDER
## OF
# MR. MA

# FOREWORD

## Beijing, 1966

Every story connects to all stories.

The country is in upheaval. The earth shakes beneath feet pounding this way and that. People rush to proclaim their purity before the other side can proclaim the same. So many are so sure, yet at such odds with one another.

Those of us who've lived long lives have seen such things before.

Over my own long life I've written many stories. But some remain untold, though they happened years ago. The time has come to write those, too. I'll put down as many as I can, relating each as I saw it. Events for which I was not present I'll recount as they were told to me. How reliable will this secondhand testimony be? As reliable as my own, I'll wager. For better or worse.

A good friend once said that no story ever truly ends. If he was correct, that must necessarily mean no story has a true beginning, either. Very well; but the one I'll now tell can be said, for the purposes of the telling, to begin in the city of London, in the year 1924, not far from the Marble Arch.

# CHAPTER ONE

## London, 1924

Leaning on an iron railing, I took in the sights and sounds of a Hyde Park spring afternoon. Yellow daffodils splashed the borders of the emerald lawn, on which picnickers sat on plaid blankets. Threading among them, giggling children chased yipping dogs. The late sun lent everything a generous honey glow.

At Speaker's Corner the Union Jack billowed in the breeze, lofted by Conservatives fixed on squelching Socialists by means of shouted slogans: "Traitors will destroy England!" and suchlike. The Socialists, stationed beside them, waved red banners and roared, "Down with Capitalism!" Young women in severe suits—and more than one in trousers—held placards demanding the full franchise, not the limited version currently on offer. Others who saw salvation in trade unions, the squelching of trade unions, Indian independence, opposition to Indian independence, the Catholic Church, atheism, the Liberal Party, or an end to the consumption of alcohol pressed their causes, while uniformed men and women banged drums and sang hymns in an enthusiastic effort toward the salvation of souls.

Ah, the British. Often wrong, but never without opinions and the zeal to express them. Possibly, I thought, as I turned to walk to my lodgings, we Chinese could take a lesson from them; though if so, I could not for the life of me discern what it might be.

As I approached the little house near the British Museum, my heart began to beat with the usual mixture of anticipation and trepidation. These two emotions shared a common source: the possibility of encountering Miss Mary Wendell.

Miss Wendell, the daughter of my landlady, was quite the most attractive creature I had ever laid eyes on. A gleaming golden bob framed her lively, rose-cheeked face; her blue eyes glowed with merriment and her movements were quick and graceful. From the moment we met she sparked such ardor in my soul as I had never anticipated finding in England.

The fervor of that moment, however, had not been mutual. When I first came to lodge with the Wendells, Mary shared her mother's disdain for the Chinese and would barely speak to me. I could hardly blame the ladies, for their heads were filled with the slant-eyed, long-nailed images of yellow-skinned horror perpetuated by pulp magazines, cheap stage shows, and moving pictures. It was only through the exhortations of the Reverend Robert Evans, a man of the church known to both myself and the Wendells, that the widow Wendell agreed to let me the attic rooms in the name of Christian charity.

In the months that I had been living there, I believed my comportment had caused the Wendell ladies' idea of the Chinese to reverse. Mrs. Wendell and I had become good friends, and Mary now smiled and winked as she rushed off to her work at a millinery shop or her worship at St. George's, Bloomsbury. I had not yet spoken to Mary about my true feelings for her, thinking the time not quite right. But I had hopes, as I stepped into the entry hall that afternoon, of her glowing smile and perhaps a brief but warm conversation.

However, such was not to be.

"Lao She!" came the voice of Mrs. Wendell. The barking of Napoleon, her little dog, joined in. I hung my bowler hat above the mirror and entered the drawing room, where I found my landlady in conversation with a red-headed young man in chauffeur's livery. The young man jumped up when I walked in.

"Lao She," said Mrs. Wendell, frowning, "this young man has come to fetch you. He says it's urgent. I trust you're not in trouble?"

"As far as I know, I am not," I replied. "How can I help you, young man?"

"I went to your office at the university, sir, but I was told you'd gone." Here was a working-class Britisher calling a Chinese "sir." I blinked.

"Yes," I said, "the spring holidays have begun." For which I could not deny I was thankful. Attempting to teach the Chinese language to people whose need to learn it far outstripped their interest in doing so was wearying. I was looking forward to some quiet weeks of work on a novel, for which an idea had yet to come to me; but I had hope.

"I telephoned my employer," the young chauffeur continued, "and was instructed to wait for you here. With the lady's permission, of course." He nodded at Mrs. Wendell. "He asks that you come at once."

"Who might your employer be, who is so anxious to see me?"

"The Honorable Bertrand Russell, sir."

"Bertrand Russell?" Hearing my voice hit a few notes above its usual tenor, I swallowed and said, "The Honorable Bertrand Russell has sent for *me*?"

"If you'll please come at once, sir."

"Mrs. Wendell," I said, befuddled but delighted, "I'm going out again."

As I walked once more into the entry hall to fetch my hat,

Mrs. Wendell's face reinstated its accustomed satisfied aspect. She patted Napoleon's head and smiled, probably as pleased as I was, though for different reasons, that her lodger had been summoned to the presence of the Honorable Bertrand Russell: mathematician, philosopher, liberal thinker, great friend of China, and—to Mrs. Wendell's mind possibly most important—the second son of an earl.

Stepping out of one's door in Peking, one was swept into a whirlpool of people, hurrying this way and that, on foot, in rickshaws or sedan chairs, or, for the moneyed, in carriages pulled by horses. The occasional motorcar inspired awe and a frisson of fear, for these machines were solely in the possession of diplomats, aristocrats, the powerful, and wealthy.

In the streets of London, however, the automobile, already on the increase before the war, now reigned supreme. Pedestrians were relegated to pavements on the edges, while horses shied and barrow-men cowered as lorries, buses, taxicabs, and indeed, the motorcars of private citizens surged past with a great grumbling of engines and bleating of horns.

In the time I had been in London I had not managed to develop an expertise in motorcars, except to be able to differentiate those of quality from the second-rate. The automobile into which the chauffeur urged me was a Morris Oxford, as befit a gentleman of Mr. Bertrand Russell's station—an excellent machine and not at all ostentatious. It hummed with quiet confidence as we made our rapid circuit of the London streets. I tried to appear to anyone gazing in the window as though I quite belonged.

We stopped in front of a dignified West End home of yellow brick and white limestone. The young chauffeur hurried to open my door, and then led me to the threshold of the house. As he pressed the bell my heart pounded almost as it had when I'd arrived at my lodgings. The Honorable Bertrand

Russell, wishing to speak to me! I'd hoped to encounter Mr. Russell at some point during my London sojourn, for I felt we had much to discuss. His writings had made clear that in his opinion China's troubles were not of China's making, but caused by those countries besetting us, each to further its own ends. England was not innocent in this regard, and I was eager to exchange views with Mr. Russell on a multitude of related subjects.

Once again, however, what I was hoping for was not to be.

The chauffeur's ring was answered by a butler, bald as a billiard ball. I presented my visiting card. The butler placed it on a silver tray while the chauffeur retired to his automobile. I was shown into a carpeted sitting room. By the room's stone fireplace a tall silver-haired man was pacing. "Sir," intoned the butler. "Mr. Lao She."

The tall man rushed across the room to shake my hand. "Lao She!" said he. "Bertrand Russell. I'm glad to make your acquaintance. Many times since I learned you'd arrived at the university I've thought to have you here, but one thing or another always interfered."

"I understand, of course, sir. I'm thrilled to meet you. I've read your books and I look forward to discussing China with you, and so much more."

"Yes, well, I look forward to those discussions also, but I'm afraid they'll have to wait for another day. Right now there isn't time. The plain fact is, I asked you here not so much to speak with you, Lao She, as to have you arrested."

# CHAPTER TWO

My heart stopped its eager pounding. In fact, it stopped altogether. Bertrand Russell wanted me arrested? What had I done?

"Oh, my dear man!" Mr. Russell started chuckling. This was too much. I was to be arrested and he found it funny? "You've gone quite pale. Perhaps I should have expressed myself differently. I need your help, you see. Your arrest wouldn't last long and would have no consequence for you aside from an hour or two in a jail cell. It would be of the greatest assistance to a friend of mine, however. Here, sit and I'll explain."

I was feeling weak-kneed, and still had no idea what he was talking about, so I welcomed the invitation and lowered myself into a chair.

"Word's come to me that my friend, Dee Ren Jie, has found himself mistakenly swept up in the arrest of a group of Chinese agitators in Limehouse. I—"

"Dee Ren Jie? The celebrated Judge Dee?" I was astounded to hear myself interrupting Bertrand Russell.

Mr. Russell, on the other hand, seemed delighted. "Yes! Do you know him?"

"By reputation only, of course. Judge Dee is in London?"

"He is, and as I say, he has got himself clapped behind bars. This would be nothing more than an inconvenience, to be sorted by your country's legation, if it weren't for the facts of his war service. Dee was at China's mission in Geneva when he was seconded to the Chinese Labour Corps in France, to resolve disputes between the laborers and the British at the front. As I understand the situation he was almost always in the right, but as I'm sure you're aware, my countrymen often put less weight on 'right' than on 'British.' The long and the short of it is, Dee made enemies. One of them, a certain Captain William Bard, is now an inspector with the Metropolitan Police in the very district where Dee sits in jail. Bard hasn't yet discovered he has Dee in a cell and I'd like to get Dee out of there before he does. Will you help?"

I hardly knew what to say. "I'm sorry, sir. Judge Dee has been arrested and in order for him to be released it will help if I'm arrested? I'm not sure I follow."

"I'm not sure I blame you. Let me propose this—we ride to the jail while I explain. If when we arrive you decline to participate, we will go our separate ways with no hard feelings. Does that seem satisfactory?"

I could only nod mutely. Apparently that was enough. Mr. Russell rang for the car and I soon found myself racing through the London streets again, this time with Bertrand Russell by my side.

He had become acquainted with Judge Dee, Mr. Russell told me, in Peking, where Dee had aided him in the writing of his famous book, *The Problem of China*. "Why Dee's in London now I don't know," Mr. Russell said, "but once he's released I expect we'll find out. Now, your part in this, my good fellow, would be simply to switch places with him. We'll go into the jail with you as my translator. My Chinese is passable, and

Dee's English is perfect, of course, but he's clever enough not to have used it within the hearing of the constabulary. We'll meet with him, you'll stay in, he'll walk out, and then I'll call the Chinese legation and inform them that a distinguished lecturer from the University of London is, through an egregious police error, being held in jail. They'll act swiftly on your behalf. I'll make sure of it."

"But why can you not use the same strategy to get Judge Dee released? Any Chinese diplomat will know full well Dee is not a Limehouse agitator."

"That's certainly true. If it were a simple matter of contacting the legation and letting the wheels of justice go round I'd do it. The complication is this. If Captain Bard wakes to the fact that he has Dee in his clutches he might be moved to settle old scores."

"Ah," I said. "You fear for Judge Dee's safety."

"Yes, but perhaps not in the way you imagine. Dee, as you may have heard, is a skilled fighter. Any physical confrontation Bard cares to initiate would be met competently by Dee. In close quarters, with no chance of escape, I fear Dee might find it necessary to cause serious harm to any man who sets upon him. This could result in a legal liability from which it would be difficult to extricate him. No, he must get out before his identity is discovered. So, Mr. Lao, what do you say? You'll likely be out in time to join Dee and myself for dinner. Does that suit you?"

To dine with Bertrand Russell and Judge Dee! What could suit me better? Yet the plan still appeared flawed. "Forgive me, sir," I said, "but can this deception succeed? Do Dee and I resemble one another to that great an extent?"

"Why, of course not! But this is England. To a certain type of Englishman, all Chinese look alike. I assure you the men of the Metropolitan Police are of this type. Also, Dee's disguised himself. An eye patch or some such." Again, Mr. Russell chuckled. "You'll put it on, and switch clothing, and I promise the constabulary will be none the wiser."

The car stopped at the gates of the Metropolitan Police district station in Limehouse. Against every grain of good sense I had, I agreed to participate in Bertrand Russell's plan. We left the car and for the third time that afternoon I approached a door with heart hammering, though now without the compensating anticipatory thrill.

The constables within were not thrilled, either, when we made our demand. "This is the Honorable Bertrand Russell," I said in my most officious manner to the portly sergeant behind the high oak desk. "We are here to speak with one of your prisoners."

The sergeant peered down at us. "Are you now?"

"My good man," drawled Mr. Russell, presenting his visiting card, "indeed we are, and my time is limited so I'd be obliged if we could get on with it."

The sergeant eyed Mr. Russell's card as if something might jump out from it. "You looking for one of them Chinamen, they're all down in the cells. You'd have to speak to Captain Bard about it, though."

"Then fetch him at once!" I commanded. I quickly felt my cheeks flush; I did not often order Englishmen around.

The other constables laughed and the sergeant's face reddened as mine had. "What did you say to me? I don't hold with no Chinaman telling me what to do!"

The others began jeers of "That's it, Tom!" and "Give him what for!" Mr. Russell rapped on the desk and said, "My good man—" as the sergeant jumped from his high stool and came out to meet us. The catcalls from the others grew. It was all I could do to keep from edging toward the door, but I couldn't countenance the idea of leaving Bertrand Russell on his own among these ruffians.

"Here! What's all this?" A new voice issued a sharp demand and all laughter stopped. "You fellows have nothing to do? I'm sure I could find something for you. Sergeant, you've left the desk. You'll be docked a day's wages. And now, you, sir. You seem to be at the center of this. What have you done to stir these men up so?"

That last was addressed to Mr. Russell. While the sergeant set his jaw and remounted his stool and the rest slunk away, Mr. Russell presented his visiting card to the new man. "Bertrand Russell," he said. "And you are—?"

"William Bard. Inspector and captain in the Metropolitan Police." So this was the famous Captain Bard. A large, fit-looking man in tweeds, with thinning hair and a thick mustache, he glowered at the card, and then at Mr. Russell, and finally at me.

"Just the fellow," said Mr. Russell, unperturbed. "You have a Chinese prisoner in your cells with whom I need a word. I've brought my translator with me. If we could trouble you?"

Bard narrowed his eyes, then shrugged. "Don't see why not. Bleedin' agitators. The upper ranks of Scotland Yard in their wisdom saw fit to assign me to this station because I speak the bloody language. Wish to hell I didn't. Why a gentleman such as yourself would want to spend time in a cell with a bunch of Chinks I couldn't say, but I suppose that's your business."

Mr. Russell smiled blandly and replied, "Yes, rather."

With that Captain Bard blew out a breath and called a man over to lead us to the cells.

# CHAPTER THREE

A rank smell informed me we had entered the cell area proper. Cries of "Hoy!" and other less polite expressions came from behind the steel doors as men leered from the small barred openings. The constable led us to one door whose distance from the others suggested a larger cell behind it. Jangling a set of keys, he worked the lock. The door creaked open to a big room holding perhaps a dozen Chinese men in varying states of injury. Clearly being an agitator was a dangerous profession.

"Rap on the door when you're ready to leave," the constable instructed as he ushered us into the cell. "Or if any of 'em gives you trouble." He glared around at all the men. When he left the door clanged shut behind him.

One of the prisoners stood. He wore an eye patch and a silk scholar's robe. Another, with white hair and beard, also wore Chinese dress, though in his case it was the cotton tunic and loose trousers of a merchant. The remainder were clothed in the same rough garb as the average British laborer.

The scholar was taller than I, broad of shoulder, and, despite the eye patch, handsome of face, with a square chin and a sparkle in his visible eye. He approached us with a small smile. Quietly, he said in English to Mr. Russell, "I see you got my note. Thank you for coming."

"Indeed I did," Mr. Russell replied, also whispering, as the man he'd come to see presumably did not speak English, hence my necessary presence. "This is Mr. Lao She. He's a lecturer at the University, a novelist, and an important Chinese intellectual here in London. He's come to take your place, after which I shall demand his release." I tried mightily to hide my pride, as well as my surprise, at being thus referred to by Bertrand Russell.

Once Mr. Russell was finished outlining the scheme, the scholar spoke. "I see. Xiexie, Mr. Lao." He folded his left hand over his right fist and bowed.

"You are Judge Dee?" I asked in Chinese.

He straightened again, his lips pursed and his nose crinkled as though encountering an unpleasant aroma. He lifted his chin and I must say he looked a touch arrogant.

"I am that man," he replied, his voice a note higher and his words a bit slower than they had been at first. He shifted his stance to hold his left hip slightly forward of his right and he bent his right arm at the elbow, his hand moving up and down in the manner of an uncomfortable fellow jiggling his hat.

He did not have a hat.

However, I did.

I realized what was happening. Dee was aping me.

I couldn't say I was flattered by his portrayal, but neither could I deny its truth. He ran a hand through his hair, smoothing it back as mine was combed, and then, with a grin, removed the eye patch and handed it to me. I put it on. He undid the silk buttons of his robe. I glanced at Mr. Russell, who smiled encouragingly, so I removed my jacket and loosened my tie. Mr. Russell put out a hand offering to hold whatever items required a temporary stop. Thus, using the Honorable Bertrand Russell as a clothes tree, Judge Dee and I exchanged trousers for trousers, and shirt, waistcoat, tie, and jacket for robe. My hat I handed Dee in payment, I supposed, for the eye patch. The other men in the cell found this process highly amusing and had to be quieted by Dee, who whispered he'd have them all out if only they didn't give away the game.

Dee, a Northerner from Shandong, had three inches the advantage of me in height and a more muscular physique than I might have expected in a member of the judiciary. His robe hung oddly on me and I had to hitch up his silk trousers. My trousers, equally, were short on him, my jacket he could not button, and my shoes must have pinched his toes as my feet swam in his slippers, but Mr. Russell assured us that in the brief time it would take himself and Dee to exit the station no one would take notice of Dee's odd attire, or mine. I attempted to pull my shoulders back and set my features in a non-committal attitude—that is, to become Dee as Dee had become Lao. Mr. Russell looked us over, gave a satisfied nod, and rapped on the cell door.

"Here! Constable!" he called. A moment later came the rattle of keys and the complaint of unoiled hinges as the door was pulled open. Mr. Russell exited the cell, followed by Dee. "This man," Mr. Russell said to the constable, pointing at me, "is no agitator. He's a distinguished scholar. You cannot keep him here."

The constable shrugged. "None of my lookout, sir."

"Well then, I shall contact the proper authorities. Don't you worry, old fellow," he said to me. "I'll have you out soon enough."

"Yes, sir, thank you, sir," I said before Dee-as-Lao-the-translator could speak—and then by the widened eyes of Mr. Russell, Dee, and the officer, I realized my mistake.

"What's this? I thought none of you Chinks spoke English!" The officer looked from me to Dee, down at Dee's ankles protruding from my trousers, and up again. He scowled.

"No, sir, I—" I broke into a sweat; I was making it worse. The constable ripped off my eye patch. "Why—"

Dee and Mr. Russell exchanged a look. "Ah, well," said Dee. "Nothing for it." He wheeled a kick into the button of the constable's jaw. The constable staggered back, grabbing for his whistle. As he sounded it Dee threw open the cell door. In Chinese he shouted, "All right, agitators. Go agitate!"

The corridor filled with Chinese and soon after, with constables. "Russell, don't get caught up in this." Dee raised his voice over the din. "Go. We'll meet you later."

I felt that to be a sanguine assurance given the circumstances, but Mr. Russell nodded and slipped along the wall. He moved quickly up the same stairs the constables were streaming down.

"Can you fight?" Dee asked me.

"Indeed I can," I replied. "I'm Manchu, born under the Plain Red Banner. There were plenty of knocks to be had in the Peking of my youth."

"Well, then, Bannerman, let's get to it."

In the scrum of constables and agitators I punched and kicked. I acquitted myself reasonably well, I thought; but in the moments I took to catch my breath I could see Dee moving like a human whirlwind. I was a pugilistic craftsman, I realized, while he, in the true sense, was a martial artist.

Dee's strategy, I soon discerned, was to leave the constables and agitators contending with one another and to edge toward the stairs. Very well; I targeted my battling to my left and made progress in that direction. I attained the second stair and looked back for Dee in time to see him sidestep two constables rushing at him. They crashed into each other and both went down. A third, however, grabbed Dee from behind. He threw an arm about Dee's neck and, choking, began to pull him away from the action. Near me was a constable at the bottom of the stairs, his back to me, his truncheon raised high. Before he could bring it down on the head of the agitator he was aiming for, I yanked it from his hand, took aim, and sent it spiraling through the air. It hit the head of the man with his arm around Dee's neck—not perhaps as squarely as I'd hoped, but with enough heft that the man's grip was loosened. The elderly Chinese merchant pulled the man away and, with a kick of economy and grace, knocked him to the floor. Dee rushed toward me. "Up we go!" he shouted, and up we went.

# CHAPTER FOUR

A s we burst into the antechamber of the district police station, Dee yelled, "Trouble below! See to it at once!" The authority of his voice caused the eyes of the charge officer to swing to the staircase door. Out of it, in our wake, erupted a torrent of agitators and constables. Dee and I sped to the entryway and made our escape.

By the time we'd hurtled halfway down the block, the agitators had surged from the station and melted into the Limehouse streets. I fancied we would do the same, leaving the constables to scratch their heads and wonder which of the many Chinese wandering this way and that they had lately had inside their cell. I was eager to put distance between myself and my first— and, I hoped, my last—visit to a jail. However, Dee pulled me into the first alley we found. "Well fought," said he, smiling. "But Lao, if we don't exchange footwear immediately I fear I will lose my toes."

I saw the wisdom in this, for I was tripping in his large slippers. As we effected the transaction a shadow fell in the entrance to the alley. I whipped my head around, but Dee glanced up and then straightened without haste. I saw the reason why: the newcomer was the man from the cells wearing Chinese merchant's garb.

This man was a good twenty years Dee's elder, and so thirty-five years or so older than myself. The snowiness of his hair and beard and the wrinkles mapping his face might have led me to expect a certain frailty of carriage, but that expectation would have been dashed. He stood erect, with the serenity of a man without fear.

"Ni hao," he said, stepping forward. "Are you Dee Ren Jie? Now Judge Dee?"

"I am, yes," Dee replied. "Do I know you?"

The man bowed. Rising up, he said, "You knew me once. I'm Hoong Liang, the third son of Hoong Pei Tie."

Now Dee's eyes flew wide. "Big Brother Hoong? Can it be?"

The man smiled. "It is. I wondered if it was you in the cell, but the eye patch and the Guangdong pronunciation you affected caused me to suspect that, if so, you preferred to remain unknown. I confirmed it was you most definitely when I saw your fighting style. The circular kick with double forearm strike—most fighters use a closed fist in that skill, but my father taught it with the open hand."

Dee now smiled also, gloriously. "He did," he said, "and my brothers and I paid dearly until we learned it. Lao, this man's father was tutor to my family. Big Brother Hoong, this is Lao She, a man brave enough to enter a London jail to rescue someone he had never met." I bowed to Hoong Liang to cover my pride at this remark. "But Big Brother Hoong," Dee said, "you left Yantai when I was a boy. To find you now in London—how is this?"

"I'll relate that tale, though it's uninteresting," said Hoong. "But may I suggest we first make our way to my shop, where you fellows can complete the exchange you've begun? It's not far from here, and while you, sir"—indicating me—"merely look ill-dressed, you, Judge Dee, look absurd."

Dee glanced down at himself in my clothing and laughed, and we all slipped from the alley onto the Limehouse streets.

The shop to which Hoong led us was, in fact, close by. I'd passed it occasionally in my months in London and each time felt immediately homesick, for Hoong's shop sold vegetables, grains, and spices such as were common enough in China but not easy to come by here. He also sold apothecary herbs and fungi; dishes, bowls, chopsticks, and fans; needles and thread; washing powder; ink and brushes; and similar goods. None of the valuable—or at least, exotic—antiquities Londoners thirsted for, as in some of the other Limehouse shops. Just everyday items of use to a Chinese clientele.

Once in the shop, Hoong Liang locked the door again, and made sure the sign reading "closed" in both English and Chinese was in place. Dee and I clothed ourselves in our rightful raiment while Hoong narrated his tale: he'd left home to see, as he said, what there was to see. He joined the army, attaining the rank of sergeant.

"Then I must from now call you Sergeant Hoong," said Dee, buttoning his robe.

"As you wish," Hoong replied with a smile. When he'd had enough of military service, he signed on as a sailor on a merchant vessel. He traveled on many ships to many countries, finally stepping ashore permanently a dozen years ago to help a cousin with a shop in Limehouse. The cousin returned to China, satisfied that Hoong had a good living at the shop.

"Of you, Judge Dee, I've heard many times over the years. I confess to feeling as proud of you as if I'd taught you myself."

"If I've done any small good in the world," Dee said, "it's due to the teachings of my father and yours."

The smiles the two gave one another, if stored in a bottle, could have lit up the Limehouse streets come nightfall.

"But Sergeant Hoong," Dee said, "how did you come to be in the jail? Were you agitating?"

"Not precisely. I'd tried to pull some of the agitators into my shop when I heard the constables' whistles. I favor the men's cause but their methods endanger them. They were having none of it, however, being determined to skirmish with the constables. The constables descended in overwhelming numbers, with truncheons, so I . . . found my role changing."

"I saw you in the jail," I said. "Your kicks and blows were admirable."

"Thank you. For an untrained fighter you acquitted yourself impressively, also." I thanked him for the compliment, though I did not enjoy his pointing out the homegrown nature of my fighting skills. "Will you gentlemen have tea with me?" Hoong asked. "We have much to talk about."

"I'd like nothing better, Sergeant Hoong," said Dee. "But we'll have to delay that to a future time. Lao and I are expected in Chelsea." He looked around. "Though your shop has given me an idea. Have you a telephone?"

"I do not. As you may imagine, Limehouse is not high on the post office's list of areas that urgently need the service. I feel fortunate the National Grid has seen fit to provide me with electricity for my lamps."

"Is that so? Well, there are other ways of communicating."

At Dee's request, Hoong gave him pen and paper. Dee wrote, then opened the shop door and gestured to one of the street urchins watching a game of flick-cards. "Here's a shilling," he said to the boy. "Take this note to Thirty-one Sydney Street and there's another waiting for you there."

The boy grinned, snatched the note and coin from Dee's hand, and disappeared.

"That's quite a distance, Dee," I said. "It will take him hours."

"Certainly not," Dee answered. "In any city you choose to name, there are none so resourceful as street children. I have employed many in my career. None has ever failed to complete his assigned task. He'll be there within the time it takes us to gather what we need."

I was not aware we needed anything, and if we did, didn't know what it might be, but Dee wandered Hoong's shop, consulting with the older man over vegetables, spices, and rice. Eventually I was dispatched to the fishmonger's to purchase a large carp, and to the butcher's for a pound of ground pork. When I returned Dee stood between two stacks of paper parcels each lashed with string.

"Ah, Lao!" he said. "Come, we must be off."

Dee thanked Sergeant Hoong for his help, promised to return, lifted the parcels by their string handles, and we left.

A TAXICAB RIDE later, I was once again on the doorstep of the Honorable Bertrand Russell. Mr. Russell met us at the door himself, with a twinkle in his eye. "Mrs. Hennessey is cross with you, Dee. She's only agreed to your proposal because she remembers meals you cooked in Peking. As payment for upsetting her plans she demands to be taught to use a cleaver as you do."

"I suspected she might not be pleased," Dee replied. "Let me see what I can do to remedy the situation."

Instead of entering the hall, Dee took the gate that led below stairs. Thus it came about that I finally sat over whiskey with Bertrand Russell, discussing *The Problem of China*.

# CHAPTER FIVE

"So, what brings you to London, Dee?"

The question came from Bertrand Russell. Dee, Russell, Russell's wife, Dora, and I were at table. We were eating, with silver chopsticks brought back from the Russells' time in Peking, a Shandong feast of Dee's creation. The Russells were both adept with their chopsticks, and seemed to be enjoying the cuisine as much as Dee and I.

It was Dee's determination to cook this meal ("To repay Russell for his efforts, Lao, and also because as many good meals as I've had abroad, there's nothing like the food of home") that had brought on the ire of the cook, Mrs. Hennessey, whose planned menu had been shunted aside for it. Her wrath had been turned away by Dee's cleaver lesson and his promise to leave with her all the herbs and spices that remained after he'd prepared the dishes. Those dishes—stuffed tofu, four joy meatballs, and now a whole ginger-steamed carp, all accompanied by a tureen of jasmine rice—simultaneously filled me with delight and deepened my homesickness. Since I'd first let rooms from Mrs. and Miss Wendell I'd generally taken breakfast and dinner with them. This arrangement offered the dual advantages of providing nourishment and affording me an opportunity to spend time with Mary. As to the latter, I hoped little by little to win Mary's affection; but in terms of the former, though I was unable to fault Mrs. Wendell's skills in what was called "plain cooking," I could not be said to be enthusiastic about the cuisine. The East End held a number of Chinese eateries and noodle bars, and I occasionally made my way to one for a midday meal. Nothing I'd eaten since my arrival in London, however, held a candle to the rough, salty meatballs or the silken sauce on the fish, the golden-brown color of the tofu squares or the rich aromas of all the dishes mingled together in the feast we were sharing tonight.

"The answer to your question, Russell, goes back to the war," Dee said. "As you know, but Lao, perhaps you don't, I was seconded from Geneva to the trenches of France to adjudicate disputes between the British military and the men of the Chinese Labour Corps. It was there that I met Captain Bard." Dee paused to sip his wine.

"Bard was a British Army officer in charge of a large battalion of Chinese laborers," Russell informed Dora and myself. "His disciplinary measures were apparently . . . harsh."

"We did not"—Dee smiled slightly—"see eye to eye. Within the battalion were smaller labor bands. One of these groups, four men, made their way to London at the end of the war."

"But Dee, that's extraordinary," Dora Russell said. She was a woman of even features and bobbed brown hair. "Quite pretty" might have been one's mild assessment until the lively beam of her dark eyes and the compassionate smile playing on her lips worked their compelling magic. "To our disgrace, Britain has been adamant about refusing to admit any men of the Chinese Labour Corps. Yet you say some are here?"

"As far as I know, just these four. Their admission here was engineered by Captain Bard."

"My," said Russell. "Do we detect remorse? An attempt with a good deed to atone for ill behavior?"

The smile Dee offered now was, I thought, a touch bitter. "If that was his intention, it will take more than a single good deed. It's possible you're right, though, Russell, because I understand he's been calling on these men periodically, to see how they're doing. Unfortunately, not all are doing well. One was murdered last week."

Dora Russell gasped. Even Russell turned pale. "Murdered, Dee? Surely not!"

"Murder?" I said, leaning forward. "Who was the poor fellow? What were the circumstances, do you know?"

Dee smiled. "Asked like a true novelist, Lao. But yes, murder." The smile faded. "His name was Ma Ze Ren. He'd set himself up as a merchant, a Limehouse dealer in Chinese antiquities. I imagine we weren't far from his shop earlier today, at the police station and again at Sergeant Hoong's." Sergeant Hoong had already been identified to the Russells as the font of the bounty before us. "When these men learned they'd be permitted to come to London at the end of their Labour Corps contracts, they were excited. It gave them the prospect of continuing to earn a good wage before returning home. But one thing still worried them.

"One of the four—in fact, this very man, Ma Ze Ren—had been wounded in a German barrage attack. Of course the contracts of the Chinese laborers with the British government guaranteed they'd be far behind the battle lines, but that provision was regularly violated. These men were all young and strong, and I'd wager, until Ma's injury, they had never considered the idea that any of them might die. Now, with a chance to spend some years in England, they sent for me in the camp. They asked, if any of them should die there, that I would undertake the arrangements to return his body to China. I agreed.

"Now that, of course, can be done from a distance through the Chinese legation. I was once again in Geneva when I was contacted about Ma's death, and I would have handled the situation in that way—but for the fact of murder. Suspecting the London authorities might not delve deeply into the death, natural or otherwise, of a Chinese, I determined to investigate Ma's case myself. I arrived last night and had barely left my hotel this morning to start my work when I was caught up in the arrest of the agitators."

"Why did you let them take you?" Russell inquired. "London constables are no match for your skills."

"I saw Bard there directing his men. He's familiar with my fighting style. If he knew I was in London—and had escaped his custody—he'd become determined to recapture me."

"Why such enmity?" Dora Russell asked.

"In France I delivered rulings in which he came out badly more than once. He had no authority over the men of the Chinese Labour Corps, yet he was determined to put them in harm's way to keep the British soldiers safe. Sacrificial lambs, if you will. He maintained that I was the one overstepping, yet in each instance his superiors accepted my judgments. The military record of disciplinary actions against him is, I believe, one reason his career in the Metropolitan Police has not gone as he would have liked since his return."

"He blames you?"

"One must always blame someone." Dee smiled, putting down his wineglass. "When I saw him this morning, I realized his focus on apprehending me would divert his attention from Ma's murder—if, indeed, he was giving that matter any attention at all—and my need to avoid him would have the same effect on me. So I decided to avoid drawing his attention and see what you, Russell, could devise."

"Seriously, Dee, all that calculation in the moments between being swept up in the protest, and your arrest?" I could not work out if he was being serious.

"Indeed. I barely had time to steal a beggar's eye patch to disguise my face."

"Dee! Tell us you did no such thing!" Dora Russell remonstrated.

"The man could use both eyes as well as you or I. I could tell by the way he walked, consistently tapping his cane onto things instead of running it into them. I tossed him a shilling for the use of the patch. He plucked it out of the air."

The entire company laughed. For myself, I was nonplussed at Dee's ability to notice the tiny detail of the cane in the middle of the swirl of agitators and policemen.

"So now that you're free," I asked, "what steps do you propose to take, Dee?" I was intrigued to hear his plan. Investigation of this nature was new to me, and Dee was renowned for his success at it.

"I'll see where paths take me, but I'll start by visiting Ma's shop. I'll consult Sergeant Hoong in the morning to see if he knows where it is. It's called 'Ten Thousand Treasures.'"

"Oh!" I said. "If that's Ma's shop, no need to bother Hoong. I've passed it many times. I can take you there."

Dee regarded me silently. Russell spoke up. "Dee, that's a fine idea. In fact, you might consider having Lao assist in this investigation. He's been in London for some time. I've no doubt his knowledge can save you time and effort." He looked to me. "For one thing, he'd have steered you clear of those agitators."

Dee lifted his eyebrows at Russell. "His knowledge is one thing. His courage is also not at issue. His ability to hold his tongue, however . . ."

I felt my face grow hot. "If you gentlemen would like to discuss my flaws and virtues, I'd be happy to withdraw."

"Oh, come, Lao," Russell said. "You have to admit it's a worthwhile suggestion."

I didn't feel I had to admit anything of the kind; but I didn't like to contradict Bertrand Russell, especially in his own home.

"Also," Russell went on, "you've said that your teaching burden at the university is not heavy, and that you arranged things that way to give you the opportunity to gather material for your novels. Although the book you told me about—*The Philosophy of Lao Zhang*, is it?—sounds delightful, I fancy a murder investigation will offer inspiration you'll not find elsewhere."

Dee's eyes were on me, but he didn't speak.

Stiffly, I said to him, "If you think I could be of use."

After another few uncomfortable moments, during which I felt like an insect under a scientist's glass, Dee said, "I do. But Lao, this will be unfamiliar territory for you. You must agree to take your lead from me."

I opened my mouth to protest, but Russell clapped his hands. "Excellent! It's settled, then. Now let's have brandy in the drawing room."

# CHAPTER SIX

The following morning I took breakfast as usual with Mrs. and Miss Wendell. As I pulled out my chair Mary looked up and frowned. "Why, Mr. Lao. Wherever did you get that bruise on your cheek?"

"Oh, it's nothing," I said, trying to hide my pleasure at her concern. "I was running for a bus and I fell."

"I'm glad to hear that," said her mother. "I mean, I'm sorry, Mr. Lao, that you're hurt, but I read in the morning paper of a shocking incident yesterday at the Limehouse police station. A group of Chinese staged a jailbreak! Agitators and ruffians all. Disgraceful. I trust you don't associate with that type of person." She peered at me, eyes narrowed.

"Certainly not," I said, busying myself with buttering a piece of toast. I tore off a corner to give to Napoleon, who was wagging his tail in expectation beside my chair.

"Well, I must be off," said Mary, jumping up. I watched her in the entryway as she pulled on her gabardine coat and fixed her hat. Today's was a pale green felt affair, its color matching her pumps. Circled with tiny yellow flowers just the shade of Mary's bobbed hair, the hat made her look like a flower herself. She turned and called, "Do stay out of trouble, Mr. Lao," waved gaily, and vanished through the door.

My heart was still singing from Mary's smile when I presented myself at Sergeant Hoong's shop in Narrow Street. Dee was already there, in fine good humor, sharing a pot of tea with Hoong. "Ah, Lao!" Dee said. He slapped his thighs and stood. "You look a little the worse for wear. I hope you're feeling up to the day?"

"I certainly am."

For all the fighting Dee had done the day before, he himself showed no visible injury. The scholar's robe he wore looked fresh as well.

"Excellent. Hoong, we'll speak later. Come, Lao." Dee exited the shop, not looking back to see if I followed.

I bristled at his high-handed attitude. At the same time, I must confess to some excitement at the day's possibilities. My duties at the university consisted of teaching the basics of the Chinese language to ambitious young men hoping to get a leg up on other ambitious young men in their international-trade firms, and to the wives of businessmen and missionaries soon to go east, whose chief concern was their ability to converse with the servants. None had any interest in the language for its own sake, or for the sake of becoming acquainted with Chinese people, or with our culture. Chinese is a difficult language, a fact my students personally resented as an unfair burden upon them. My work, in short, presented the occasional challenge to my good nature, but rarely any to my intellect. It also, as Bertrand Russell had mentioned, did not occupy a great deal of my time. I had turned, therefore, to the writing of novels and essays. I had gained some ground on that front, but, having finished one manuscript, was at a loss where to begin the next. A totally unfamiliar exercise such as this might be just the thing to strike a match.

DEE AND I walked through the Limehouse streets. This area, so close to the docks, always carried the odor of the sea. Around us bustled men with handcarts, or barrows, or with poles across their shoulders hung with parcels on each end. The occasional horn blast announced the incursion of a car or lorry on streets barely wide enough for three men to pass. But pass they did; here English sailors crossed paths with Chinese, Lascars with Arab merchants, and dark-skinned Caribbeans with long-bearded men of the Hebrew faith.

The murdered man's shop, Ten Thousand Treasures, was indeed not far from Sergeant Hoong's. When we arrived it was shuttered. Sergeant Hoong had told Dee the shop assistant, a man named Li, was in the process of packing away the goods. Hoong believed the shop's contents had been sold on as a single lot, although he didn't know who the buyer was.

"I suppose if all you're doing is packing up, no reason to get here at the crack of dawn," Dee said, seemingly unfazed by this obstacle. "We'll speak to Li when he arrives."

"What shall we do until then?" I asked.

"We'll visit the widow."

"Where will we find her?"

"I think, right here." He stepped to a set of temple wind bells dangling in a small doorway beside the shop. Shaking them, he sent their ringing through the street until a window opened above and a pale freckled woman stuck her head out.

"All right, all right, keep your hair on." She looked us over. "Yes?"

Dee stepped back and craned his neck. "I am Dee Ren Jie. I was a friend of Ma Ze Ren, from our time in France during the war. This is Lao She. We've come to offer condolences."

"Oh." She smoothed her chestnut hair, piled loosely atop her head. "Oh, that's kind. Please come up."

She dropped a key and Dee caught it.

"That's Ma's widow?" I whispered as Dee unlocked the door. "She's—"

"An Englishwoman, yes. I understand Ma met her at a nightclub, where she worked as a dance hostess."

We entered and climbed a narrow staircase. The widow Ma was waiting at the door to the upstairs flat. Dark half-moons sat below her eyes and her smile was wan. A plumpness to her belly and cheeks indicated that the lady was in general good health, though losing her husband had obviously struck her a blow.

"Please come in." She closed the door behind us. "I can put the kettle on if you'd like tea."

"Please don't trouble yourself, Mrs. Ma," said Dee. "We won't stay. I can see you're busy."

Indeed, if packing up was the theme of the day for Ma's shop, the same could be said of the flat above. Boxes, cases, and a steamer trunk lay in various stages of overflow, as did the chest of drawers and the wardrobe. Mrs. Ma looked around, gave us a helpless smile, and sank onto a settee. "I'm sorry about the jumble. I'm leaving London tomorrow, going back to Norfolk by train. I thought I'd be further along by now, but I don't . . . feel my best."

"Nothing to apologize for," said Dee.

I looked closely at the young lady. "You do look delicate," I said. "Shall we send for a doctor?"

"No, no," the widow said. "I'm just . . ." She dropped her gaze.

"I can easily imagine," said Dee, "that losing Ma Ze Ren has been very hard."

"Well, if you knew him, Mr. Dee"—she sighed—"you know what a kind man he was. He took good care of me."

"And the police have no idea who committed this crime?" I said.

Dee shot me a look as Mrs. Ma answered. "They've hardly investigated. Well, you wouldn't expect them to, would you? A Chinese shopkeeper? They have ever so many more weighty things on their minds." Bitterness tinged her words. "The inspector who came said it must have been another Chinese. Because of the sword, you see. With that, he washed his hands of it. 'Never catch 'em,' he said, and walked away." She shrugged. "He may be right. I don't suppose it matters now."

Dee said, "The weapon used was a sword?"

"Something called a butterfly sword. Ze Ren said it was"— she furrowed her brow—"a short-bladed dao? It was for sale in the shop. It's missing."

"Could the killer have been trying to steal it?" I asked. "And Ma came upon him?"

That got me another look from Dee.

"I don't know," said the widow. "I suppose. I spent hardly any time in the shop. It upset the British customers to see me there. We English girls are supposed to keep ourselves pure for our brave boys back from the war, you see. Well, my brave boy didn't come back. Lots of others didn't either. I don't know how it is in China, but it's hard for a woman alone in England, I can tell you. Dancing with men in a nightclub for pay—it's not much of a life, is it? Men purchase a dance and they think they've bought . . . other things. You're supposed to keep a smile on your face while they touch you and speak to you in such a way! Then they offer you more money to meet them in the alley, and expect you'll be grateful it's you and not another girl."

"How appalling!" I began stoutly. "It is never right to treat a woman that way, no more here than in China. As equal citizens—"

"Lao," said Dee. "Perhaps we can address the rights of women another time?"

I was drawn up short. "Yes. Yes, of course."

"But Ze Ren," Dee said to the widow. "He was not like that?"

"Oh, no!" She smiled sadly. "Ze Ren was different. Sometimes he didn't even want to dance, just sit and talk. His English was lovely! After a while he started asking me if I'd walk out with him of an afternoon. Just to walk, and to have tea. In a proper tea room! When Ze Ren asked me to marry him I felt like the luckiest girl in the world."

"He was, indeed, a fine man. And the shop gave you a good living?" Dee inquired.

"Ze Ren had great hopes for it, but it hadn't come up to them yet. Still, he'd go down immediately after breakfast. I'd shop, and cook, and go about my wifely work." She gave the wan smile again. "Ze Ren and Mr. Li, the shop assistant, were very busy, dealing with customers and merchandise all day. I wouldn't see him again until he came back up in the evening. I'd make his tea." She blinked away a tear and touched an embroidered handkerchief to the corner of her eye. "Ze Ren said he liked English food, as long as I cooked it." She raised the handkerchief to her eyes again. "I'm sorry."

"No, no," said Dee. "We apologize for intruding at this time. Mrs. Ma, when we were in France Ze Ren had asked me, in the event of his death, to arrange for his body to go home to China. I've come to London prepared to do that, but in light of your marriage, perhaps you'd prefer to bury him here?"

"I . . . I'd been thinking to take him to Norfolk with me, but he wasn't a Christian and I'm not sure they'd let me lay him to rest in the church graveyard. I know how much he loved his country." She lifted her eyes to Dee's. "Maybe it's the right thing to do, for you to take him home."

Dee nodded. "Very well, then. I'll make arrangements. My condolences, again. We'll see ourselves out."

Exiting the widow's flat, we made our way down the rickety stairs and into the street. The shutters on the shop window had by now been secured back and a man could be seen moving within. Dee knocked and the door was opened.

"I'm sorry, gentlemen, but this shop is no longer doing business," the young man at the door began. Although Chinese, he was dressed not in the merchant's trousers and tunic, but in the suit-and-tie apparel of a British clerk in a respectable shop.

"We're not here to buy," said Dee. "I'm Dee Ren Jie. This is Lao She. We—"

"Lao She?" The young man's eyes widened. "Of course! I recognize you, sir. I attended a lecture you gave at the University just recently. 'China in the Great War.' Engrossing. I'm Li Zi Rong. I was Ma Ze Ren's assistant. How can I help you?"

Dee gave me a look of appraisal, then turned back to Li. "I knew Ma and his friends in France, during the war. I'd like to ask a few questions, if I may."

"About his death?"

"And his life."

"Of course. Please, come in." He shut and latched the door behind us. "I'm sorry you find the shop in such a state," he said as he cleared three porcelain stools of their occupants: a bronze Buddha statue, a set of temple bells very like the ones outside, four delicate teacups, and a trio of silk fans. "The contents have been sold. I'm packing them for delivery. Please, gentlemen, sit."

Dee and I did as invited. Dee said, "You must be an efficient young man, to have so quickly found buyers." I opened my mouth to remind Dee of what Sergeant Hoong had said, but Dee spoke again before I could. "I commend you."

Li Zi Rong said, "Thank you, sir, but it's a single buyer, and it has nothing to do with me. Colonel Livingstone Moore, a longtime customer. When he heard about Ma Ze Ren's passing he made the widow an offer for the lot." He lowered his voice. "Between you gentlemen and myself, I tell you he's got a bargain. I suggested to Mrs. Ma that she could get a better price, or even that rather than selling on we keep the shop open. It's quite a good living here, you know. I'm always surprised at the end of the month when we go over the books at how well we've done."

Remembering the widow's words about Ma's hopes for the shop, I again started to say something, but once again Dee spoke first. "Ma—assisted by you, of course—must have become an able and persuasive salesman since he came to England. I remember him having many excellent attributes, but a silver tongue wasn't among them. Li Zi Rong? Why do you smile?"

Still smiling, the young man replied, "Ma Ze Ren had, as you say, many excellent attributes, but few that were valuable in the running of a shop. When he started out he expected to spend his day as dealers in antiquities do in China: drinking tea with customers, discussing philosophy and art. He'd been a shop assistant in China before the war, you know, and that's what he'd experienced. But it's not the British way. Here they come, they look, they buy or not, and they're off. Luckily there's a fashion now in London for Chinese goods, so our merchandise was its own salesman. Ma Ze Ren expressed his disappointment to me often. He spent very little time in the shop."

"But the widow said—" I began, to be cut off yet again by Dee. He slapped his knees and rose.

"We must be getting on. Thank you, Li Zi Rong. You've helped me with a picture of my friend's life in London. I do have one last question. Or rather, two. He was killed with a short-bladed dao?"

"Yes. We'd only recently got it in and it was on the table with the other new inventory."

"And do you have any ideas about who might have committed this crime? The police say it was a burglar, another Chinese. Do you also believe this?"

Li shook his head. "I can't say I do. The killing happened at the end of the day. I was in the back room and Ma Ze Ren had recently returned. The shop was still open. What burglar would enter an open shop? Why not wait for nightfall? And why, if Ma confronted a burglar, would he not cry out for me? Yet I knew nothing until I came out of the back and found him. It was . . . It was quite a horrible sight. I'm sorry, sirs." The young man turned his back to us, stood for a moment, and then faced us again. "No, I don't see how the idea of a burglar makes sense."

"And you told this to the inspector who came?"

"Of course. An Inspector Bard. He apparently knew Ma Ze Ren in France, also."

"Yes, I know the man also, from the war."

"As an old acquaintance of the victim he offered Mrs. Ma his sympathies, but he said if Chinese were going to go around with knives stabbing one another there was nothing he could do."

# CHAPTER SEVEN

Dee strode up Church Lane in the direction of Commercial Road. I wondered where we were going next. I'd have asked, but I fell behind as he slid along the crowded pavement like an eel through reeds, while I was continually jostled and bumped. When I caught him up, it was as before: I had no chance to speak because Dee spoke first.

"Lao," he said, in deliberately patient tones, "I recognize you're unfamiliar with even the fundamentals of investigation, but surely you possess more common sense than you've so far displayed."

I was stung. "I don't know what you mean."

"When we were with the widow," he said, "the questions you asked led her in the direction of your thinking." He wove around two ladies and their shopping baskets. "You will learn a good deal more if you keep your theories to yourself and allow your subject to choose the path." Three laughing street children chased each other past us. "Then, when we were with Li Zi Rong, you almost blurted that what the widow told us contradicted what he had just said. Do you deny it?"

I drew myself up. "I do not 'blurt.' That aside, what harm could there be in his knowing their recollections differ?"

"Perhaps none. Or perhaps, a good deal. Knowledge is power, to be guarded until its use is necessary." A young man on the pavement stumbled into us, apologized, and went his way. "Also," Dee continued, "you must be aware of your surroundings at all times."

"Really, Dee. As a writer, I like to think my powers of observation are a cut or two above the average."

"Ah. Then you will have noticed your wallet has just been lifted."

"I—what?" I thrust my hand in my jacket pocket. It was empty.

Dee was off like a shot. I attempted to follow closely but abandoned the idea when I saw Dee leap in the air, seize a lamppost, and swing himself over the heads of several people. He dropped down and disappeared. I continued along in a more conventional way, making for the disturbance I could hear rippling through the crowd ahead.

NOW HERE WE come to the first of those episodes about which I warned you at the opening of this book. I was not present for the chase and capture that led to the retrieval of my wallet. Retrieve it Dee did, and I will paint you the picture of how he went about it. Because I didn't observe the events myself, this picture is necessarily speculative, and with Dee I had a further difficulty: it wasn't easy to persuade him to describe to me the proceedings I hadn't witnessed. In his eyes these events had no bearing upon our quest for justice for Ma Ze Ren (although as we shall eventually see, they did yield other fruit) and therefore, once completed, were no longer of interest. By the time I'd found him and he'd handed me back my property, Dee was anxious to reach our next destination.

It was only in short bursts as we hurried along that he told me what had happened. This disjointed account I have stitched into a workable narrative, enabling me, before I recount our next interview, to bring you the wallet adventure.

DEE WAS OFF like a shot.

Leaping, he seized a lamppost, swung himself over the heads of several people, and landed lightly on the pavement, to the astonished gasps of men and women (and the dumbfounded delight of two small boys) who'd never before seen a robe-clad Chinese man fall from the sky. He spotted the thief and raced after him as the young man turned a sharp corner into a winding street. Dee put on a burst of speed and grasped the fellow by the shoulders. He spun him around and threw him to the ground.

No sooner had he done so than he found himself surrounded by a gang of hooligans. Stepping from the doorways and curbs where they'd been loitering, they threw away their cigarettes and flexed their hands.

"'Ere!" called one of them. "Wot's this?"

Dee, standing over the thief, looked about him and smiled. *First,* he recounted having thought, *I was arrested and rescued by an aristocrat and a countryman. Then I encountered Sergeant Hoong, and now here is a situation for which Hoong's father so well prepared me. Truly, London is a wondrous place.*

He pointed at the ruffians one at a time and counted aloud: "Yi, er, san, si, wu, liu."

Perplexed, they stared. "'E's a right queer Chinaman," said one. "Come on, lads. Let's give 'im a good thrashing."

With that, they began to close in.

Avoiding the fellow on the pavement, whose mouth hung agape, Dee stepped back into a bow stance, stretching his right arm behind him, hand in a fist, and his left to the front in the tiger claw bridge. In his mind he heard Master Hoong's words: *When confronting multiple opponents, the long-handed technique of the swinging wave punch should be used to its maximum potential.*

The biggest of the gang, the one who'd suggested the thrashing, snorted and came at Dee with a wild kick to the midsection. Dee shifted his body left to avoid the kick and smashed his forearm just under the man's kneecap. The ruffian gave a high-pitched yelp and swung a furious right-handed haymaker. Dee ducked, followed with a swinging punch, and then slammed his right and left hands successively under the chin of his opponent. He delivered the coup de grâce of a tidal wave punch upon the hooligan's jaw.

The big man fell to the pavement, knocked out cold.

Dee straightened and spoke to the rest of the gang. "Shall we stop this?"

All the thugs hesitated. After a moment one of them stuck his chest out. "Like 'ell we will!" With that, he and a second man exploded toward Dee.

Dee shrugged, then used his left forearm to deflect the oncoming blow of the first attacker. He snagged the man's hand and smashed his arm. The second thug lunged in. Dee spun between the two. They stared in disbelief as he unleashed a double whipping strike, left and right arms outstretched. Catching each in the back of the skull, he sent them both face down into the muck and mire of the cobblestone street.

Another assailant, not as tall as the first but heavier by half, charged in. Dee deflected his punch with a swinging left hand and slammed the lumbering man in the groin with his right. Swiftly, Dee spun behind him, executing a crashing elbow strike to his head. The moaning man dropped to his knees, hands between his legs.

Dee fixed his gaze upon the remaining two members of the gang, prepared for the next attack. The pair looked at each other. As one they turned tail and dove into the crowd.

IT WAS AT this point that, pushing through the spectators, I finally reached Dee, and thus am now able to continue my narration.

I found Dee standing over the supine figure of a thin, cowering young Englishman—none other than the man who had stumbled into us. Four other men, more bruisers than he, lay on the cobbles in various states of disarray, while two more toughs could be seen slinking away through the crowd.

"Please, sir!" the quaking young man said. "I didn't mean no 'arm! Your friend there"—he nodded at me—"'e was just such easy pickings. And I 'aven't eaten a proper meal in days, 'ave I?" From his position on the stones he reached out to Dee, my wallet prominently in his hand.

Dee took the wallet and said, "Is it your habit to commit a crime each time you're hungry?"

"It ain't an easy life, sir."

"No," said Dee. "I imagine it isn't. I should summon the constabulary on behalf of my friend here."

"Oh, no, please, sir! The nick don't suit me, that it don't."

"Does it not?" Dee gave the man a thoughtful look. "Well, there may be another way. If you were employed, I suppose you would have no reason to steal?"

"Oh, no, sir. If I could fill my belly with an honest day's labor—"

"You can. I am engaged upon an investigation of a serious nature. There will be certain information I'll need and you may be in a position to obtain it. If you bring me reports from time to time on subjects I'll ask about, you'll be rewarded. How does that sound?"

"Why, it sounds first-rate!" The thief jumped to his feet. "'Ow will I find you?"

"If I need you, I'll find you. What's your name?"

"Jim, sir. Jim Finney, but the lads call me Jimmy Fingers."

"And where do you live, Jimmy Fingers?"

"Silver Street, sir. In Stepney. Ain't that a joke? 'Aven't seen a piece of silver since I came there, that I 'aven't."

"All right, Jimmy Fingers. Now take this." Dee unsnapped my wallet's purse and took out half a crown. "Here's silver. Go fill your belly."

"Yes, sir! Thank you, sir!" The thief turned to go, and then turned back. "And may I say, sir, watching you fight and leap and swing through the air—even though it were me you was chasing—it were a privilege. Until I saw you was Chinese, I thought you was Spring'eel Jack 'imself."

"Who is that?" Dee inquired.

"Oh, come now, sir. Surely you'll 'ave 'eard of Spring'eel Jack, the Terror of London?"

"No," said Dee. "I haven't. Perhaps that's a deficit I ought to remedy. Come, Lao." He handed me my wallet and proceeded through the crowd. Yet again, I hurried after.

# CHAPTER EIGHT

"Dee!" I said as we hastened along the crowded street. "The half crown you gave that thief came from my purse."

"You offered him much more by making your wallet so tempting to steal."

I buttoned my jacket with the wallet inside. "You also suggested you could give him honest employment. I venture to say that young man hasn't spent a day in honest labor since he was in short trousers."

"The labor he'll do for me will be honest. On other occasions I've found that to be enough to start a man down a different path."

"You've employed lawbreakers before this?"

"Many times." I supposed I appeared as discomfited as I felt by this easy acceptance of iniquitous behavior, for he continued, "Successful thieves, Lao, tend to be knowledgeable and daring men. When these attributes are turned to honorable uses they can prove quite valuable." Dee looked me over. "Also, it's my practice to make use of whatever tools present themselves."

I wasn't pleased with the implications of that statement,

but I followed him as he stepped into the street and hailed a taxicab.

We soon arrived at the Mayfair home of Colonel Livingstone Moore, the buyer of the contents of Ma Ze Ren's shop. The house was a fine limestone structure on Berkeley Square, not perhaps the oldest or the grandest, but an imposing edifice nonetheless. Above the doorway loomed a large shield with a hippogriff rampant. On the door, a bronze lion's head held a ring in its mouth. The butler who answered Dee's use of this ring raised not an eyebrow at the sight of two Chinese on his master's doorstep. I had my university calling card at the ready and was, if truth be told, looking forward to whatever silver-tongued explanation Dee would offer for our presence. Beyond announcing our names, however, he needed none, for the butler took my card and, placing it on a silver tray, conveyed it and us through the entrance hall. Opening a door to a drawing room ornamented with Chinese goods and antiquities, he intoned, "Mr. Lao and Mr. Dee."

A portly gentleman in an old-fashioned smoking jacket rose from a wingback chair, removing a large gray cat unceremoniously from his lap. The cat took offence and stalked from the room. The gentleman lifted my offered card from the tray. "Thank you, Perkins," he boomed. "That will be all." The butler withdrew.

"Livingstone Moore," the gentleman said, at a volume well suited to being heard over the crash and clatter of artillery. "Colonel, Durham Light Infantry, retired." His blue eyes glittered and when he smiled, his side-whiskers parenthesized his fleshy lips. "Delighted to make your acquaintances. Always glad to meet a scholar, always glad. You're Lao?" He beamed at Dee.

"No," said Dee. "He is Lao. I'm Dee Ren Jie, at your service."

"Ah. The robe, that's what confused me. Chinese scholars, robes, you see. Well. I suppose you've come to see my collection? Happy to show my beauties, always happy."

I was about to correct the colonel when I realized I didn't know exactly why we'd come. Dee said, "Indeed, sir, that's a part of our purpose. We understand you to be quite a connoisseur of Chinese art."

"That I am, yes, yes." The colonel nodded sagaciously. "Quite the aesthetes, you Celestials. Impressive, I say. Come, let's start here." While his misuse of the word "aesthetes" grated on me as much as his form of address to us, I held myself in check as I supposed Dee wanted me to do. The colonel led us to a table by the window. For the next half hour he discoursed upon platter after brush painting, bowl after fan, bronze urn after clay horse. I followed Dee's lead and listened silently, though more than once I was forced to bite my tongue. I was no scholar of Chinese art, but I could tell the Tang from the Ming, differentiate a Yongle reign mark from that of a later period, distinguish between an incense burner and a wine cup. Colonel Moore seemed to have no such insight. Some of the items in his collection he described correctly, others in a garbled way that indicated his understanding of Chinese culture to be minimal at best. Nevertheless, he showed us around with a good deal of pride.

Finally, Dee said, "Thank you, Colonel, for this edifying tour. We won't take up any more of your time. You must be busy preparing for the arrival of your new acquisitions."

The colonel's eyebrows knit together. "New acquisitions?"

"The contents of Ma Ze Ren's shop."

"Ah! Ah, yes, of course. Terrible shame, that. A good man, Ma. Good man."

"Yes, it is a shame. I suppose the widow was too distraught to consider keeping the shop open."

"Oh, yes, quite. That's why I offered to buy the contents as one. Save her the burden of managing their disposition, don't you know. You'd think, being married to a Chinaman—but no, poor girl has no idea, when it comes to Chinese antiquities she can't tell a hawk from a handsaw."

*Nor can you*, I thought to myself.

Dee said, "But the young shop assistant—he seemed knowledgeable. She gave no thought to keeping the shop open under his management?"

I fancied I saw the colonel's eyes flash, but perhaps not, as his manner remained affable. "I really couldn't say. Always struck me as unreliable, that fellow. Running off to lectures here and there. Probably a Bolshevik, a Chinese Bolshevik, yes, that's it. No, no, better this way, much better. Well, gentleman, if there's nothing else?"

"No, nothing," said Dee. "Thank you, Colonel. We'll be off."

And off we were.

"WELL, LAO," SAID Dee, as we walked, "what did you make of that?"

"The man's a fool. Connoisseur my foot! Chinese goods are all the rage in London and so he amasses them. His collection is probably the talk of his club, where men as ignorant as he discuss his treasures in weighty tones. When the fashion winds shift I wager he'll sell everything and collect the art of the Bantu or the Cherokee or whatever craze follows next."

"I don't disagree. But as relates to our investigation?"

I thought back. "I'm sorry," I said. "I don't see—"

"No, I thought not. It didn't strike you as odd that I had to remind him of his new acquisitions? And when we met Li Zi Rong at the shop, did you notice anything about him that implied he might be a Bolshevik?"

"Rather the opposite," I admitted. "He seemed keen to keep up the shop's capitalist business. But Dee, what does all this mean?"

"I don't know. It's important, when investigating, not to make judgments on the basis of incomplete information."

We walked on, discussing the incongruity between the fashion in England for artifacts of Chinese antiquity and the present-day striving in China for modernity. This discussion absorbed us until Dee stopped. I looked around; we'd walked for some time and without my noticing the change, we had crossed into Whitechapel. Puddles stood on the shadowed streets and the smells of old cabbage and rotting fish permeated the air.

"Why have we come here?" I asked. "What are we investigating? This area is most unsavory."

"We're investigating nothing. I was thinking to change into European dress. This is my hotel." Dee pointed to the building outside of which we stood. Its peeling paint, canted staircase, and general ramshackle appearance did not bode well for the interior, or for the nature of the other guests.

"Dee! Why here?"

Dee's smile was wry. "I'm a Chinese who needed lodgings in London. Hotels at this season are in demand and hoteliers are able to pick and choose their guests. This was all I could find. The current fashion for our art does not, it seems, translate to a fashion for our persons."

"How well I know that!" I replied. "But really, Dee. You cannot stay here. I shudder to think of the state of the rooms, nor can I imagine the meals are palatable." I paused in thought. "Why not prevail upon the Russells? I'm sure they'd be delighted to have you as a guest."

"Very possibly. But as the circumstances under which you and I met would indicate, investigations can be thorny things.

The Russells would, I'm sure, affect to take no notice of any disrepute my work might bring them, but I won't allow it."

"I see." A fishmonger's lorry rumbled by, swaying side to side on the uneven pavement. A half-grown cat, ribs prominent, dashed across the street. I looked once more at the decrepit building before us, and I shuddered.

I had known Dee for less than a day. During that time I had been in a jail cell, got involved in a fight, and had my wallet lifted. I had also had dinner with Bertrand Russell, and had met an Englishwoman who had clearly loved a Chinese man, dead though he now was. Thinking about that last filled me with such buoyant hope that before I realized it I had come to a decision.

"I lodge in Bloomsbury with Mrs. and Miss Wendell," I told Dee. "My rooms are quite large enough for two. You will share them as long as you are in London."

"No, Lao, I couldn't—"

"Yes, Dee, I insist. I shall go now to make things right with the ladies. You take what time you need to pack up your possessions. Here is the address. I'll expect you in an hour."

# CHAPTER NINE

I hurried off to the little house by the British Museum, absurdly pleased at the idea of sharing my rooms with a fellow Chinese. The Chinese population of London tended to break down into two groups: students, who were younger than myself and from such wealthy and powerful families that they could afford to indulge in the radicalism—indeed, the proto-Bolshevism—shaking China in those years; and sailors and dockworkers, the uneducated sons of peasants who had boarded ships in the hope of escaping the poverty of home, and now lived in the poverty of a foreign port. Of course there were also a few dozen shopkeepers, like Sergeant Hoong and Ma Ze Ren, and a small number of restaurant owners, men of business, and even performers; in addition, a handful of academics like myself, and the diplomats of the legation. But among none of these had I, with my natural reticence, found a companionable spirit. I had been lonely; and though Dee's manner could be haughty and the pathways of his mind were still a mystery to me, I found, to my surprise, I'd been enjoying our time together.

As I walked I gave thought to how I would introduce the

idea to Mrs. and Miss Wendell. Mary, I was sure, being caught up as she was in the affairs of the millinery shop where she worked and the church where she worshipped, taught Sunday school, and sang in the choir, would have no objection. Mary, however, was not the decision-maker in this regard. I settled upon a plan and began its implementation as soon as I had hung my hat in the hall.

"Mrs. Wendell," I hailed, entering the drawing room. "And Mary! How nice to see you both." The little dog came running over, madly wagging his entire back half. I rubbed his head. "And Napoleon," I added. "I trust you're all well?"

Both ladies smiled, Mary's impish grin sending arrows to pierce my heart. "Quite well, thank you, Mr. Lao," the mother replied. "And you are, also?"

"Indeed!" I sat on a brocaded chair. "I'm quite pleased. I've run into an acquaintance. A judge."

"Oh, my, Mr. Lao. Yesterday an Honorable, and today a judge. You will soon be too grand for us."

"That will never be the case, Mrs. Wendell," I said, not sure if the lady was serious. "As a matter of fact, I was saying to the judge not an hour ago how fortunate I am to lodge with two ladies of such style and refinement."

"Why, Mr. Lao." The mother blushed, as the daughter laughed a silvery laugh.

"Style," as concerned Mrs. Wendell, might have been an exaggeration. Her skirts, cinched at the waist, rode barely four inches above the ankle, and dark blues and browns were her shades of choice. Her shoes were of the Oxford type, black, with sturdy, low heels. I suspected, aside from the token adjustment in length, that her garments differed little from those she had worn before the war.

Mary was a separate case entirely. The mannequins in Selfridge's window, re-garbed monthly though they were, followed no more closely the fashion of the moment. She favored dresses that fell loosely from shoulder over torso and hips, ending a scant three inches below the knee. Their jolly plaids, tender pastels, and bow-trimmed striped fabrics set off her vivacious silhouette in a way that would make any man's heart flutter.

Mine was fluttering at the moment, equally from trepidation as admiration, as I went on. "Now I must tell you, the judge—and I—are in need of the assistance of you two fine ladies."

Mrs. Wendell's eyebrows went up. "What assistance could we possibly offer a judge?"

"Regrettably, he has found no place to lodge," I said. "As he will be in London for no longer than a fortnight, I thought I might prevail upon you to allow him to share my rooms."

"How is it that he can find no place?" Mrs. Wendell narrowed her eyes in suspicion. "London is full of hotels large and small."

"True," I said. "But sadly, some have turned him away, and those that will have him are quite beneath his station."

"Why would a judge have been turned away?"

"It can happen," I said, "if the judge is Chinese."

Mrs. Wendell lifted her chin and pursed her lips, her expression telling me she had found her suspicions confirmed.

Mary, however, gave out with a tinkling laugh. "A Chinese judge!" she said. "Whoever heard of such a thing? Your country has judges, then, Mr. Lao?"

"Of course we do." Such sweet ignorance! "The legal system of China is quite ancient and sophisticated. In the days before the reign of the first Qin emperor—"

"Oh, Mum, let's do it! A Chinese judge, in our own home. How exotic!"

"Mary, please!" said Mrs. Wendell. "No, I'm sorry, Mr. Lao. I don't think such a thing will be possible."

"I would, of course," I hastened to add, "expect to pay an increase in rent for the time Judge Dee is here, to cover the cost of any additional burden his presence creates. Also"—it occurred to me to say—"the judge is a friend of the Honorable Bertrand Russell. It was he who introduced us." I did not think it necessary to add, *Only yesterday, and in a jail cell.*

On hearing these two pieces of news, Mrs. Wendell stayed silent for some moments, petting the dog, who had jumped into her lap. "Mr. Lao," she finally said, clearly lacking her daughter's enthusiasm for the idea, "this judge—he does not wear his hair in a pigtail, I suppose? Or keep his fingernails long and sharp?"

"Certainly not." I attempted not to bridle at this offensive image. "He is a representative of Modern China. As am I."

"Oh, Mum! You must!" Mary exclaimed. "The judge is respectable, Mr. Lao promises"—she winked at me, and I felt my cheeks redden—"and it would be an act of Christian charity to give the poor man a place to lay his head. It's only temporary, isn't that right, Mr. Lao?"

"No longer than a fortnight," I asserted again. "Perhaps less."

Mrs. Wendell continued to look displeased.

I said, "Let me propose this. I have invited Judge Dee here and he will arrive"—I lifted my watch from my waistcoat pocket—"very soon. If after you've met him you find him in any way objectionable, you may, of course, send him packing. I am confident, however, that you will discover him to be a man of education and refinement. Much like myself."

Before the ladies could respond, the brass knocker on the front door sounded three jaunty raps.

"Don't trouble yourselves, I'll go," I said. Scooping up Napoleon, who was running toward the noise with warning yips, ready to discharge his guard-dog duties, I hurried into the hall and opened the door.

It was, as I expected, Dee who stood before me, but a Dee transformed. He had washed off the dirt of the day's adventures to the point of burnishing his skin. His carefully combed hair sat beneath a fashionable fedora which itself complemented his suit-and-tie ensemble and wingtip shoes. As in the jail he had become first a half-blind scholar and then a fair representation of myself, here on the Wendells' doorstep he was a cheerful, strong-jawed, respectable man of the modern Chinese variety. He held a large leather valise in one hand and a bouquet of irises in the other.

"Best behavior, now, Dee," I whispered as Napoleon bared his teeth at the stranger. "Mrs. Wendell is not convinced."

Leaving Dee's hat and valise in the hall, we entered the parlor. I deposited the dog on the carpet and he ran to Mrs. Wendell, leaping into her lap to protect her from danger.

Dee beamed a glowing smile at the two ladies and presented his flowers to the elder.

"Ah, Mrs. and Miss Wendell," he said, his English now the posh tones of the Oxbridge-educated—very like Bertrand Russell's. "I am Dee Ren Jie. This is an honor. My friend Lao has told me so much about you. He failed, however, to fully communicate your loveliness, and how much daughter resembles mother."

Mrs. Wendell blushed as she accepted the flowers. I could see her opinion on the lodging question was being swayed. My eyes, though, were on Mary, whose own eyes seemed to have come alive in a new way at the sight of Dee.

"Mary, put these in a vase, will you?" the mother—whose resemblance to the daughter was more evocation than fact—requested. "Mr. Dee, or I suppose I must call you Judge Dee? Please come and sit."

Dee smiled again. "I am a judge in my own country, but I have no titled position here. Mr. Dee is quite appropriate." He sat, crossing one elegantly trousered leg over the other.

I sat also, though I suspected that had I left the room my absence would not have been noticed, so captivated were the ladies by Dee's broad shoulders and easy gallantry. Mary did leave the room, as it seemed to me reluctantly, to return almost immediately with the irises in the household's best cut-crystal vase.

"So, then, Mr. Dee." I could not fail to notice Mrs. Wendell's smile was warmer than the one bestowed upon me when I first made her acquaintance. "Mr. Lao tells us you are a friend of the Honorable Bertrand Russell."

"Mr. Russell and I have known each other for some time. We met while he was living in Peking, researching his book *The Problem of China*. I was able to render him some small service."

"Small service!" I said. "He credits you with nearly half the book! He told me so yesterday," I added, to remind the Wendells that I, too, knew Bertrand Russell.

"He is a generous man and a true friend of China."

"And what brings you to England?" Mrs. Wendell inquired. "It must be an important errand, to cause you to undertake such a long journey."

"Not so long as it might seem. I didn't come to London from China, but from Geneva. I've been attached to the Chinese legation to Switzerland for some time." As he smiled I could see Mrs. Wendell absorb this information, which implied—not by accident, I was sure—a certain diplomatic status.

"Geneva!" said Mary, clapping her hands together. "Do you simply devour the chocolates? In the winter, do you ski?"

It was thus that Dee came to share my rooms in Bloomsbury.

THAT FIRST EVENING, however, he did not share the Wendells' table. "I won't impose," said he to the ladies, after we'd got the rooms set up for two, with linens for Dee upon the daybed in the study. "You did not expect an extra mouth to feed, and I have some small errands to attend to. I'll take dinner out and return afterwards." He smiled at the ladies, bent down to pet the dog, and took his leave.

# CHAPTER TEN

Dinner with the Wendells that evening was a matter of ham and potato stew, bread and butter, and endless questions about Judge Dee. Unlike my co-lodger-to-be, I had no objection to British cuisine strong enough to risk offending my landlady by declining to eat her cooking. Of course I missed the tastes of home, but Mary's company at table was usually more than adequate compensation.

At that meal, however, I became exhausted with singing Dee's praises. The mother's questions were in the service of further allaying her apprehension about the new lodger. Mary's could clearly be chalked up to fascination.

"He was in France during the war?" Mary exclaimed, when I reached that part of Dee's biography. "A battlefield judge? How courageous! And you say he is famous in your country?"

"I said, 'well-known,'" I corrected. "Not, perhaps, famous."

The mother, for whom fame carried the whiff of immodesty so distasteful to the British middle classes, asked, "For what is he well-known, Mr. Lao?"

"He's said to have an unerring sense of justice and fair

play, paired with a dogged determination to find the truth of whatever matter is before him."

Mary said, "How wonderful!" but her mother took a different view.

"Are these qualities so rare in your country, then, as to make a man famous who has them?" she asked.

"By no means!" I replied heatedly. "China's long tradition of law and justice—"

Fortunately, for I felt myself on the verge of delivering a lecture, we heard Napoleon's sharp yapping and the sound of a key being inserted at the front door. Moments later Dee stuck his head in the dining room from the hallway. "Good evening, all. I won't disturb you," he said. "I'll just go up—"

"Oh, Mr. Dee, do stay and have coffee with us!" Mary insisted. "I'm anxious to hear about your wartime adventures."

A shadow crossed Dee's face, though I venture to say no one saw it but myself. He smiled and joined us at table, however, and as Mary poured coffee he began a tale of humor and derring-do.

After a second such account, begged for by Mary and followed wide-eyed by her mother, Dee pleaded fatigue and declared his intention once again to make his way upstairs. I thanked the ladies for an excellent meal and joined him in bidding them good night.

As we reached my rooms, Dee said, "Your landladies are exhausting, Lao."

"If you don't want to be in such demand, Dee, you ought not to be so charming. You've quite won them both over."

"The British are oddly vulnerable to charm. I've found that in England it's often the easiest path to one's objective. And hurts none along the way."

Dee and I went about our ablutions, with Dee returning

from the water closet with this remark: "Do you know, Lao, that in France the British forces referred to that room as a loo? They probably picked it up from the French soldiers, who with circumspection called it the 'lieu,' the French word for 'place,' but the Tommies found the connection between 'Waterloo' and 'water closet' highly comical, and used it to tease the French."

I regarded him. "Am I to understand you have a store of this type of intelligence, and will impart it at a moment's notice?"

"I'm afraid so." He sat on the daybed and from his toiletry bag extracted a bottle and a spoon.

"Dee!" I eyed the bottle. "Is that laudanum?"

"It is," he said calmly. "I prefer to smoke my opium when I can, but the aroma of the air in even the finest establishment for that purpose clings unmistakably to clothing. Had I returned scented with it I think the Wendell ladies would have found me considerably less charming."

"But Dee," I protested. "Smoking opium? Or taking it as laudanum, which is hardly better? Is this wise?"

"Wisdom does not come into it." He looked up at me, standing aghast in my nightshirt. "Stories of comedy and adventure aside, Lao, war is a bad business. The contracts of the Chinese Labour Corps guaranteed the men would not be required to work near the front, much less in actual battle, and having been hired as laborers, not soldiers, they had no weapons. But in the event, the contracts were ignored. Many men were injured—including Ma Ze Ren—and many killed. More than once I protested this situation on behalf of the men. More than once I was . . . disciplined for my protests, although no Western government had a right to lay hands on me."

"Oh, but I've seen you fight," I said. "Surely your martial skills could easily have kept you out of anyone's hands."

"Indeed. But had I refused British authority the British would have refused mine. At that point I'd have become useless. I'd been sent to France to serve my countrymen. My ability to do so rested on the British and the French acknowledging that my judgments were legitimate, even if they considered that my protests were not."

"So you submitted yourself to violence?"

"It would not have been my first choice of strategy, I assure you. I saw no other way."

"And the laudanum?"

"A British nurse, as an act of kindness, administered opium when I was in hospital. It was effective. But it had residual costs. As you see."

"But Dee," I said again. "Does this habit not . . . diminish the faculties?"

"You may judge," Dee responded. "We've been investigating together all day. Do my faculties, mental or physical, appear diminished to you?"

I had to admit they did not.

"Well, then," he said. He poured out a spoonful of the tincture and swallowed it, then did the same with a second. "Good night, Lao." After a moment's consideration he poured a third spoonful and swallowed that, too. With a small smile and a distant look in his eye he said, "Thank you for inviting me to share your rooms." Stretching out on the daybed, he opened a small book with a lurid cover.

"What are you reading?" I asked.

"The exploits of Springheel Jack, the Terror of London."

I retired then to my bedroom, closing the door between us. Even so, for some time before I fell asleep I could hear Dee cackling with laughter as, under the influence of his laudanum, he followed the escapades of a madman.

# CHAPTER ELEVEN

The next morning when I opened the door between our rooms I found Dee dressed, shaved, and continuing his reading. He looked up. "Ah, Lao! Are you ready for another day of investigating?"

"I must dress and have my tea first," I replied, perhaps a bit more irritably than I intended, "but yes, I'm looking forward to it."

"Are you?" Dee's eyebrows rose. "Fine, fine."

THE DINING ROOM was deserted when Dee and I entered. Mrs. Wendell came out from the kitchen with a pot of tea and a rack of toast when she heard us.

"Good morning, Mr. Dee," she said. "I hope you slept well your first night with us? Good morning to you also, Mr. Lao."

We greeted her and she poured tea.

"Has Mary left for the hat shop, then?" I asked casually.

"She's first gone to a meeting with Washington Jones, the music master at the church."

"Ah. Very dedicated to her choir responsibilities, Mary."

"Oh, yes," said her mother. "Oh, yes, very."

I beheaded the egg in my eggcup and began to eat. Dee drank a cup of tea and immediately poured himself another.

"Look at this." Mrs. Wendell placed a folded newspaper on the table. "A Chinese man was murdered yesterday."

Dee and I glanced at one another. Ma's murder was a week in the past, so it could not be he to whom the story referred. I craned to read the newsprint. It seemed a fellow called Ching, a dockworker, had last night got himself stabbed.

"I don't know what your people are up to, I really don't," Mrs. Wendell said, shaking her head. "A murder last week, and a riot at the jail, and now this. I tell you, an Englishwoman can't feel safe in the streets."

I was struck by the coincidence of timing in Ching's and Ma's deaths, but I couldn't let the lady's remark go unprotested. "Now, Mrs. Wendell," I said, "it's not Englishwomen who have been the victims of any of these crimes."

"Not yet, perhaps, but I'm sure that can be laid down to nothing but chance. Let some poor innocent cross the wrong path and I guarantee she'll soon learn what trouble is. Here," she said, "you don't know this Ching fellow, do you?"

"Of course not. Not all Chinese in London are acquainted, you know. Dockworkers like Ching—"

"I knew him," said Dee, who had been writing something in a notebook. He looked up from the newspaper and pushed his chair back. "Come, Lao. We have work ahead of us."

"Why, you've eaten nothing," Mrs. Wendell said as Dee went to the hall for his fedora. I scrambled to follow him, lifting my own bowler from its peg. "And you, Mr. Lao—one egg? No toast? Not a clementine? I'd hardly call that breakfast."

"I'm sorry, Mrs. Wendell. We mean no offense to your cuisine," Dee said. "But we must run. Thank you." And he was out the door, with me at his heels.

"Dee!" I said. "You knew that man?"

"Ching Pan Lu. He was in France with Ma Ze Ren and myself."

"My condolences, then."

"Thank you. Of course you noticed how he was killed."

"The article said he was stabbed."

Dee, still striding, turned his head to me. I must have looked mystified, for he continued, "The article made note, toward the end, of the jagged nature of the wounds. You did read that far?"

"Of course I did. The writer speculated that fact implied a great deal of anger on the part of the killer."

"The writer is incorrect." Facing once again the direction of our travel, he said, "The butterfly sword is an invention of the monks of the Shaolin Temple. In harmony with Buddhist teachings, the weapon was designed for parrying and disarming, not for killing. The blade is sharp only along half its length. It's a slashing weapon, not a stabbing one. If someone unfamiliar with the butterfly sword were to stab someone with it, the wounds would be . . . rough and jagged."

"Oh," I said, as the import of this intelligence dawned on me. "You believe, then, that Ching was killed with the same weapon that killed Ma?"

"I do." Dee increased his pace.

I did the same. "Where are we going?"

"Back to see Ma's widow."

.

# CHAPTER TWELVE

D ee and I made our way through the bustle and buzz that is London on a fine spring morning. This daily jumble of sights, sounds, and smells—lorries, buses, and motorcars rumbling and honking; schoolchildren laughing and calling on their way to their lessons; nannies crooning to their charges; men of business striding to workplaces; bakeries and florists' shops releasing filaments of fragrance into the still-clear air—filled me, as usual, with an agreeable expectancy, a sense of hope and options, very different from what I found in the streets of home. China at the time—much as now—was convulsed with revolution, rebellion, rending, reversing, and retrenching, producing nothing so much as uncertainty and a desire to keep one's head out of the line of fire. The future might indeed hold a good deal of promise, we thought then, but we could not see it from our position in the present. Much as now.

Dee, I was learning, generally preferred his own feet over other forms of transportation. As I hurried after him, I reflected that his physical training at the hands of Sergeant Hoong's father had perhaps given him a different understanding of the nature of walking from my own conception of the process. I was well pleased whenever we were forced to halt for a bus or a lorry to rumble past, opportunities I seized upon to catch my breath.

I was never able, however, to feel sufficiently restored to hold a conversation, and so was unsure what Dee intended our interview with the widow to produce. Thus when we arrived at Ma Ze Ren's shop in Limehouse I determined I would be content to observe.

Which, I was sure, would fit in with Dee's preference.

And much there was to observe. Sweating men carried the widow's furniture, trunks, and boxes down the narrow staircase and loaded them onto a removals lorry, under the supervision of the shop assistant, Li Zi Rong. The widow herself, seated on a chair outside the shop, watched with interest but left the instructing of the men to Li, who was efficient and decisive. Two of the laborers were Chinese and the third, if one could tell from the vocabulary of his muttered curses, was Irish. Li switched back and forth between Chinese and English with admirable ease.

"Good morning," Dee said, sidestepping a chest of drawers being juggled by the two Chinese workers.

"Mr. Dee!" said the widow. "And Mr.—Lao, is it? How nice to see you both. Forgive me if I don't rise. I'm not feeling myself this morning."

"Of course," said Dee. "Good morning to you, too, Li Zi Rong."

"Good morning, gentlemen. You've found us at rather a busy time, I'm afraid. Mrs. Ma is traveling by train to Norfolk later in the day."

"Yes, I know. That's why we've come now, hoping to catch you." Dee addressed himself to the widow. "We won't interfere with your work, but I do have a question, if I may?"

"Of course."

Dee withdrew his notebook from his jacket pocket. "I have here three names. Could you tell me, please, if you recognize any of them?"

Mrs. Ma leaned closer to see what was written on the page. Her pale brow furrowed. "I think they sound familiar, but I can't be sure. Possibly they were friends of Ze Ren's."

"Would you know where I might find any of them?"

"No, I'm sorry. Ze Ren's friends would come to the shop, or we'd meet them at restaurants or nightclubs for an evening out. I never knew their homes or workplaces. Is it important?"

"It might be," Dee said, "but please don't worry. Li Zi Rong, may I ask you to take a moment and look over this list as well?"

Wiping his brow, Li looked at the paper. His eyes meet Dee's and he dropped his voice. "I don't know any of them," he said softly, glancing at Mrs. Ma, "but I read in this morning's newspaper that a man named Ching Pan Lu was murdered yesterday."

"Yes, I know," Dee replied, also quietly. "He was stabbed. Most likely, with a butterfly sword."

"Was he?" Li's eyes widened. "Then the killings must be related, don't you agree?"

"I'm sure they are. But you have no idea where any of these men might be found?"

"No, I'm sorry."

"Very well," Dee said. "We'll explore other avenues." Raising his voice to its normal tones again, he said to the widow, "Mrs. Ma, I wish you the most pleasant of journeys. I hope your good health returns soon."

"Thank you, Mr. Dee."

"Have you an address in Norfolk where I might contact you when I've made the arrangements for Ma Ze Ren's body?"

"No, I'm afraid I don't have a new home yet." She smiled weakly. "Perhaps I can get in touch with you?"

"You can reach me in care of the Chinese legation here in London."

"I shall do that, then. Thank you again for being so kind."

I echoed Dee's wish for Mrs. Ma's return to health and we bid the two goodbye, to the tune of grunting workers and thumping boxes.

"Well, Lao," Dee said as we walked away. "What do you think?"

"I don't envy the lady the necessity of traveling in her condition."

"No, nor do I," Dee said. "In her condition. Now, Lao, as Mrs. Wendell observed when we left this morning, I have eaten nothing. You yourself were wrenched away from your accustomed breakfast. Allow me to make it up to you. I'm sure you know the area well enough to recommend an establishment where we might take a meal. My only requirement is the cuisine must be Chinese. I've been in England for only three days and I've had quite enough of British food for a while."

Pleased that Dee was asking me for advice, I responded, "It's a bit early for the larger restaurants to be open, but there's a small, pleasant shop three streets over that does a creditable job on noodles, congee, and the like."

"Just the thing." Dee rubbed his hands. "Let us stop in on Sergeant Hoong briefly and then head directly there."

Hoong's emporium stood not far off our route. We were greeted with a wide smile by the proprietor.

"Well, Judge Dee! Mr. Lao! Good morning to you. Come in, have a cup of tea."

"I'm sorry, Sergeant Hoong, but we're following a trail unswervingly. It leads to breakfast. Will you join us?" said Dee.

"Then I'm equally sorry. I'm awaiting a delivery from the docks. What progress have you made in your investigation?"

"We've made some, indeed. Perhaps you can help us now. Do you know any of these men?" Dee showed Hoong the notebook page.

After a moment: "I do not. Ching Pan Lu—is this the man who was killed yesterday?"

"Yes. I'd very much like to speak to these other two men if they can be found."

"Well then," Hoong said, taking out a pen and paper and copying down the list—but into Chinese characters, "you gentlemen go off to breakfast while I wait for my goods. If I learn anything I'll let you know."

"Very well." Dee smiled. "Thank you, Sergeant Hoong."

"Judge Dee," said Sergeant Hoong, also smiling. "It's a pleasure to have you in London."

THE TEA SHOP to which I led Dee was one of my favorites in London. Not that the city presented one with a broad array of Chinese cafés from which to choose. Of those available, however, Wu's Garden offered the best food in the most agreeable surroundings. It was popular with London's Chinese academics, merchants, and diplomats, and also with a certain class of Britisher whose conception of the Chinese race, though usually far from accurate, had at any rate moved on from the devious and debased villain of Sax Rohmer's stories. Though it was said that Sax Rohmer himself took the occasional meal here at Wu's Garden.

Dee and I seated ourselves at a table under a paper lantern. Painted scenes of ducks and drakes, pine trees, and peony flowers covered the walls. The scent of noodle broth and the sound of clicking chopsticks reminded me satisfyingly of home. "Ah, Lao," said Dee, sniffing the air. "I believe you've chosen wisely." He perused the day's menu, written out in quick calligraphy on paper strips tacked to boards hanging from the molding. Some of the dishes were also listed in English for the benefit of the British clientele, which at the moment included two tables of office clerks; a table of three well-dressed ladies attempting to be discreet as they glanced around at and whispered about the exotic surroundings they had been liberal-minded enough to brave; and a middle-aged gentleman sitting with a younger man at the far end of the room, finishing a meal, their table a wreckage of bowls and bones. The Chinese diners varied from a table of diplomats in their bespoke three-piece suits to two Chinese opera stars, he in a midnight blue velvet jacket and red tie and she in a green silk frock that set off her porcelain skin and was short enough to show a bit of knee as she sat.

The waiter came with tea and Dee requested the menu items that appealed to him. I poured for Dee; he tapped the table with one finger in response, as has been done in China since the days of the Qianlong Emperor. "Dee!" I said. "You have no idea what joy it brings me to see you do that. It's a habit of which I've had to break myself, as table-tapping in England is not a sign of thanks, but a bad-mannered request for more. Mrs. Wendell used to think it rude of me to demand more tea, as though I considered my cup not full enough."

"Did you explain the custom to her?"

"Yes, of course, to both ladies. Mary thought it charming. Still, one does get weary of changing one's habits, and certainly one wearies of explaining things to the British."

"Yes, one does. Ah! Here are our jiaozi."

I allowed Dee one entire beef-and-carrot dumpling and a bite of a second before I said, "Look here, Dee. That list you showed Mrs. Ma and Li Zi Rong, the list Sergeant Hoong copied from you. You wrote it out when you saw Ching Pan Lu's name in the newspaper. Who are the men on it?"

Dee finished his second dumpling as the leek cakes and dried tofu skins with seaweed were delivered to our table. "Those men," he said, reversing his chopsticks to lift a square cake onto his plate, "are the other three who, along with Ma Ze Ren, came to London from the trenches of France. Now two of the four, Ma and Ching, have been killed—identically."

"Is it possible," I said, "that some madman is going about killing Chinese men, and happened upon two who knew each other? Having killed Ma and stolen the dao, he then went on to find another man to kill, and the connection between the two men is coincidental?"

"I suppose that hypothesis must be considered," said Dee. "In that case, another man may shortly turn up dead. Possibly you or I."

"I should like to see him attempt it!" I said stoutly. "I can assure you—"

"Excuse me, gentlemen," said a new voice, in the accents of American English. Dee and I looked up to see the middle-aged man who had been breakfasting across the room. He wore a sharp beard and a black velvet jacket. A cravat wrapped his throat and a sea of black hair waved atop his head. The younger man beside him was clean-shaven, sandy-haired, and handsome of face, if a bit haughty of bearing. His pale worsted suit, in contrast to the other's theatricality, was of this year's fashion, and his white collar spotless. His French cuffs, also dazzlingly white, were set off by rather plain gold cufflinks.

"I'm Ezra Pound," the bearded man said. He spoke as if he needed no other introduction, as indeed he did not. Though he had abandoned London for Paris a few years earlier, the shadow Pound cast in the literary world here remained long.

"Mr. Pound!" I started to rise. "This is an honor." In truth I found Pound's translations of classical Chinese poetry took rather too many liberties, but the man was inarguably a great poet in his native tongue.

"No, don't get up, gentlemen. This is Roger Whytecliff." He indicated his companion. "He is a viscount or some such." Pound waved away Whytecliff's claim on the British peerage. Whytecliff, for his part, seemed to find this amusing. "More important, he's a poet. He was rather a protégé of mine when I lived here in London. We spotted you across the room, Mr. Lao, and wanted to come pay our compliments. We attended your university lecture of a fortnight ago. 'China in the Great War.' We're both admirers of your culture. Whytecliff is a collector of porcelains and paintings—"

"Jade also," said the younger man offhandedly. "And the occasional bronze."

"Quite." Pound continued to address me. "We found your comments intriguing, Mr. Lao. Though I, and I believe I speak for Whytecliff also"—Pound looked to Whytecliff for confirmation but went on without waiting for the younger man to supply it—"find myself uncomfortable with the spirit of rebellion and the disregard for the glories of China's past that we see in the founding of the Republic and more recently in the May Fourth Movement. If it's true, as you said in your remarks, that the eyes of the leaders of that movement were opened to the ways of the Occident by the men of the Chinese Labour Corps as they returned home, then I fear China will have reason to regret that those men ever left."

Dee's face betrayed no emotion, but I felt I must speak. "But sir," I said, "with all respect, would you have China remain in the past while the Western world races full speed into the promising future?"

"If the alternative is to throw upon the ash heap the beauty, grace, and complexity of five thousand years of Chinese culture, then yes, I believe I would."

"Indeed," agreed Whytecliff. "I've seen nothing made in China since the establishment of the Republic that rivals any art produced before that. Not a bowl or a bracelet that I'd add to my collection."

"Although," Pound said drily, "perhaps, Whytecliff, if you spent less of your time in gambling halls you'd be able to spend more of your wealth on a better class of treasure."

Whytecliff rolled his eyes; this was obviously a familiar scolding from Pound. "If I, the Viscount Whytecliff, were to be found unfamiliar with the newest games sweeping London—at present, Mei-jongg," he said to Dee and myself, "a fast-moving contest whose cards are beautifully painted and depict various picturesque locations throughout China—no, the shame of it would be too much to bear. But you needn't worry about my means, Pound. The straits I'm in are temporary. I've proposed marriage to an unappetizing American, Miss Clarissa Porter. She'll marry me for my title and I her for her money. We'll be very happy together, I'm sure."

Now it was time for Pound to roll his eyes. "Whytecliff's weaknesses—and his vanity—aside," he said, "and returning to our original subject, the overthrow of the emperor will prove to be the undoing of Chinese culture, I'm afraid."

I hardly knew how to respond, and was on the verge of pointing out the obvious—that the Republic had not been established for the purpose of producing art for export—but Pound smiled at his protégé, bowed to us in an old-fashioned, slightly mocking way, and said, "Good day, gentlemen." The two turned and took their leave.

Dee's eyes met mine. "Lao," he said with great seriousness, "I think you and I have earned a platter of ground pork chow fun after that." He beckoned to the waiter and requested the dish. "He is a famous writer, is he not, this Mr. Pound?" he asked after the waiter had gone.

"Indeed. A famous lover of China, also. Although apparently if given his way he would love us all the way back to the Xia dynasty."

"And the other gentleman? The viscount? He seems quite the model of young British manhood."

"Yes, I can well imagine him provoking appreciative, though of course discreet, glances from the young ladies he passes in the street."

"Or meets in the gambling hall. And he is a connoisseur of the art of our nation, also."

"Let us hope his connoisseurship is on a higher level than that of Colonel Livingstone Moore."

Dee smiled and shook his head. "Ah, well. Their ignorance only reflects upon them. We have work to do, Lao. And," he said, turning his attention once more to the dumplings, leek cakes, and seaweed-draped tofu, "food to eat."

# CHAPTER THIRTEEN

The platter of sizzling noodles arrived quickly thereafter. Dee and I made short work of it and whatever remained of the other dishes. We swallowed the rest of the tea and Dee settled the bill.

"Thank you for a fine breakfast," I said. Leaving Wu's Garden, we exchanged the smells of noodle broth and roast meats for the scents of the river and the rotting sewers along the streets of Limehouse.

"Thank you, Lao, for introducing me to a place in this fine city where we can get such a breakfast. Now if I'm not mistaken, we can continue our investigation."

"How are we to go about finding the men on your list?" would have been my question, but Dee was already nodding in the direction of the answer, which walked toward us in the person of Sergeant Hoong.

"Ah, Sergeant. Your goods have arrived, then?"

"Three kinds of tea, two of ginseng; pepper, soy sauce, wood ear fungus, dried wolfberries; various bamboo cooking utensils and a number of woks; bolts of silk in black and red; and a crate of trousers of the type the seamen like to wear. All waiting to be shelved, but I thought your errand more urgent."

"I'm grateful. Have you had success?"

"Only with one name so far. But he might lead to the other. Guo Song. I'm told he works in an opium establishment not far from here."

"Does he now?" Dee smiled. "Guo was always enterprising. I confess to looking forward to seeing him again. Lead the way, Sergeant Hoong."

"But Dee—" I protested.

"Lao, I know your views on opium. If you'd prefer not to accompany us, you and I can meet later in the day. Though I can't say when that would be or where my talk with Guo might lead."

"But Dee," I repeated, and then, crossly, "oh, very well," for I did not intend to be shut out of the investigation just when it seemed progress might be made.

Hoong led us past laundries and butcher shops, fishmongers and hardware stores, to a corner where a Chinese cobbler sat on the curb in front of an Irish barber's. Hoong and the cobbler nodded to one another and Hoong turned down the narrow alley. From behind the various tumbledown doors came the smells of cooking. We walked through the intertwined aromas of the cuisines of many races, for though most of London's poor Chinese lived in Limehouse, the residents of the area, though all poor, were by no means exclusively, or even predominately, Chinese. To our ears came the sounds of argument, of laughter, of talk, of song, in languages as various as the cooking scents.

Hoong stopped at a door near the alley's end. He rapped a patterned knock, and when the small wooden window in the door was slid over he said, "Qi yu." This was apparently the watchword for admittance, because the door opened to us. We slipped inside.

The sickly sweet smell overwhelmed me immediately. Neither Dee nor Hoong seemed even to notice it, and it occurred to me to wonder whether Hoong, also, was an opium user. I hoped not; the every-Chinaman-a-dope-fiend notion that reigned in England at the time was hard enough to counter without finding out that, among those Chinese of my acquaintance, it was true.

A Chinese man of indeterminate age, small, obsequious, and none too clean, emerged from under a staircase that disappeared up into darkness. He came to us holding out three pipes. With a thin smile he waved his hand toward a set of couches in an alcove. I looked about me. Of the patrons sprawled in various states of disgrace, no more than half were Chinese. Though it does me no credit, I confess I felt pleasure at seeing this. I decried the indulgence in opium in any of its forms by any user; and yet, as the drug had been forced upon China by the British sixty years earlier, causing inestimable damage to my countrymen, I could not help but be bitterly gratified to see Britishers falling prey to it, also.

Dee glanced at the pipes and shook his head, though it seemed to me not without regret. "Thank you," he said politely to the small man, "but not today. I'd like to speak with the proprietor, if I may."

The man surveyed us, his smile fading, and glanced across the room. Catching the eye of a man tall, pale, and thin, he inclined his head at our trio. The tall man wore merchant's dress, as did Sergeant Hoong, but unlike Hoong's serviceable cotton, this man's tunic and trousers were silk. He crossed the room without haste.

"I'm Chin Peng Da," he said, wrapping left hand over right and lifting his hands to each of us in turn. "Is there some way I can help you gentlemen?"

"Dee Ren Jie," said Dee as we all returned the gesture.

"These are my companions. We need a word with one of your employees, an old acquaintance of mine. Guo Song."

Chin regarded us, Dee clothed in the latest London fashion, myself a bit more conservative but still wearing Western dress, and Sergeant Hoong, older than we and in his worn shopkeeper's garb. "I'm sorry, sirs. No one of that name works here."

"I'm sorry, also, but that isn't the truth. I assure you we wish Guo no harm. Our errand is urgent. Please don't delay us."

"I have no desire to delay you, but I can't help you."

"Sir. I am an official of the Chinese government and I must speak to Guo Song."

Chin's lip curled. "Which Chinese government would that be?" he sniffed. "Cao Kun's in Peking, bought and paid for? Sun Yat Sen's in Guangzhou, isolated and useless? Wu Pei Fu's, wherever he may be this week? Or perhaps Zhang Zhuo Lin's, behind the scenes of all the others? No matter, gentlemen. Whichever of China's contending powers you represent, it has no authority here. This is England and no one named Guo Song is employed in this establishment."

"I'm afraid I must insist. As I said, we don't intend trouble for Guo Song. Nor for yourself, or any of your honored patrons." Dee looked around, as though recording in his head the names of the slack-faced clientele. Some of the habitués had not the wit even to notice us but others had begun to watch us with groggy suspicion. "However, you give us no choice. If you don't know Guo Song, it's possible one of your patrons might. Sergeant Hoong, ask that gentleman over there. Lao, approach that lady."

"You will do no such thing!" Chin snapped.

Dee had chosen two of the more aware Britishers. As Hoong stepped toward the indicated man's couch the fellow lurched up and stumbled out the door. I attempted to appear as menacing as Hoong and apparently I succeeded, for the lady, though she did not seem able to rise, cowered in fear before me.

"Stop this at once!" Chin commanded, but Sergeant Hoong started across the room toward another customer, who was already groping under his couch for his shoes. "I will not have this!" Chin shouted. "Rui! Fa! Show these gentleman out!"

A pair who clearly were not gentlemen arose from the shadows and marched toward us. Both were large; one was scarred on his face and the other missing a number of teeth. Dee and Hoong watched them with no change of expression. Then one laid a hand on Dee.

Dee reacted to the touch on his arm almost before it happened. Dropping his right foot back into a cross position, he entwined his left hand around the toothless assailant's arm like a python. When his hand reached the back of the man's neck he applied a vise-like grip, locking his shoulder and forcing him down. Dee sent his right palm crashing into the assailant's ear.

"Chang! Lu!" yelled Chin, the proprietor. "Take that one!" He pointed to Hoong, probably thinking that Hoong, being older, would be easy to defeat.

Dee called, "Sergeant Hoong! Subdue them without grievous injury. They may be hooligans, but they remain our countrymen, and furthermore they may have information important to us."

"Very well," Hoong called back. "I'll use Father's broken row palm." Hoong stood, feet planted in a wide stance, as the two thugs closed on him.

I moved to help Hoong but Dee waved me back. One of the thugs came fast at Hoong with a succession of left and right punches which Hoong first diverted. Then he trapped his opponent's hand. He rose up with a palm strike to the base of the man's jaw. While the thug was reeling Hoong extended his hand in a hooking position, captured the back of the hooligan's head, and dragged him down, finishing with a thrusting palm strike to the base of the skull.

Another attacker took a running leap and tried to pounce on Hoong. Hoong came in swiftly from underneath, catching the man on the throat and the groin with his tiger claws. The assailant hung suspended in the air. Hoong, shifting his body, threw the man across the room, where he crashed into a pair of bewildered opium smokers just rousing from their stupor.

From the corner of my eye I saw the scarred man rush at Dee. "Take care!" I cried. Dee spun and stunned the man with a heel kick to the center of the chest. The hooligan flew up into the air and landed on top of a tea table, smashing it to pieces.

I looked around to see if I could spot the next attack. Skulking in the corner was Chin, the proprietor, sucking his teeth in bafflement and anger. He barked a loud order. I assumed he was calling for more men. Not waiting to see himself obeyed, he bent to grab the leg of a shattered stool. Slowly, with an ugly smile, he walked toward me. I heard a door open upstairs and feet clatter along the hallway overhead. I prepared to defend myself.

In youth, being Manchu in a Han world, I had of necessity been a street fighter. Pugnacity, however, was not in my nature and I was never trained as Dee and Hoong had been. I understood and could even label the various techniques the two used, but I did not possess those skills myself. The battle yesterday at the jail had been my first physical confrontation in years. Now I was involved in a second skirmish in as many days.

"Bannerman!" Dee shouted, his eyes on Chin. "First dissipate his energy, then return it in kind!"

I nodded to acknowledge the instruction.

Chin swung at me several times with his makeshift club. Each time, I brushed the club away, diverting it side to side. Finally, perceiving that Chin was starting to breathe heavily, I shifted to my left and stepped in quickly with a short, high stance. I delivered a straight arrow punch squarely to Chin's nose. Chin stood staring at me in amazement, and I must admit I felt some of the same. Then his knees buckled and he crumpled to the floor.

I held up my fist and shouted across the room to Dee, "Success!"

Dee grinned. A moment later, still grinning, he swiveled, his attention drawn by a group of men galloping down the rickety stairs.

The first of them was armed with two daggers.

That man leapt toward Dee and slashed at him diagonally three times. Dee effortlessly slapped away each slash. With the third attempt the assailant spun around, trying for Dee's head with his left dagger, then his right. Dee blocked both strikes with a circular bridge hand. When the assailant spun again and slashed at the top of Dee's head and swiftly at Dee's feet, Dee ducked and jumped with the agility of a cat.

"Hurrah!" I called.

The assailant went red with fury. He sliced at Dee with both daggers. Dee intercepted his arms, spun him around and shoved him. Stumbling backward, he made one more attempt at Dee's head and then aimed a thrust at his thigh. Dee sidestepped, deflecting the thug's forearm with his shins. He caught the assailant's wrist and twisted his arm, forcing him to drop one dagger. The man turned and came at Dee with the other. Dee withdrew his torso and used both right and left hand to snap the wrist of the assailant, sending the second dagger flying. It landed with a *thunk* in the door.

Disarmed, the thug aimed a left-handed strike at Dee. Dee

captured wrist and elbow, digging his vice-like fingers into the joint for a dragon locking claw. Yanking the thug forward into a piercing heart kick, Dee dropped him to the ground. He lay in a heap and moaned.

As Dee glanced around for the next wave, I looked across the room to see Hoong making a clean sweep of two more assailants. One came at him with a right punch followed by a left kick. Hoong stepped back and smashed his forearm down on both punch and kick in a single chopping motion. His opponent stumbled forward. Hoong rose up and unleashed three enormous uppercut punches to the assailant's torso and chin. Teeth flew and the thug crashed down. Hoong gestured at the other toothless attacker laid out on the floor and said, "Now you're a matching set."

At that moment two more assailants charged at Dee from left and right, reaching for him simultaneously. He clutched both their arms, slid his hands down to the wrists, jerked them both in swiftly, then thrust a hand out to either side. He captured each man at the throat with the double eagle talon. The energy from their bodies drained under Dee's iron grip and they crumpled to the ground like rag dolls.

We three surveyed the room, on the alert for more attacks, but no one moved. Amidst the damage the couches stood empty. The patrons had all fled, with the exception of one who, smiling in his opium reverie, seemed oblivious to everything that had gone on.

"Gentlemen," said Dee, "I think we've made our point."

Righting a stool, Dee sat and slapped his hands onto his thighs. I did my best to tidy my clothing and smooth back my hair while my breath returned. Sergeant Hoong lifted a moaning Chin by the collar and dragged him across the floor to deposit him before Dee.

"Chin Peng Da," Dee said to the bloodied man, who peered

blearily up through the swollen eyes my blow had provided him. "In China I am a judge. In a situation such as this I would now pronounce sentence; and as you operate an opium establishment, refused a lawful request, and ordered your men to attack a government official without provocation, your sentence would be death." He paused. "In such circumstances, if you were to tell me where to find Guo Song, it might be possible I'd commute the sentence to one hundred lashes."

A whimper escaped the prisoner.

"However," Dee went on, "as you pointed out, this is England. Opium is not illegal here, so I must remove consideration of your trade from my verdict, thereby precluding a death sentence. As I'm in somewhat of a hurry—the more, now that you've delayed me—and even fifty lashes, the slow, deliberate way Sergeant Hoong delivers them, with the prisoner allowed time to fully experience each fall of the whip and then to wait in anxious agony for the sudden slash of the next," he paused again as the prisoner began to shiver, "even fifty lashes take a good deal of time. Thus I'd advise you to give me the information I require. If you do that, your sentence will be limited to the damage already done to your person and your establishment."

Chin opened and closed his lips but no sound came.

"But perhaps leniency doesn't interest you," said Dee. "Very well, then. Hoong, will you—"

"No!" the prisoner croaked. "Please! Oak Lane. A boarding house with a green door. Across the lane from a pub."

Dee stood. "Come, gentlemen. Chin Peng Da, I suggest you be civil to government officials in the future. It will save a great deal of trouble."

I walked behind Dee through the tangle of overturned and broken furniture, with Sergeant Hoong bringing up the rear. In case any of the toughs had not had quite enough I kept a vigilant eye. None of them made any motion toward us, however, and the only unexpected thing I saw was Dee, just before we reached the door, bending quickly over one of the abandoned couches. He emptied its two unsmoked opium pipes into his hand, wrapped the contents in his handkerchief, and slipped the folded cloth into the pocket of his pleated trousers.

# CHAPTER FOURTEEN

The gutters and coal smoke of Limehouse were as fragrant as fresh country air to me after the suffocating atmosphere of the opium room. As we walked toward Oak Lane, however, I was still bothered by something Dee had said.

"Sergeant Hoong," I asked, "do you really whip men in that slow, cruel way when carrying out a sentence? And fifty lashes, Dee—is this not excessive? For China to enter the modern—" I stopped because both men were laughing.

"I have never taken the whip to a man in my life," Hoong said.

"And whether or not he had," Dee said, "Sergeant Hoong and I have not seen one another in twenty-five years. I would have no idea of his methods. You'll find, Lao, that the threat of pain is often better than the thing itself as a technique of persuasion."

"Well," I said. "Well. I am relieved to hear it."

At the green-doored boarding house we found the landlady mangling a tub of washing in the street before her establishment. No technique of persuasion beyond the shilling in Dee's hand was required to induce her to mutter, "First floor, rear on the left," when Dee inquired after Guo Song. In fact, eyeing Dee's fine, if now slightly creased, clothing, she volunteered, "But I 'aven't seen the gent all day."

Dee handed her the shilling and we entered and mounted the stairs to the first floor.

The stale, close air inside the house was as unappealing as that in the opium room, though without the stench of iniquity. This was merely the scent of the poor, the ill-fed and unwashed, those whom life had tossed upon rocky, barren shores. That they had come to inhabit this sad cove was no fault of their own.

Except for Guo Song, who after all worked for an opium dealer.

Dee's rap upon the door to which we had been directed yielded no response. "Guo Song!" he called. "It is Dee Ren Jie. I must speak with you upon an urgent matter." When another knock and another call were also met with silence, Dee turned the knob.

The door swung open.

Dee put out a hand to stop Hoong and myself from entering. He made no move either until he had surveyed the room from the doorway. Then, grim-faced, he nodded to us and stepped inside. We followed.

A man lay sprawled across the bed in the small, untidy room. "Is this—"

"Guo Song," Dee affirmed.

I might have taken the man's stillness for sleep, or an opium stupor, if his shirtfront had not glistened with a wide stain of blood. Guo Song had been killed, and if I was not mistaken, with the blade of a sword.

I looked at Dee, who had gone pale. "He was . . ." Dee shook his head as if to clear it. "In the trenches, he would act the clown, to calm his fellows. He told stories, pulled pranks. He has—he had a younger brother. He was sending the boy to school with his war wages. Coming to London, he thought, was great good luck. It meant he could continue—" Dee drew a breath, uttered a curse, and turned from us. Head bent down, he placed his hands on the wall as though to steady himself. "He . . . They . . . Ma, Ching, now Guo! They survived the war, and thought that luck had found them. And now . . ." After a long pause, Dee turned and said bitterly, "Well, Lao, I suppose this puts paid to the coincidence theory."

I had to admit that it did.

Dee spoke again. "Sergeant Hoong, I'll call upon you in the shop in an hour or two. Lao, I'll find you later in the day."

"But Dee," I protested.

"But sir," said Hoong. "Are you well?"

"No, Hoong, I am not. I recommend you two slip out past the landlady without letting her catch sight of you. The less she remembers about any of us the better." Dee looked once more at his slain companion. Then he opened the room's single window, allowing in the powerful smell of stabled horses from the lane behind. Dee dropped from the window into the small rear yard and nimbly scaled the fence.

Sergeant Hoong and I exchanged a look, then did as Dee had suggested, creeping quietly down the stairs. From just inside the doorway Hoong tossed a stone from the street toward a tippler at the table outside the public house. It struck the man on the arm.

"'Ere!" the red-faced fellow said indignantly to one of his companions. "'Oo do ya think yer pokin'?"

"I never poked you, you old souse."

"You did and I'll thank you not to do it again!"

The landlady's attention turned toward this quarrel and Hoong and I made our escape.

AND WHAT OF Dee? For the answer to that question, I must again venture from the clear path of my own experience into the thicket of that which was told to me. As I relate what followed I'm confident you will find it somewhat bizarre, as did I. But though he was not averse to the use of falsehood in the service of an investigation, never in all our acquaintance did I know Dee to distort the truth in order to make himself appear more impressive. Rather the opposite, in fact. Thus I am forced to credit this tale as he told it, and I hope you are able to do the same.

DEE DROPPED FROM the window into the small rear yard and nimbly scaled the fence.

He made his way past four horses at their trough and into the stable. Waiting in the shadows until a young groom turned away, Dee slipped into an untenanted stall. From his pocket he withdrew the handkerchief holding the contents of the opium pipes from Chin's establishment. Using his thumbnail he cut a corner off one brown, viscid lump and placed the fragment in his mouth. After a moment he swallowed it down. Carefully rewrapping the remaining opium, he restored the handkerchief to his pocket.

Dee stayed in the shadows of the horse stall for some minutes, until, as he told me later, the visions from the trenches had begun to fade. For this was what had driven him from our company: the sight and smell of blood, the screams of men and the concussion of bombs, the pulse of mud and metal raining down. "These memories come upon me," he explained simply. "The opium pushes them back into darkness. For a time."

The sensations waning, Dee peered out from the stall. He could hear the groom in the yard talking to the horses. Dee walked quickly through the building to the stable door and out into the lane.

Crossing into Stepney some few minutes later, Dee inquired of a cockle and mussel seller as to the location of Silver Street. Reaching that place, he asked a boy playing with a whirligig whether he was familiar with Jimmy Fingers.

The boy stared at him. "Are you a Chinaman?"

"I'm Chinese, yes," Dee replied.

"Ain't never seen a Chinaman in such fine clothes," said the boy. "You look a proper gentleman, you do."

"Thank you, my boy. I have a gentleman's purse, also. I'll give you a shilling to lead me to the home of Jimmy Fingers."

"I'm yer boy for that, Mr. Chinaman," said the child, jumping up. Then he added casually, "But 'twon't do you no good, for he ain't there."

"Is he not? Where is he, then, do you know?"

"I do," the boy said slyly.

"Can you take me there?"

"I can. Will I get the shilling?"

"You will."

"Then"—the boy grinned—"follow me, Sir Chinaman."

The boy led Dee to another lane, where stood a pub, the Mermaid and Seahorse. The boy marched through the open door, announcing grandly, "Make way, make way! My Lord Chinaman, come to see Sir Jimmy Fingers!"

All heads turned. "What are you on about, young Bobby?" inquired the ruddy-faced woman behind the bar. The boy might have answered, elevating Dee to royalty, but a man stood from a group of others at a table by the wall.

"Mr. Dee!" said the man, who was indeed the young thief, Jimmy Fingers. "An honor, sir! You, Bobby, go on now."

Dee gave the boy the promised shilling and he ran off laughing.

"Lads, this is my employer, Mr. Dee," the thief then said to the three other young men at the table. They nodded, displaying various levels of suspicion and distrust. "Will you take an ale with us, sir?" Jimmy Fingers continued. "Or 'ave you come with a charge for me? I stand ready to do you any service!"

"The answer to both your questions," Dee said, "is yes. I'd be happy for an ale, and it would be my privilege to stand a round for you and your companions." This suggestion greatly increased Dee's stock with the men, who all agreed the offer was most generous and it was upon them not to be so rude as to turn it down. "In return," Dee said as he signaled to the barkeep for drinks, "I'd like you, Jimmy, and your friends if they are willing, to talk to me."

# CHAPTER FIFTEEN

Once Hoong and I parted, I went to the university, for I felt I had been neglecting my duties there. I applied my energies to correcting some short essays written by my students before the spring holiday upon the topic of "The Chinese in Britain Today." The work was not engaging, as I was the only Chinese person most of them had ever met. Their poor choices of characters to express their thoughts and the appalling calligraphy they applied to those they selected made me wish for distraction, with which I supplied myself by considering questions arising from the day's investigation. Not the least among these was, where had Dee gone? The answer to that, however, I was not to be granted until the following day, when the account I offer below, a continuation of Dee's adventure, was reported to me.

MORNING HAD GIVEN way to midday by the time Dee once more walked into Hoong's Limehouse shop.

"Dee!" said Hoong, turning from his shelves, where he'd been placing the goods he'd received earlier. "What's happened? Are you all right? Have you found anything?"

"Nothing, except a way to engage the Metropolitan Police Force in our investigation. I'll need some lengths of your new black silk, and a tailor. The tailor's work needn't be fine, but it must be durable. And quick."

"The silk's right here," said Hoong, pulling down a bolt. "And there's no swifter seamstress in Limehouse than Mrs. McCarthy in the next lane. I've been told, though I haven't seen it myself, that a newly acquired Singer foot-pedal machine is the secret to her speed."

True to Sergeant Hoong's account of her, Mrs. Moira McCarthy, an Irishwoman plump of figure, cheek, and hand, was prepared, once Dee had explained his requirements, to give the project her all. Her only comment on the unusual nature of the work was, "You're queer ones, ain't you, you Chinese?" She made this remark cheerfully as she measured, cut, and pinned.

"I expect so," Dee replied.

The lady called on her daughter, a lass of twelve, to help with the simple parts of the work, as Dee had urged speed. Dee retired to Sergeant Hoong's shop for a cup of tea. Less than ninety minutes passed before the young girl was at the door, requesting Dee's presence. Dee left with her for the tailor shop.

A quarter of an hour later, Sergeant Hoong finished serving a customer and, that gentleman having left, turned to replace on the shelf a bowl that had been rejected. When he turned again a figure all in black darkened his doorway, cape spread wide over outstretched arms. Black gloves hid its hands and its face was disguised by a black mask with a terrifying grimace fixed upon it.

"Who are you?" Hoong said in a quiet but ominous tone. He spoke in English, judging this odd figure unlikely to be one of his countrymen. He shifted his weight to balance on the balls of his feet, in case the stranger desired a violent encounter. "What do you want?"

"Oh, come now, sir," the masked stranger replied, the sound of a sneer ringing in his reedy voice. "Surely you'll 'ave 'eard of Spring'eel Jack, the Terror of London?"

"I have not. If you are he, you're preventing customers from reaching my shop."

"Oi! Can't 'ave that, can we?" With a cry, the black-clad man threw a paper-wrapped parcel at Hoong and vaulted up to grab hold of the beam overhead. He swung onto it and lay along it, his masked face leering down.

Catching the parcel easily, Hoong stared up at the creature. Then he slapped his sides and laughed. "Dee! Is this what you've made of my fine silk?"

The masked figure leapt lightly to the shop floor. He peeled off the mask and with it made a large, sweeping, Continental bow. "Spring'eel Jack, at yer service," he said, and it was, of course, Dee.

"A very effective costume," Hoong said, "though I can't say I understand the purpose of it. Nor for that matter do I follow the change in your speech. You talk now like one of the Cockney toughs who wander these streets, causing trouble when the mood strikes them."

"Oh, now, Sergeant, the lads ain't so bad. 'Twas from them I learnt this manner of talkin' and it cost me nobbut a few rounds of ale. But now I must be off. Three men have been murdered and the coppers don't think their deaths worth the paper to write home about them. No Chinese is about to convince 'em otherwise. But I'll wager they'll listen to Spring'eel Jack!"

With that Dee pulled the mask back on, said, "Keep that parcel in yer shop for me, Sergeant, there's a good bloke," and sped out the door.

UMBRELLA IN HAND (for the sky threatened rain), Captain William Bard stepped from the Limehouse police station, turned on the pavement, and strode resolutely along. It was that hour in the afternoon when a copper will be wanting a pint to wash away the troubles of the day. Captain Bard was making for the Copper's Beech, a pub whose cheeky name announced its friendliness to the Force.

He did not attain his goal.

As he reached the mouth of an alley, powerful hands grabbed his shoulders and yanked him backward into the shadows. Stumbling, Bard relied upon his umbrella for support. When he straightened and spun about he found himself facing an apparition: a hideous face topped a black-draped, caped being.

"Just a brief word with yer, that's all's I want," said the fiend.

"I'll not parley with the likes of you, whatever you are!" Bard's words were strong but his voice was not. He swung his umbrella as a club at the creature before him.

The creature stepped back, avoiding the umbrella with preternatural speed. It drew its palms together in front of its chest, as in prayer.

"'Ere, me copper, Jack doesn't want to fight yer, just to talk."

Bard swung the umbrella again. He missed as the creature stepped back once more, but he kept swinging. The fiend sighed. "Well, then, if I must." The prayerful hands suddenly thrust straight out, allowing the creature's forearms to parry the next two strikes.

Bard lunged into a straight-on stab. The black-clothed figure sidestepped, caught the umbrella on its inner forearm, and grasped it. "Captain Bard, come now, I ain't meaning to 'urt yer."

"Hurt *me?* I'll teach you about hurt, you villain!"

Bard tried to wrest the umbrella from his opponent's grip. The creature tugged back and with a foot sweep knocked Bard off-balance. Bard staggered and found the umbrella pulled from his hands. Catching his footing, he raised his fists in a boxing posture. "Come at me, then, ruffian! You'll find yourself dealing with the boxing champion of my secondary school!"

Bard launched a left jab and right cross, which the creature parried, using the umbrella like a staff. Then, rolling its wrist around the umbrella, it extended the handle and ensnared the inspector's ankle. One tug and Bard's legs flew out from under him. Landing unceremoniously on his posterior, he watched the fiend twirl the umbrella about. Bard found the umbrella's tip lightly touching his chest, just above his heart.

The masked creature spoke. "Surely I'm known to yer, Captain William Bard."

"That you are not," said Bard, breathing heavily. "But whoever you are, I'll have you up on charges for manhandling a member of the London force. I—" Bard's words stopped as the figure dug the umbrella deeper against his chest.

"Well, then, allow me to introduce meself. I'm Spring'eel Jack, I am."

"You never are!"

"I am, and yerself, Captain Bard, 'ave caused me considerable worries. A man lies dead not three streets from 'ere, and yet I see yer going off to the pub as though yer 'adn't a care in the world."

"What man? Dead where?"

"In Oak Lane, in a boarding 'ouse with a green door, on a bed in a room on the first floor. On the left in the rear, I might add, as I want to be 'elpful. What would be *most* 'elpful would be for yerself, Captain Bard, to investigate this death as is yer right and proper responsibility."

"And just who is this dead man in Oak Lane?"

"Guo Song was 'is name, when 'e was living." The creature stepped aside, allowing Bard to rise.

"Oh, bloody hell! A Chinaman? Another dead Chinaman?" Bard stood, dusting himself off. "Come now, Jack, or whoever you really are, I've had two dead Chinamen this week already. You can't seriously expect that I'll waste my time on a third." He reached to wrench his umbrella from the creature's grip.

Jack danced aside, laying hold of Bard's arm and twisting it behind his back. Bard cried out. Jack released the pressure slightly and said, "I expect that yer will do yer duty, Captain Bard. Investigate the death of this man—and the others. Or as sure as I'm whisperin' in yer delicate ear, more men will die."

Jack unhanded the inspector. Bard turned to face him, his countenance a sputtering, angry red. He poked a finger into the black-clad figure's chest. "I do not take orders from civilians, and certainly not from the likes of you, whoever you are. I'm tired and I want my pint. Your dead Chinaman will bloody well keep until tomorrow. Now move aside."

In a flash Jack grabbed the hand poking his chest and snapped the smallest finger back. A cracking noise and a yowl from Bard were simultaneously heard. "It ain't a bad break," said Jack. "Think of it like yer makin' an investment in them other nine fingers. Now, Inspector, go inspect! And keep in mind, Spring'eel Jack has his eye on yer!"

Jack vanished back into the shadows while Bard clutched at his injured hand.

From the rooftops Jack paralleled Bard's path. It led back to the Limehouse police station, from which, a few minutes later, two constables emerged, followed by Bard, his left hand now bandaged. Back then to Oak Lane, where Bard and the constables were met by the coroner's van.

Dee found it interesting, he reported to me in recounting

this tale, that Bard had chosen not to verify for himself that a body was in fact to be found before sending for the coroner.

"Well, Dee," I said on that occasion, "perhaps breaking a man's finger leaves him more willing to be convinced of the truth of your assertions. I feel I must ask, what became of the threat of pain being more efficacious than the thing itself?"

"The threat," Dee said, "was to the rest of Bard's fingers."

BUT THAT CONVERSATION came the following day. That evening, as the clouds began to spit rain, Dee, in Springheel Jack's black suit and cape, watched from the rooftop across the lane as the coroner's men took the body of Guo Song out through the green door.

# CHAPTER SIXTEEN

Driven by a heavy wind, the rain began in earnest. As the red taillights of the coroner's van disappeared through the storm, they mixed in the mind of Dee with the ambulances of the Western Front. The foot-slaps of people running for shelter became the sharp sound of rifle fire, and the sight of Guo Song on the stretcher transformed into visions of the torn and bloodied bodies of countless men, some European and some Chinese, some carried away across muddied fields and some abandoned to die where they fell.

"THESE RECURRING MEMORIES," Dee told me later, "come unbidden and replace all that is before me. As you know, during the war I served in France in the Chinese Labour Corps camps and also at the front lines—wherever complaints arose that involved our countrymen. I was, as is my habit, strict but fair, both in my rulings in disputes between Chinese, and in those between our countrymen and the British or the French. In such cases I would rule for the Europeans if their causes were just. Most often, however, they were not, and I supported my countrymen. Many of them had signed contracts with clauses they did not understand, some because they could not read—a fact of which the labor contractors were well aware.

"The men in the trenches respected me, Lao. My support of them even at the price of an occasional beating, my continuing presence, and my insistence on discipline in my work all allowed for a certain level of order to prevail in that disordered time.

"The cost to me, though, was greater than I knew. I remained composed in the midst of chaos as I felt my role required. It was only after the war, when I returned to China and was sent thence to Switzerland, that these visions began. They are quite horrifying and do not stop. However, they can be made to vanish handily, though temporarily, by the administration of opium. Thus, Lao, my fondness for the substance which you hold in such contempt."

ALL THIS, AS I said, he told me later, and we discussed his declaration at some length. At this time, though, I knew nothing about it, and Dee stood on the roof opposite the green-doored house, watching the body of the third of his companions to recently die being removed to the morgue. The sights and sounds of the battlefield bore down on him together with the heavy pounding of the rain. Dee crumpled to the roof slates, leaning his back against a chimney to stop from sliding to the street. For a moment he held his head in agony. Then he unwrapped the opium from the handkerchief in his pocket. Unlike he had earlier, he didn't bother with the nicety of cutting off a fragment. He took one of the chunks and swallowed it whole as rain streamed down, thunder crashed like falling bombs, and lightning blazed through the heavens.

SOME TIME LATER, as rain continued to fall from a sky completely dark, Dee awoke to find himself shivering on the slates of a rooftop. Not sure where he was or how he'd come to be there, he blinked his eyes and tried to throw off the familiar stupor of an opium sleep. The roof ridge wavered before him and a vertiginous sense caused him to press himself once more against the chimney and shut his eyes. The world began to spin. A loud crack of thunder shook the very air around him and then, more loudly still, he heard his name.

"Dee Ren Jie!" a voice called. "You are summoned to trial!"

Dee's eyes flew open. To his surprise he was no longer on the roof, but in a battlefield judge's chambers similar to his own former chambers on the fields of France. But these chambers, erected in the middle of a muddy ground of carnage where cold rain fell on lifeless bodies, were not Dee's. Nor was he in the judge's tall chair, which stood high on a platform. He was kneeling before the bench as a prisoner, and the judge, looming over him, was Lin Tse Shu.

Commissioner Lin.

"Dee Ren Jie!" Commissioner Lin's voice, deafeningly loud, boomed out over the battlefield. "Three men known to you have been brutally murdered. It is your duty to investigate these crimes. Yet here you sit in the rain paralyzed by opium. Do you deny it?"

"No, Commissioner Lin." Dee's voice was torn away by the wind, so that he barely heard himself.

"Dee Ren Jie, I dedicated my life to the cause of ending opium use among our people. It is a vile drug which renders the best of us—men like you," Lin said sternly, "incapable of action. Why, then, do I find you in its thrall?"

"Commissioner, the effects of the battlefield have not left me."

"Many men were on the battlefield and still feel its effects." Commissioner Lin's voice softened somewhat. "I am aware of what you suffered, and that your first taste of opium was not from your own choice, but was administered to you as an intended kindness." Lin paused and glowered down on his prisoner. "But the war is five years over, Dee Ren Jie! Three of your companions who survived the battlefield have now lost their lives in peacetime, in a foreign country. Your craving for this drug prevents you from fulfilling your responsibility to them and to justice. Tell me, should I not condemn you to death? Should I not have you thrown from a roof into the street below?"

Dee could make no answer.

"Dee Ren Jie, in view of your life of service I will grant you a reprieve. But you must put the opium aside and *do your work.* I leave you with a single question: What is the value of a life?"

Dee, though he did not fully comprehend the question, still attempted to form a response. But the sky once again exploded in flashes of lightning and booming thunder, and Commissioner Lin vanished into the swirling rain.

# CHAPTER SEVENTEEN

The trill of a lark brought Dee back to awareness. He still sat on the roof, still leaned his back against the chimney, but the sky, just beginning to pale, had been scrubbed clear by the previous night's storm and the temperature had begun to moderate. In the predawn air Dee tentatively stretched his limbs. Finding them a touch stiff but in working order, he let himself down from the roof along a drainpipe. He was seen by none but a souse whose sleep Dee disturbed when he dropped beside the man into an alley. The sot's eyes widened at the sight of the mask and cape, and he searched the cobblestones for his bottle which, once found, he rapidly raised to his lips. Dee left him to his addled dreams and made his way to Sergeant Hoong's shop.

"Dee!" Hoong said, opening his door in response to Dee's rap. "What has happened? Are you hurt?"

"It's possible, Hoong, that I am dead. If you ascertain that not to be the case, perhaps you would offer me a cup of tea and return to me the parcel I left with you."

"The parcel is over there," Hoong said, letting Dee into his shop and closing the shutters once again. "And the kettle is already on."

"Thank you. I won't be a moment." Dee took the parcel into the rear of the shop and, though he was in fact a number of moments, by the time he returned to the front room dressed in his jacket and trousers, the tea had finished steeping and was ready to warm him.

"This costume," Dee said, hanging the Springheel Jack regalia on a hook on the rear wall to dry, "has proven to be not only useful, but durable. Please convey my compliments to Mrs. McCarthy until I find it convenient to do so myself."

"I'll be glad to." Hoong poured tea and set out a plate of biscuits. "Has the terrorizing identity you've assumed helped in the investigation of the murders?"

"Springheel Jack has impressed upon the Metropolitan Police in the person of Captain Bard that these murders must be investigated despite the fact that the victims are not the sort whose demise troubles the captain unduly. Whether that will result in anything useful I don't know, but it does put him on notice. Meanwhile we must continue our own work. I will consider what avenues I shall pursue. For your part, I trust you'll find the time to keep searching for the last man on the list?"

"Indeed. Although, whatever your next steps, I might suggest you stop off at your rooms first and replace your suit and shirt. Yesterday's activities and the night your apparel spent wrapped in a parcel have not been kind."

"Ah, yes, Hoong, always concerned with my sartorial state. I thank you and will do as you suggest." Dee finished his tea and stood. "Once the Springheel Jack ensemble is fully dry, would you kindly wrap it into a parcel, also? I'm sure to have need of it again."

"Yes," Hoong said, "I rather imagine you will."

IT IS AT this point that I am able to resume the narration of events in which I was personally involved, for as I sat at breakfast with Mrs. and Miss Wendell, Dee's key was heard in the lock.

"Good morning, Dee," I called. "You managed to catch the early train from Sevenoaks, then?"

"I did." Dee emerged into the dining room, rumpled but cheerful. "It was full to bursting with men of business getting a leg up on the day. Mrs. Wendell, if you'll forgive the appearance of a man well-soaked in last night's storm and furthermore unexpectedly forced to spend the night without his toiletries, I'd greatly enjoy a cup of tea."

Both women beamed as Dee pulled a chair to the table. The black variety of tea the British prefer is similar to pu-erh and can be bracing. I noted that Dee drank three cups. After recounting the amusing events of his ill-starred, though fictitious, journey to visit a retired diplomatic acquaintance in Sevenoaks, the idea of which I had planted in the Wendells' heads that morning and that Dee had picked up seamlessly, Dee and I thanked the ladies and returned to my rooms.

"Ah," said Dee, throwing himself into the easy chair. "Well done, Lao, with the Sevenoaks ruse."

"Thank you," I said coldly, unmollified by his compliment. "Fortunately, as I am a writer, creating fictions comes easily to me. I was forced to invent some excuse for you because I feared exactly what in fact came to pass—that you would stroll in the door during breakfast looking like a vagabond who had spent the night in the open. Dee, where were you?"

"Lao," Dee said gravely, "I spent the night in the open. Now"—and he erupted out of the chair—"I shall change my suit and we can continue our investigation. Brother Hoong is hard at it, searching for someone who can cast light on the location of the remaining man. We must try to do the same."

"How will we do that?"

"Unfortunately," he said, removing his rumpled jacket, "I have no idea."

LEAVING DEE TO his transformation, I returned downstairs to the parlor, hoping for a bit of pleasant conversation with Mary before she left for the hat shop. I found her with her mother, conferring about such things as women discuss among themselves. They looked up with smiles as I walked in, though Mary's welcoming expression faltered just slightly upon seeing that I was alone. Dee, I reminded myself, was a new and exotic creature to the ladies, while I was, by this point, a well-known and well-liked friend. I believed my position would be ultimately more conducive to sparking in Mary the ardor that I hoped, eventually, to generate, a devotion that would match that which I felt for her.

Also, Dee would be leaving London soon.

"Where are you and Mr. Dee off to today, Mr. Lao?" Mary inquired.

"I'm not quite sure," I said. "Dee has many errands he wishes to accomplish in the short time he'll be in England, before he returns to his work in Switzerland and, ultimately, to China."

"And when will that be?" she casually asked.

"The moment his business here is finished. I'm sorry I can't be more precise than that, but I know he's anxious to be off."

Mary stood. "Well, I'm off also, and I wish you a good day. I must speak to Washington—Washington Jones, the music master, you've met him, Mr. Lao—at St. George's. Oh, Mr. Dee, you look quite a changed man!" she exclaimed as Dee appeared in the parlor doorway. "I was just saying to Mr. Lao that I must leave early, as I need to stop by the church before I go to work. I'm to sing a solo part with the choir at next Sunday's service. Oh! Perhaps you gentlemen would come worship with us? Mr. Lao, we have not seen you in church in an age!"

My heart itself sang at the invitation. Though I had been baptized in Peking and felt an abiding love for Jesus, in whose image I strove to live, I had little patience with the trappings of Christianity as they manifested in the Occident. The music was lovely, of course, especially when given voice by such a clear, light soprano as Mary possessed; but the elaborate ecclesiastical buildings, the long-winded clergymen and their recondite sermons, the pre-meal saying of grace by those not remotely grateful for anything, the parishioners bent devoutly over prayer books on Sundays after mistreating tradesmen and servants the rest of the week—all this I could not countenance. Thus my absence at regular worship services, as noted by Mary.

Still, the invitation to hear Mary's voice raised in song was most appealing. "I would enjoy that greatly," I said. Suddenly a thought dawned. "Your church is St. George's, Bloomsbury, and my friend the Reverend Robert Evans is your rector, if I'm correct?"

"Yes, of course. Such a learned man. His sermons are most inspiring! Although occasionally, I admit, difficult to follow. But it was he who brought you to us, Mr. Lao, for which we all must be grateful."

"Indeed, I owe the Reverend Evans a great debt. Come, Dee, let us escort Miss Wendell to the church." Dee frowned and began what was sure to be an impatient response but I spoke again, for—possibly inspired by the knowledge that once the investigation was successfully concluded he would be on his way back to the Continent—I had been struck by an idea. "The Reverend Evans," I said, "spent some years in China—"

"As a missionary," Mary put in, fixing her cloche hat in the mirror.

This statement did not seem to enhance Dee's outlook so I hurriedly continued. "Yes, well, for whatever reason, the reverend knows a good many members of the Chinese community in London. He may be able to help us in our quest for the remaining man on your list."

Dee raised his eyebrows. Whatever he'd planned to say went unuttered. Instead he looked from me to Mary, then replied, "An excellent thought, Lao. Miss Wendell, may we have that honor?"

Mary smiled, and again my heart sang. I opened the door. Mary went out, Dee went out, and I followed, my joy barely diminished when, though he did not offer it as a gentleman should, Mary, as I shut the door, took Dee's arm.

# CHAPTER EIGHTEEN

"My dear boy! Come right in, come right in!" The Reverend Robert Evans, a tall, pale man with hair as white as snow and a nose as large as a turnip, ushered Dee and myself into his study. We'd left Mary to consult with the young music master, Washington Jones, over the fine points of her upcoming performance. "And you've brought a colleague! Delightful! The Reverend Robert Evans, sir." Evans thrust a large palm out to Dee.

"Dee Ren Jie." The two men shook hands.

"Sit, sit. I'll ring for tea. How are you getting on at the Wendells', Lao? I haven't seen you here in church lately, so I haven't had the opportunity to inquire. Such good Christian ladies both, and the daughter so vivacious. I trust your situation is to your satisfaction?"

"Please, no need for tea," I said. Dee had remained standing and I perceived he was anxious to continue our work. "Yes, I'm greatly enjoying my time with the ladies, and I'm indebted to you for making the introductions. In fact Judge Dee is staying with me just at present."

Evans turned to Dee. "Are you indeed? And you are a

judge? Well, sir, I'm honored. Are you sure you won't have tea with me? I'd very much like to discuss the troubling situation of Christians under Chinese law. I understand that at this moment in Peking—"

"Thank you, we can't stay," I said quickly, for Dee's eyes had begun to narrow and his mouth to set into a line. "Reverend Evans, we've come to ask for your help. We have the names of some men of Dee's acquaintance whom we'd like to locate. We're also interested in any friends these men might have, or anything at all you can tell us about them. I thought, with your knowledge of London's Chinese community—"

"I see." The reverend's face fell. "Yes, of course, I'd be happy to help. Who are these men?"

Dee produced the list and Reverend Evans studied it. He glanced up. "Ma and Ching—those are the men who were recently murdered, are they not?"

"I'm afraid so," I answered, not mentioning that Guo was now also in that category.

After another few moments Evans said, "Well, I'm sorry, but I can't help you." He handed the paper back to Dee. "It's entirely possible, I suppose, that one or another of these men have come to our Christian Mission for meals. We make rather a point here at St. George's of feeding the poor three days a week and many Chinese are among the supplicants. Rice Christians, we called their kind back in China, as they would allow themselves to be baptized to partake of the meals we offered." He smiled diffidently, as though refusing praise for his munificence, praise that a glance at Dee showed was unlikely to be forthcoming. "Some of them made honest conversions, of course," continued the reverend, "and became active in the church. Some do the same here. As for the others, well, at worst they've been exposed to the Gospel. But if these men on your list have come here, they haven't become converts and they've not identified themselves."

"Thank you," Dee said stonily, replacing the paper in his jacket pocket. "Come, Lao. We will continue our search elsewhere." He turned on his heel and stalked from the study.

"Oh, my," said the reverend, gazing after him. "Have I somehow given offense?"

"I apologize," I said, feeling myself flush. "Dee can be . . . somewhat short-tempered. He's anxious to continue our work and no doubt disappointed. Please forgive him. Thank you, Reverend." I replaced my hat and hurried after Dee.

"Dee!" I said when I caught him up outside the church. "What do you mean by treating the Reverend Evans with such discourtesy?"

"The troubling situation under Chinese law! Rice Christians!" Dee retorted. "Damnable! The learned and inspiring reverend offers food to our starving countrymen and mocks them for accepting it. China cannot be rid of his sort soon enough for my taste."

"You judge him too harshly," I said. "He has done a great deal of good in China. I've taught at the school that he founded, and it was who helped me come to England."

Dee scowled. "That a man has been useful to you personally does not make him a good man, Lao."

"Here in London he directs a mission shelter which houses the indigent. And he continues to offer meals to the poor."

"The way a householder places cheese in a mousetrap."

"Dee!"

"Why is it, Lao, that you feel called upon to side with the British against the interests of your countrymen?"

"Side with the British! Hardly that. Nor am I opposing my countrymen when I contradict you, Dee. In this instance I believe you are wrong. The Reverend Evans—"

"The Reverend Evans." Dee fairly snorted the man's name.

"Dee, you are not yourself. I really cannot—"

"Judge Dee. And Lao She," came another voice. "I was hoping to find you here."

We both turned to see Sergeant Hoong approaching. He had, I was beginning to sense, a disconcerting habit of appearing out of nowhere.

"I went to your lodgings and was told you'd gone to the church," Hoong said. "I believe I may have located the last man on your list. Jiang Gwan Li." He handed a paper to Dee on which was written an address.

"Ah, Jiang," said Dee, nodding. "Always a volatile fellow. This approach will need to be made with care. Come, Hoong. And Lao? Will you join us? Or do you have some more British business to attend to?"

"Dee," I said, falling into step with them, "you can be a most infuriating man."

# CHAPTER NINETEEN

The address Hoong had provided we found attached to one of those unlikely, dilapidated dwellings one finds near the docks: buildings that appear to have been mistakenly left standing when, well over a century ago, the warehouses went up by the wharves. According to Hoong, this one was now a rabbit-warren of a rooming house. Jiang Gwan Li lodged on the first floor.

"Now Jiang," Dee said as we approached, "is a skittish fellow. His time in the war only increased his inborn wariness. He was"—he eyed me sidelong—"the only Christian among the company. Not, I'm sure, that that fact bears any relevance to his constant unease. In any case, if Jiang has heard about the violent deaths of his companions he's sure to have taken measures to protect himself. We must approach with caution."

"But Dee," I said, with great Christian forbearance ignoring his jibe, "why not just announce yourself? Surely he'll remember you and know you mean him no harm."

Though the day was not particularly warm, Dee removed a handkerchief from his pocket and wiped droplets of sweat from his brow. "Three men of Jiang's Labour Corps company have been murdered," he said. "It would not be amiss to conclude that the company is, for some reason, being targeted. Jiang will certainly remember me, but as to my trustworthiness, in his position I'd be suspicious."

A sudden thought came to me. "Do you suppose it's possible that for some reason Jiang has killed the others himself? In that case he most certainly would fear your arrival."

"Very good, Lao." I didn't care for Dee's sardonic tone but had no chance to protest as he continued, "I do, though, intend to announce myself. I'd like you and Hoong to be in place before I do. If Jiang takes it into his head to bolt one of you will then be in a position to stop him. If you are up to it?" Dee looked at me the way a man would look at another over pince-nez, though he wore none.

"Of course I'm up to it," I said, frowning. "You, however, look a bit pale. Are you sure—"

"Yes, Lao, thank you, completely sure," Dee said, turning his back to us to survey the rickety pile and equally to dismiss my concerns. "This building was clearly here long before indoor water closets became common. It will have been built with a rear entrance to allow access to a WC in the yard. Hoong, if you'll find your way around to that entrance, and whistle when you're in place? Very good. You, Lao, will come with me. When I go up to find Jiang you'll remain at the front door. I hope he'll be willing to converse with me, but if he distrusts me and runs and I'm unable to stop him, you each must be prepared to prevent further flight. You'll have the element of surprise, both of you, and I'll soon join you in attempting to restrain him. Are we all in agreement?"

We were. Hoong turned the corner and soon came his whistle. I took a position just inside the front door, in a hall where no ray of light found entry and no bad smell, it seemed, had for years found egress. The creaking of Dee's footsteps receded up the stairs.

FROM HERE, I must offer you the following as told to me by Dee—told with a certain irritability, the reasons for which you will soon perceive.

AS DEE'S STEPS creaked on the narrow staircase, he heard what sounded like a faint, maniacal giggle from somewhere above. *A strange energy in this place*, Dee thought, and felt his senses tingle. At the top of the stairs, he stopped and spoke. "Jiang! I am Judge Dee. You remember me. I need to talk with you."

"You've come for the money! I don't have the money. Go away. Leave me alone!"

Dee had had little hope of being welcomed, but his greeting had served its purpose. He now knew which door was Jiang's.

He gently tried the knob, but the door was locked. Removing from his pocket a set of pick-locks, Dee made use of a skill I hadn't known he possessed until he told me this tale. The lock gave way in a matter of seconds.

Entering the room, Dee saw no one, yet he sensed a presence. *Jiang must be concealing himself,* he thought. A wardrobe stood against the wall, large enough for a man. Dee made his way there. He stealthily turned the latch, and heard a soft click as he opened the door a quarter inch. Stepping lightly to the side, he yanked the door fully open, using it to shield himself.

Three pub darts whooshed from the wardrobe and thumped into the opposite wall.

Giving the door a final yank to be sure no dart remained, Dee crossed the room. He pulled a dart from the wall and was examining it when he sensed a movement behind him. He spun to see Jiang, skeletally thin, slipping not from within the wardrobe, but from behind it. Jiang sped to the door, danced in a strange manner across the corridor, and dove out a rear window.

A call came from Hoong: "He's here! He's running up a staircase that goes to the roof."

Dee heard Jiang cackling, then shouting to Hoong, "You'll never catch me, old man!"

Dee ran his gaze over the corridor Jiang had so oddly traversed. Some of the planks were visibly uneven. He touched his foot to one. An ominous creak came and Dee reared back just in time. Three loud booms shook the building. As the smoke cleared Dee saw that shotgun shells had been rigged to go off under the slightest weight.

He made a fast survey of the uneven boards and, shifting his weight again and again, worked his way across avoiding further catastrophe by the use of precise footwork.

Slipping out the window, he perched on the sill. "Take care!" Hoong called from below. "The manner in which Jiang climbed makes me feel something is wrong with the staircase to the roof."

Dee glanced at the ramshackle assembly. Something was indeed wrong. The stairs had been sawn apart in a way so skillful as to be invisible to an eye less keen than his own.

The handrail, however, was intact.

"Thank you, Big Brother Hoong, for the warning. I'll use my lightness skill."

Dee gathered himself and leapt. Easily balancing, he sped up the handrail without sway or misstep, aware of Hoong below and Jiang above watching in amazement. When Dee reached the roof landing he jumped lightly from the railing. With his eyes locked on Jiang's he stamped his foot. In a series of cracks and creaks, the entire exterior staircase shattered. Dee said, "Jiang! I just want a word!"

Jiang whimpered, "The money! You're after the money!" and dove through a gable window back into the house.

Dee shouted to Hoong, "Come inside and come up! But take great care. Jiang is unhinged and very clever." Hoong, with a nod, disappeared inside the back door.

AND HERE IS where my own sad part in this affair comes into play.

At my post inside the front door, I was fretting. I heard explosions, creaks, and shouts. My nerves in a jagged bundle, I felt I could wait no longer in the literal and figurative dark. When Hoong raced past me and took the stairs two at a time, I reasoned that our quarry was above and I would therefore be more useful on the stairs than at the door.

"Sergeant Hoong!" I called. "Wait for me!" I started forward.

"Stop!" Hoong answered, looking down at me from the first-floor landing. "Everything is booby trapped. Don't move."

I watched Hoong touch a cautious foot to the first step of the next flight.

Immediately, glittering blades plunged from the ceiling with a woosh. On ropes of varying lengths, they swung to and fro above the stairs like lethal pendulums.

Hoong stood motionless for a moment and observed. Then he leapt into the moving maze of metal and wove as nimbly through it as a bird between branches.

I looked on in astonishment. I knew I couldn't do the same, and therefore had no access to the second floor; but as Dee and Hoong had both gone up to the first floor by way of the stairs I saw no reason I shouldn't go at least that far. I would then be in a position to help if Jiang somehow escaped both of my companions above.

Grasping the railing, I started my ascent. Only as I felt the railing plunge beneath my hand did I realize that neither Dee nor Hoong had touched it.

A loud clap was followed by a series of others. Each step in the staircase flattened into the next, creating something akin to a funhouse slide. I lost my balance and tumbled back into the entrance hall.

The flight of stairs Hoong was halfway up had suffered the same fate, and Hoong, in addition to ducking the oscillating knives, now had to throw himself down and haul his body hand-over-hand by inserting his fingertips into the gaps between boards. This was effective until a viscous liquid began to flood from the gaps.

Hoong shouted, "Bean oil!" before losing his grip and sliding, finally tumbling to a stop on the first-floor landing.

"Hoong!" I cried, seeing a movement behind him.

Hoong jumped to his feet. Before him stood Jiang, clothed only in leather gloves, fabric shoes, and a pair of cotton drawers. His bare skin glistened in the dimness. Swift as the wind, Hoong leapt for him. Jiang danced back, but Hoong clasped onto his arm—which slithered out of Hoong's grip.

Jiang threw back his head and laughed. "Bean oil!" he shouted, in a precise imitation of Hoong's own tones. His foot flew out and hooked Hoong's, and Hoong, bean-oiled as he was, crashed down onto the lower staircase-slide and skidded down headfirst to land in a heap at my feet.

Jiang slammed a gloved hand onto the railing of the stairs—now the slide—to the second floor. The swinging blades immediately retracted. Nimble as a monkey, Jiang scrambled up the railing. Standing on it, he pushed a trapdoor leading to the attic and vanished through the opening.

FROM HERE, THE remainder of the tale is short, and belongs once again to Dee.

DEE, ON THE roof, had heard the commotion below. Again wiping his brow of unaccustomed perspiration, he had just determined to reenter the building when a section of roof slates popped up and from this hatch burst Jiang. Dee stared at the glossy, emaciated specter before him. Jiang Gwan Li's features were barely discernible in the creature's eyes and mouth. For his part, Jiang, equally surprised to find Dee standing upon the roof, emitted a screeching cackle.

"Jiang Gwan Li!" said Dee. "I am Judge Dee. You remember me."

"I don't have the money! Go away!"

"I'm not after money. This is of utmost importance."

"Then catch me!" Jiang spun around like a mad harlequin on one foot.

Dee pounced on Jiang but found himself holding only empty air, hands slippery from bean oil. Jiang danced to the edge of the roof.

"Jiang!" Dee shouted. "No!"

"You won't get me, you won't!" With another loud cackle, Jiang sprang high in the air. Arms flailing like windmills, he landed on the very edge of the roof across the alley. He tottered there and Dee held his breath. Finally Jiang threw himself forward onto the slates. He found no handhold and slithered down, disappearing behind the fence enclosing the rear yard.

Dee considered the leap; uncharacteristically, he didn't attempt it. He chose, instead, to slide down a drainpipe into the yard, vault over the fence, run across the alley, and clamber over the fence Jiang had vanished behind. The building's rear door was open and, breathing heavily, Dee dashed inside. The front door also stood wide. Muddy footprints led from back to front. Emerging onto the street, Dee listened for the commotion a half-naked greased Chinese man would surely occasion as he ran; but the rumbles, rattles, shouts, and horn blasts of everyday life made any particular turmoil impossible to distinguish.

Disgusted with how the episode had ended, Dee circled the block and entered the rickety building, where he found me kneeling over Hoong at the bottom of the staircase-slide.

"Sergeant Hoong!" I was saying to the fallen man. "Are you all right?"

"Clearly, Lao, he is not," snapped Dee. "Hoong! Big Brother Hoong, can you hear me?"

"I . . . Did . . ." Hoong blinked. "Yes. Yes, Dee, I can hear you. Equally well, I can see you. I've had the wind knocked out of me but am otherwise complete." He moved to sit up and was aided by Dee. Hoong peered around. "Jiang?" he asked.

"Gone. We so very nearly had him. If you had only attained the roof—"

"I'm afraid I'm to blame," I said. "Sergeant Hoong was on his way to you, but I triggered the oiled stairs."

Dee scowled at me. "Bannerman, I'm disappointed. At the jail you fought so well."

"I'm sorry," I said. "I can make no excuse. I only wanted to join you and help."

"Indeed. Well, you're admitting to it like a man and I suppose I can wish for no more." Dee stood and examined the staircase. He pressed on the depressed section of railing. It clicked and rose back up, and as it did the slide transformed back into stairs. Dee nodded. "The denizens here will have to clean the oil off it, but at least they'll have stairs. Come, Hoong, let's get you back to your shop."

"I'm quite capable of returning there myself," Hoong said, rising to his feet.

"Of course. Nonetheless."

We three made our way through the Limehouse streets to Hoong's shop. Dee wiped his brow once or twice, and although he strode along with his accustomed determination, he slowed his pace, throwing anxious looks at Hoong and the occasional reproving glance at me. Hoong ignored Dee's concern. I attempted to do the same with his disappointment. Although my tumble had granted me some bruises and lumps, I refrained from complaint, which I had a suspicion would be ill-received.

As we rounded the corner where the shop stood, I was hoping Hoong would be in a mood to offer tea. I would welcome a few restful moments.

Blocking the door, however, we found a Chinese man crouched on his haunches, smoking a cigarette.

Immediately I leapt in front of my companions. "You there!" I pointed at the fellow. "Who are you and what do you mean by this intrusion?"

Smiling, the man stood. He spoke, but did not answer my questions. "Hello, Dee," he said.

# CHAPTER TWENTY

Dee's face took on a look of amazement and pleasure. "Captain Lu! In London! I thought you went back to China when the war ended."

Dee and this new fellow bowed deeply to each other.

"At the last minute I was granted permission to come here with the men," Lu said.

Dee turned to Hoong and myself. "Lao, there is no need to guard against this man. Lu Yan was captain of the Labour Corps battalion that included the company of men on our list. Captain Lu, this is Sergeant Hoong Liang and this is Lao She."

We all mutually bowed. The captain, a lanky man, was closer in age to Hoong than to Dee, if his graying hair and weathered face could be relied upon. "A pleasure, gentlemen."

"I apologize for my impolite greeting," I said. "But you see, we have—"

"If I had known you were in London I'd have looked you up immediately, Lu," Dee broke in. "Yet here you are on Sergeant Hoong's doorstep, seemingly waiting for us. Or am I wrong? Did you come here for a purchase and this is just the luckiest of chances?"

"Whatever the answer," Hoong said, "may I suggest we discuss it over tea?" With that he unlocked his shop and we all entered. Leaving the "Closed" sign upon the door, Hoong locked up again and put the kettle on. He prepared the teapot while the rest of us positioned ourselves on carved stools around the low table, I feeling miffed at the interruption.

"Hoong, are you sure you're well?" Dee asked, as Hoong, moving perhaps a bit more slowly than usual, set the teacups on the table.

"Dee," Hoong said in tones of warning.

"Yes, all right," Dee responded quickly. He actually sounded chastened. Well, I reflected, this man's father was his tutor in China. If Dee respected any man, it would be Hoong.

Dee turned his attention to Captain Lu. "So, Captain, am I correct? Were you waiting here for us?"

"I was waiting for Sergeant Hoong, but you were my ultimate goal, Dee. I'd heard you'd arrived to collect Ma's body." He smiled sadly. "I knew you would. I'd have made an effort to see you in any case before you left England again, but when I read of Ching's murder, and now Guo's, I knew I must speak to you. I made inquiries and learned that you and Sergeant Hoong were acquainted. So I came here hoping he could tell me where to locate you. I didn't expect that he'd bring you straight to me."

"I'm very glad he did, and glad to see you again, Captain Lu, even in these sad circumstances. You've been well, here in England?"

"Very well, thank you. As I think you know, I have no family left in China. I have some small means and I found in France that the adventure of a foreign country suited me."

"I'm glad to hear it. Though I can't help but notice how thin you've become."

Lu laughed. "As much as I'm enjoying my sojourn in

England, our time in France, though fraught with daily dangers, offered much better food."

"I cannot deny it."

"And you, Dee?" asked Lu. "Have you been well? You yourself seem a bit . . . drawn."

And out of sorts, I could have added, but it wasn't my intention to interfere in the reunion of old squad-mates.

"Yes, yes, Lu, I'm fine. We can talk at length at another time, but I'm anxious to hear what it was about the murder of the men that has brought you to me."

Hoong, carrying the teapot, came and seated himself with us. He poured tea in the order of the age of his guests, as was proper, serving himself last.

Lu said, "Of the men who came from France, sadly only one from the company remains, besides myself."

Dee nodded. "Jiang Gwan Li. We just left Jiang's lodgings, where we failed in our attempt to speak with him." Dee briefly related the tale. To my surprise he laid no blame on me for Jiang's escape. "Jiang, more than once in our encounter," Dee said, "shouted about his fear that I was after the money. I tried to assure him I didn't know what money he referred to and in any case money was not my reason for coming to see him, but he could not be calmed. His traps prove he's as creative as ever, and even more suspicious."

"I believe I can account for his behavior," said Lu.

"Is he by any chance the killer himself?" I interposed. Dee frowned but said nothing.

"It is possible," said Lu, "as you will see when I explain. Though I very much doubt it. He is—was a staunch friend of the others." He looked around at us. "Are any of you familiar with the institution referred to as a 'tontine'?"

Hoong and I looked blankly at each other. Dee considered. "A tontine, if I'm not wrong," he said, "is a form of private mutual insurance. Individuals contribute an agreed-upon sum. More can be added, but none removed. The total amount is to be collected by the last surviving member. Are you saying, Captain, that these men were part of a tontine?"

"I am saying that, yes, and furthermore, I'm in it also. Private, informal mutual aid is of course common in China. Farmers pool their money to help one of their number buy seeds. He, after the harvest, returns the money with interest so it can be loaned again. That sort of thing. A tontine is more formal. It's a European institution. The men were introduced to the idea by one of the British officers in France. They were taken with it and those four who were permitted entry into England decided to form one here. Its object is to provide a sum of money to be used in old age by the member who, by definition, is most likely to require it."

"Well, that certainly gives Jiang a motive for killing his fellows," I said. "Perhaps he didn't want to wait for old age."

"Perhaps," said Lu. "But this tontine is held by a bank—the Hong Kong and Shanghai Bank, in the Gracechurch Street branch. As is standard practice in a tontine, the bank has brought in additional members. Their identities have been kept from us, as ours will have been from them. This is done routinely to prevent any tontine member from getting it into his head to arrange to be the last survivor. However," Lu said drily, "it appears it may not have worked."

# CHAPTER TWENTY-ONE

Captain Lu left soon thereafter. "Dee, we will have a longer visit when your pressing business is resolved. I wish you well in your investigation, gentlemen. I don't expect to live forever, but I would rather not be murdered."

"We will do our best to prevent that," said Dee.

After the captain was gone, Hoong poured out the remainder of the tea and rose to make another pot.

"Don't trouble yourself, Sergeant," said Dee. "Lao and I must leave to pay a visit to the Hong Kong and Shanghai Bank branch in Gracechurch Street."

"Dee," said Hoong, "are you sure you don't want a brief rest? Perhaps a meal? As Captain Lu said, you appear drawn. I think the night you spent in the storm has perhaps affected you more than you know. You're not quite yourself."

"Am I not? And this from a man who an hour ago was flat on his back with his mind spinning among the stars?" Dee laughed, though to my ears the sound was strained. "If I'm not myself, still, whoever I am is on his way to the Hong Kong and Shanghai Bank. Lao, he could use your help, if you choose to accompany him."

The change in pronoun confused me but I stood when Dee did.

"Very well," said Dee. "You, Hoong, are the one who needs a rest. Put some herbs on that bump on your head and return to your shopkeeping. You'll hear from me, or whomever this is, soon enough."

And with that Dee and I left the shop.

AS WE WALKED, I hazarded expressing my own opinion on Dee's condition. "Dee," I said, "two men whom you esteem have said you do not appear to be at the peak of health."

He threw a glance at me. "No, Lao, not you, also."

"Yes, I confess I feel the same. My error at Jiang's lodgings would not have signified had you been your usual self. In addition," I went on as he opened his mouth to speak, "since Captain Lu told us about the tontine I've felt you to be distracted. If I'm to continue as your associate in this investigation I must be allowed to express my concern. Your state of health may have a direct impact upon our work. Also, I would appreciate being apprised, when you find a development troubling, of your reasons for making such an assessment."

During this speech Dee's eyebrows rose so high they wrinkled his forehead. I had a suspicion he was amused, but he did not say so. He waited another moment to be sure I had finished. His reply was not what I was expecting.

"Lao," he said, "I have had a dream."

I stared. "A dream. I announce that I'm concerned for your health, and also that I'm troubled about the lines along which our association is proceeding, and you respond that you've had a dream. Dee, it must be clear even to you that you're not well."

"Perhaps I'm not, although if that's the case, the rain that drenched me on the rooftop is not the reason. In my dream I encountered Commissioner Lin."

"Commissioner Lin?" In my own dreams I had never met so much as a minor official. As a modern man I put no stock in dreams, and yet I was impressed.

"He had two things to say," Dee continued. "He told me I must give up opium."

"I'm glad to hear death hasn't changed his attitude on this important point," I said. "Of course he's correct."

"And he also asked me a question. He asked, 'What is the value of a life?' I've been puzzling over his meaning. Now, entirely unexpected, Captain Lu appears, to tell us the men in the tontine have placed a literal value on their own lives. The confluence of these facts accounts for my unease."

"I see." After considering this a moment I asked, "And what have been your thoughts on Commissioner Lin's first message?"

"Since he delivered it I've had no opium. It's an odd thing, is it not, Lao, that it was in an opium dream that Commissioner Lin chose to appear, to tell me I must stop taking opium? I was on the point of persuading myself he was a hallucination attributable to the drug, and therefore it would be permissible to ignore what he'd said, when Captain Lu made his revelation. Now, Lao, you see my dilemma. If I've brought Commissioner Lin out from my own mind, as the doctors of Vienna would claim, or if he came to me from the world beyond the grave, his message is the same. And it was delivered along with another message that seems to have a bearing on our case.

"As a result of the dream I did not take opium this morning. In this abstinence lie the roots of the diminishment of my faculties you've correctly noted, and also any irritability I've displayed. Ridding oneself of opium is an unpleasant process,

Lao, and one I'd not have undertaken in the midst of a case but for the insistence of Commissioner Lin, wherever he came from, and the simultaneous appearance, in the form of Captain Lu, of a directional arrow for the investigation. Now, if you're satisfied as to my current state—and my heightened need for your assistance—perhaps we can proceed."

Dee strode on. For a few moments I was frozen, open-mouthed, on the pavement, staring after him. Then I hurried to catch up.

Judge Dee had a heightened need for my assistance. I would do my utmost to prove valuable to him.

# CHAPTER TWENTY-TWO

The branch of the Hong Kong and Shanghai Banking Cor-
poration in Gracechurch Street stood as nobly as any in
London. Stone formed its façade, in alternating smooth and
rusticated bands. Three grand arched doors and several high
windows proudly bore the bank's name in bronze letters above
them.

"I see Stephen and Stitt are not in evidence," Dee said as
we approached.

"Who are they?"

"The lions who guard the bank's entrances in Shanghai. I
thought perhaps the branches in London would have them,
also. They're named for two of the senior managers."

"The managers? That shows rather a lack of vision, don't
you think? Why not name them for virtues the bank would
like to encourage in its depositors? 'Patience' and 'Fortitude,'
for example."

"An excellent suggestion, but for the fact that virtues are
not prized at the Hong Kong and Shanghai Bank."

The deeply recessed entryway led to heavy bronze doors,
which in turn led to a sumptuous interior of high ceilings,

marble columns, elaborate mosaic floors, and dark wood paneling. Grand half-dome lamps, now electrified, hung from the ceiling's coffers, and smaller ones with green glass shades lit each clerk's desk. Wide interior windows surrounding the manager's office overlooked the comings and goings of clerks and patrons.

Dee and I had discussed as we hurried here what our plan would be. As an innately reticent man, I found my part unnatural to my temperament, but Dee assured me it would be the fastest way to our goal. "You are capable of this, I have no doubt, Lao," he said. "You may even find that you enjoy it."

On Dee's second point I felt myself unconvinced, nor did I entirely share his sanguinity on the first. Nonetheless I undertook to play out my role honorably.

Or, scandalously; for my function in our scheme was to create rather an embarrassing disturbance.

The Hong Kong and Shanghai Bank catered to Londoners of all stripes, but as its name would imply, the bank had from its founding permitted itself to attract a Chinese clientele. While to be Chinese in London at that time was to be an object always of curiosity, often of suspicion, and occasionally of ridicule, all the same the diplomats, scholars, and artists of my homeland required banking services. Where there is money to be made, a bank will always find a way.

Therefore it was no difficult matter for Dee to enter, return a few minutes later to say to me, "The situation is ideal. Whenever you are ready, Lao," and once again walk in through the bank's doors, with not a soul taking notice of him.

Nor of me, upon my own entrance a few moments later. I spotted Dee at the center counter among other patrons both British and Chinese filling out deposit slips, or withdrawal requests, or any of various other papers. Dee noted my presence, I was quite sure, but did not acknowledge me. I likewise ignored him and focused on my mission. Taking a few deep breaths, I stalked to a teller's window and began my show.

"I must see the manager!" I demanded in a raised voice. "This situation is intolerable! Summon him now, young man. I cannot permit this state of affairs to continue, that I cannot. Where is he? Send for him!" I pounded my fist on the marble counter.

"Sir, I—" said the startled fellow.

"Do not 'sir' me. Give me no excuses. The manager it must be, and at once!"

All eyes turned to me. I continued my shouted demands and, as Dee had predicted, the manager himself emerged from his office in short order.

"Here, here. What's all this?" The stocky man, whose forehead was rather too high for his face, crossed the banking hall. Taking a tone of simultaneous cajoling and command—an impressive feat—he asked, "Sir, what can I do for you?"

I drew myself up. "Are you the manager of this bank?"

"I am. Jeremiah Stone, at your service."

"Yes. Well. Mr. Stone, I must insist. Indeed I must. It's a most perilous situation. Most unsafe, sir!"

"I'm sorry, I don't take your meaning. To what situation are you—?"

"Your tontine, of course! This bank holds a tontine of which three members have been murdered! Murdered, sir, dispatched in cold blood! My uncle is a member. Captain Lu Yan. I demand that you remove him from this deadly agreement immediately! You must return his investment and expunge his name from the list. I won't stand idly by while my relatives are murdered, sir. No indeed, that you cannot expect."

"Sir," said the manager, "please lower your voice. I understand your concern. We at the bank have heard about these . . . sad incidents."

"Sad! A most delicate term to use in reference to murder, sir!"

"However," he continued, attempting to mitigate the clamor of my voice with the soothing tones of his own, "regrettably, but for reasons I'm sure you comprehend, no member can be removed from a tontine once it's established. Except, of course, by death."

"Yes! By death! The very thing I'd prefer to avoid in my uncle's case! Your refusal is unacceptable, Mr. Stone. Surely something can be done. This is not a normal situation—at least, I hope it isn't. I had not understood London to be a hazardous place before this, but my good man, your city is presenting a most frightening aspect now!"

Naturally, though Mr. Jeremiah Stone pleaded with me to lower my voice, I did not. In fact I grew louder and more wild-eyed. This guaranteed that customers and employees alike all were staring in my direction when Dee slipped like a shadow into the manager's office and positioned himself in the armoire.

The location of this piece of furniture, in which hung, no doubt, the manager's greatcoat and a supply of fresh shirts, was, I perceived, one of the things Dee had meant when he said the situation was ideal. It stood behind the manager's desk, and thus would be the perfect place from which to observe Mr. Stone's actions, through doors now cracked the tiniest bit by Dee. This alteration in the wardrobe's usual state was unlikely to be noticed by Mr. Stone through the press of other matters occupying his mind, among which my demand, if not the most important, was certainly the most insistent.

Seeing Dee safely situated, I angrily gave Mr. Stone to understand he would be hearing from my solicitor. I then spun on my heel and marched out the heavy doors.

I walked to the corner, turned it, and stopped out of sight of the bank. I consulted my pocket watch. Dee and I had agreed that if our plan were to work at all, five minutes would be sufficient. I spent that time in a blend of the idle observation of my fellow pedestrians, some anxiety for Dee and the results of his efforts, and an unexpected though undeniable exhilaration as I contemplated my own performance.

When the time had expired I retraced my footsteps and entered the bank again. Once I had ascertained that the manager had returned to his office and that Dee was not yet out on the banking floor, I approached a different teller and once more demanded to see Mr. Stone. As expected, upon hearing my voice a second time he emerged rapidly.

"Sir!" he said when he reached me. "Really, I thought I'd made the bank's position clear. If you continue in these disturbances I'll have no choice but to summon a constable."

"Summon anyone you wish," I said haughtily. "I'll see you in court."

Once more I spun around and left, for Dee, of course, had made his escape from the manager's office as soon as the man's back was turned.

# CHAPTER TWENTY-THREE

As agreed, I hurried down the pavement and stopped again around the same corner, this time to wait for Dee. He turned the corner himself not a minute after I'd arrived.

"Come," he said as he passed me, not breaking stride. I fell in a few steps behind him and we continued in that fashion until we'd reached the next block, well clear of the bank. Only then did I catch him up. I was on the point of asking him what he had accomplished when, glancing over at him, I realized his face was lit in a broad smile.

"Lao," he said, "you were superb. I think perhaps you've missed your calling. You may have been born for the stage."

"I'm pleased that my efforts proved satisfactory," I answered, trying to hide a swell of pride.

"Oh, beyond satisfactory. You upset the poor man so badly that after you left he didn't stay a minute on the banking floor to calm nervous patrons, nor did he permit his assistant manager to do so. He beckoned the assistant to join him in his office, where he immediately opened the safe. Incidentally, Lao, should we require any large amounts of cash for some aspect of this investigation, I now have Mr. Stone's combination."

"Dee!" I said, shocked. "You cannot be serious."

He grinned. "No, of course not. Though I do have it. In any case, Mr. Stone withdrew a ledger book from the safe and opened it upon his desk. Really, it could hardly have been more convenient if he'd secretly resolved to help me read over his shoulder. He turned to the page listing the tontine. Ma's, Ching's, and Guo's names have been crossed out. Jiang's name is there, along with Captain Lu's, which he pointed out to the assistant manager as belonging to the uncle of that ill-mannered man who had just left."

"Ill-mannered!"

"Surely that was the impression you were hoping for? Mr. Stone said something to the effect that they needed to look into the situation, as the bank's reputation could be tarnished with too much unwanted attention."

"All very well," I said. "But the list? Did you find that the tontine had, as Captain Lu said, other members? And did you discover who they were?"

"I did," Dee said in a tone of triumph. "Two others. We are on our way to speak to one of them right now."

TWENTY MINUTES' WALK (at Dee's infernal pace) brought us to Denbigh Place in Pimlico. The pleasant street lined with tree-shaded terraced houses occupied a solid economic position, if not a geographical one, midway between the poverty of East London and the affluence of Mayfair. For people of this station in life, new neighborhoods and entire new towns were rapidly rising in the suburban areas; still, some preferred the city life and enclaves such as this remained. Dwelling here would be shop owners, university lecturers, young doctors and solicitors and professionals of all kinds, some in flats and some in private homes. Our first quarry, it seemed, was one of the latter. We found the house number we sought and Dee was about to pull the bell when I stopped him.

"Give me a moment to catch my breath," I said. "I haven't ever known a man to move as fast as you do without running—or without a motorcar."

"I apologize. I've told you I'm attempting to rid myself of opium. I find that physical exertion is a great help in distracting myself from some of the more unpleasant side effects of this process."

"I see. Well, perhaps I should find something of which I wish to rid myself, and then I'd be able to share in the allure of all this activity."

"I could suggest," said he, with a sly look, "you might attempt to divest yourself of any fondness for Miss Mary Wendell save that appreciation felt by a tenant toward an amiable landlady."

My face grew warm. "Dee," I said, "I fail to see how my feelings for Miss Wendell are any business of yours."

"You are deluding yourself into thinking she is capable of returning your affections. I don't like to see any man deluded."

"You're wrong. I believe she cares for me."

"Oh, no doubt. She also cares for the little dog, Napoleon. She's a kind young woman, but a British one. Like her fellows, she can see Chinese people only as interesting oddities. That, of course, is the best of her fellows; many others think of us in terms considerably worse. Her affection for you, though it clearly exists, is of the same nature as that she would bestow upon a trained parrot."

"I will not have you insulting Miss Wendell, Dee."

"I wouldn't consider it. I associated her with the best of her fellows, did I not? My argument is merely that your hopes for her romantic regard can only result in disappointment."

"You are wrong," I said.

"I think I am not, but I hope for your sake I am."

I fervently did, also.

After another long look at me, Dee said, "Are we ready now to call upon Shin Xiao?"

"Who is—oh, is that this gentleman's name? Yes, let's do that. I would greatly prefer continuing our investigation to any further discussion of my personal affairs. Although," I couldn't help adding, "you did not seem to object when I *deluded* Mr. Jeremiah Stone."

Dee nodded. "That is an excellent point. Perhaps it's only my friends whom I don't like to see in that state."

With that he turned to the door and pulled the bell. It was fortunate that he didn't wait for a response, for I was speechless.

In short order the door was opened by a woman of young middle age. The most marked feature of her pretty face was that she was neither British nor Chinese, but had that rich, dark skin that speaks of the Indian subcontinent. "Yes?" she inquired of us, seeming only slightly surprised to see two unknown Chinese men upon her doorstep.

"Is this the residence of Shin Xiao?" Dee asked.

"Indeed. Are you friends of my husband?" Her speech also carried the lilt of India.

"We'd like a word with him. My name is Dee Ren Jie and this is Lao She."

"How like him," the lady said with curled lip, "to invite friends for tea and forget to mention it to me. And on the maid's afternoon out! If he won't work he might at least consider lightening my load."

"Your husband doesn't work?"

"We live on the allowance provided by his father, who appears to understand that he raised a lazy son."

"Well, don't worry, we haven't come for tea," Dee said,

smiling. "We just need a word or two with Shin Xiao and we'll be on our way."

This assurance seemed to improve the lady's mood a bit. "Please, come in." She stepped aside to allow us to pass. "I'll fetch him. Please wait here."

We stood in a wallpapered entrance hall furnished in the British manner, with side tables, mirrors, and lithographs of pleasant gardens. The tabletops held porcelain figurines, brass ashtrays, and family photographs. An elaborately figured Persian runner stretched along the parquet floor.

From what I took to be the kitchen at the back of the house came the sounds of young children playing. A door opened from that area and we were joined by a stocky, distracted Chinese man in Western dress. He offered the left-over-right-hand greeting and we did the same.

"You are Shin Xiao?" Dee asked.

"Yes, I am. You wished to speak to me?"

Dee introduced us once more as he had to Shin's wife. Shin invited us into the parlor, but Dee said, "Thank you, but we don't wish to interrupt your tea. We're making inquiries about a situation that has come to our attention. I'm wondering if you, Shin Xiao, are a member of a tontine held by the Hong Kong and Shanghai Bank?"

"The tontine? Why are you asking about that?" In answer to some words from the kitchen he called over his shoulder, "I won't be a moment." To us again, "I'm sorry, what did you ask me?"

"The tontine," said Dee. "A friend of mine is a member and he has some questions that need to be resolved."

"Are there irregularities at the bank?" Shin sounded alarmed.

"No, no, nothing of that sort. You are a member, then?"

"Yes, I am. When I learned about it, I thought, I'm healthy

and strong. My father still manages his furniture factories in Shanghai at the age of ninety-two." He rubbed a hand over his head, leaving his hair all askew. "The investment is not large, though I understand at least one of the other members has increased his pay-in. Members can do so at any time, you know. Other members are encouraged but not required to match the additional funds. The interest, of course, accrues on the entire amount. If I'm not the man who collects in the end, I won't have lost much, and if I am it will be a tidy legacy for my children while requiring no effort from me."

Dee glanced at me, then back to Shin Xiao. "Do you by any chance know who the member was who increased his investment?"

"No, I'm sorry, I don't know the names of the other members. It's considered dangerous if that information is shared." The smile Shin Xiao offered us was slightly embarrassed.

"I'm afraid that's not an idle worry, Shin Xiao. Are you aware that three members of the tontine have recently been murdered?"

The man's face paled. "Murdered! No! How can this be?"

"We're attempting to determine the circumstances. In the interim I'd recommend that you take precautions."

"Precautions? What are—yes. Yes, of course. Precautions. Against murder! Who could have imagined? Thank you, gentlemen. I . . . Yes, thank you."

Having thoroughly disconcerted Shin Xiao, Dee and I tipped our hats and withdrew.

We resumed our perambulation to a destination known only to Dee, though we were heading back in the direction of the East End. Dee was silent beside me for a short time, then said, "What did you make of Shin Xiao?"

I told him I had difficulty believing a man that befuddled— and lazy—could be capable of these calculated murders. "Even his beleaguered wife believes he might forget he invited guests for tea."

Dee nodded. "I agree. Also, living as they do from his father's largesse, their home seems prosperous and settled. They have a maid. If Shin is in financial straits dire enough to drive a lazy man to this level of violence, I saw no sign of it."

"Nor I. Also, if his confusion and alarm when you told him of the murders wasn't real, then he is the one who was born for the stage."

"Quite. So let us suppose for the moment we can discount Shin Xiao. The tontine has three other living members."

"Jiang, Captain Lu, and the second added man," I said. "If we are correct that the tontine is the motivation behind the killings, the murderer must be one of them."

"Precisely. I believe we can also exclude Jiang from our suspicions. If he himself was the killer, why lay so many traps? When I confronted him he seemed genuinely terrified to the point of incoherence. And in the time since he escaped our grasp no one else has been murdered. No, I think he's gone to ground and is not our man."

"Well," I said carefully, "that leaves only the added man, and the captain."

Dee shot me a sideways glance. "Your tone tells me you think I may have dismissed Captain Lu too soon."

"I understand your loyalty to the man—"

"Possibly not entirely. Captain Lu risked a good deal in the trenches of France to keep his men alive—these four among them. In addition to his brave deeds, his repeated protestations to the British authorities earned him beatings of the same kind I experienced. I find it difficult to credit that, having endured what he did, he would now take to murdering these same men for the tontine money. I suppose it's possible, but my eye is now upon this last added man."

"Your logic is compelling," I admitted.

"Yet you aren't entirely convinced."

"Having not shared your experience with Captain Lu, I am perhaps more dispassionate. I shall take my lead from you, but at the same time, I suggest we totally dismiss neither the captain nor Jiang from suspicion."

"That seems eminently reasonable."

After a time the look of our surroundings began to be familiar, as did the aroma. The streets had narrowed and developed angles. The structures had either shrunken, if shops or homes, or swollen to mammoth warehouse size. The scents of water, fish, and bilge were everywhere.

"Dee," I said. "We've come back to Limehouse. Is this where the second added man is to be found?"

"No, though he lives not far from here. If I'm correct about his guilt, I think it might help to have the satchel I left with Sergeant Hoong."

"What is in the satchel?"

Dee smiled. "That, Lao, you will discover."

# CHAPTER TWENTY-FOUR

"Judge Dee! Lao She! Please, come in and tell me all you've been doing. The kettle has just boiled." Sergeant Hoong turned the sign on the door to read "closed," shot the bolt, and began spooning tea into a pot.

"No, Hoong, thank you, there's no—" Dee stopped. He looked at Hoong's face, and then at mine. Hoong's expression was displeased and mine, I'm sure, was imploring.

"Dee," I said, "this physical exertion of yours is all very well, but I'm merely human. A cup of tea and a chance to sit and rest, however briefly, would be most welcome."

"I must insist," Hoong added before Dee could speak. "If I may be blunt, sir, you look worse now than you did when you left this morning. From the peaked expression on poor Lao I imagine you've eaten nothing. You cannot continue in this manner. Especially," he added, "if you are attempting to free yourself from the chains of opium."

Dee stared.

Hoong shook his head with a smile. "You can't imagine yourself to be the first man I've seen in this state. The pallor, the beads of sweat, the tremor that starts and stops . . . Sadly, many of our countrymen find the burden of long separation from home and family too much to bear, and turn to the pipe to ease the pain. Eventually some find their way to my shop for herbs to help them gain their release from its hold. I don't know what made you first opt for the drug, Dee, but if you're now set on breaking from its grip I have some herbs you'll find helpful."

"I'm glad to hear this, Hoong," I said, "for Dee's overall state—"

"Enough!" snapped the subject of our scrutiny. "Very well. For Lao's sake—and yes, yes, Hoong, for my own—I'll consent to a brief intermission in our investigative activities. I confess to simultaneous senses of agitation and fatigue which as a combination is supremely unpleasant. If you can offer me something to alleviate that, Hoong, I'd be most grateful." With that, Dee dropped himself onto a stool and sat, hands on thighs, looking around expectantly like a patient visiting an herbalist. Which, I suppose, he was.

I sat also, while Sergeant Hoong went about spooning a different tea into another pot. That he placed in front of Dee, while from the first he poured for me and himself. While Dee's tea steeped Hoong brought over a tin of biscuits. "These are not bad," he said. "Too sweet, in the English fashion, but as neither of you has eaten lately I imagine you'll find them acceptable."

I bit into one of the currant-filled biscuits and thought it as good as anything I'd ever eaten. The pale green liquid in my cup also seemed particularly delectable. "Have one, Dee," I urged, taking a second biscuit.

"I have no appetite, thank you." Dee sipped at the thick dark tea Hoong had poured into his cup. "Hoong," he said calmly, replacing the cup on the low table, "I must congratulate you. If anything worse has ever passed my lips I can't remember it."

"That is the opium in your body enlisting your tongue to help fight its enemy. You must drink all the tea in the pot."

"Surely not."

"Surely, or I won't unlock the door."

"Big Brother Hoong"—Dee eyed the older man—"you have much of your father in you. I suppose that's a good thing, though right now I can't say I feel that it is." He once more lifted his cup. "Lao, why don't you bring Sergeant Hoong up to date on what we've accomplished while I try to ingest this vile liquid."

As I relayed my tale and Hoong listened, we did our best to keep our eyes fixed on one another, so as not to appear to be watching that Dee didn't pour his "vile liquid" out on the floor. I felt a slight twinge of guilt as I ate a third tasty biscuit and washed it down with more clean, astringent tea; but Dee had brought this upon himself, I reflected, by his continuing indulgence in the scourge of opium. I felt a swell of moral superiority, which I attempted to tamp down. Dee was, after all, an exceptional man in so many ways. His reliance on opium was a weakness in him I could not understand.

"Well," said Dee, slapping his thighs, though not with quite the snap I'd seen before, "I've finished your ghastly brew, Hoong. I feel no better, though I trust I shall, for if I don't I'll consider this an unpleasant hoax perpetrated by a man I've been thinking of as a friend. Lao, if you've downed enough tea and biscuits that you're fortified for the afternoon, perhaps we can continue our work? Hoong, if you'll be so kind as to hand over my satchel and unlock the door, I'll be most grateful."

At the end of this speech Hoong looked for a long moment at Dee. He went behind his counter and withdrew a leather case. "Your satchel is here. Unless you mean to don its contents now, I'd be pleased to carry it for you. It's no use frowning in that way, Dee. I'll be accompanying you. From what Lao has told me this next man you're calling on may well be a cold-blooded murderer. He'll have nothing to lose by fighting capture as violently as necessary. Another pair of hands and eyes can do your errand no harm and may prove very useful."

"So you think the hands and eyes of myself and Lao are not up to the task?"

Hoong remained silent. Finally Dee sighed and said, "Very well, Hoong. As the hands and eyes to which you refer are yours, I suppose I can't object."

Hoong locked up the shop and we three set off.

IT WAS NOT a long walk—especially at Dee's pace—to Cyprus Street in Bethnal Green, the residence of the second man added to the tontine and our suspect in the killings of Ma, Ching, and Guo. As we approached I felt my body's energy, renewed by the victuals Hoong had supplied, rising toward a sizzling peak. I was to participate in the capture of a killer! Hoong and Dee together presented quite a formidable force, but I trusted that my own contribution would not prove wholly insignificant.

Partway to the address we were making for we came to an alley. "Here, I think," said Dee. Hoong handed Dee the satchel. Dee disappeared into the shadows.

"Hoong," I said, "what's going on?"

"He'll just be a moment."

After a number of moments Dee had not yet reappeared. I said, "Really, Hoong. I cannot be of much use if you and Dee shut me out of aspects of the investigation."

Hoong smiled. "Dee?" he called. "Are you ready?"

"Dee?" came a voice from the alley. "Oh, 'im? I've eaten 'im!" Then from the shadows burst a figure of terrifying aspect. All in black, with raised wings and a dreadful fierce face, it screamed, "And I shall eat you too!"

I leapt back, wondering whether to run or fight. As I'd never battled a supernatural entity before and could conceive of no dependable strategy, I chose retreat. I'd turned to flee when I realized Hoong was laughing. Another familiar laugh joined his. My heart pounding, I looked over my shoulder to see the monster's face in its hand, replaced in the usual spot by Dee's amused features. "It's nobbut me, Spring'eel Jack," said Dee.

I turned and looked squarely at him, attempting to draw even breaths. "That was unkind, Dee," I said. Observing him, I realized that the ghastly face was a mask, and the wings a cape stitched to the costume's arms. "And what is this regalia you've got yourself up in?"

"I apologize," Dee said, sounding once again like himself. "Springheel Jack has demonstrated an ability to frighten British policemen. I wondered whether he would also be effective against courageous Chinese."

"Don't attempt to flatter me," I said, my heart returning to its normal rhythm. "And please conduct your experiments upon another subject from this point on."

"Of course," said Dee agreeably. "Now, if you gentlemen will proceed to our destination—I'll do the same meself!" Delivering that last in the creature's voice again, he placed the mask over his face and leapt upward. He reached for a roof gutter but nearly missed it. At the last moment he was able to grab hold. With a grunt he swung himself onto the slates, and was gone.

"Hoong," I said, my eye on the gutter that had almost eluded Dee's grasp, "how difficult is it to free oneself from the grip of opium?"

"From what I've seen in my customers, it is extremely arduous. Many don't succeed, or seem to but slip back after a time and must make the attempt again, sometimes more than once. The Western powers did China no favors when they forced opium into our ports."

I agreed with him upon that point, because who could argue the opposite? Even the British, whose ships brought the cursed drug from India to China's shores, and who, save those clashes fought by China under Commissioner Lin, won every battle in the wars to force China to accept it, never argued that there were benefits in that trade to any but themselves.

I said to Hoong, "Dee claims to have been visited in a dream by Commissioner Lin, who told him he must give up the drug."

Hoong glanced at me. "Did he? That's a good sign, then."

"So you believe in ghostly visitations from the other side?"

"I believe, Lao, that a man receiving instructions from Commissioner Lin in a dream was predisposed to follow that advice before it ever came."

As we neared Cyprus Street I heard the sound of police sirens. "Hoong!" I said. "Springheel Jack has been spotted!"

We quickened our pace.

"Not that they'll be able to take him," I reassured us both. "Dee is more than a match for the London constabulary."

"At his best, he is," Hoong agreed. "But right now he's not at his best. It's possible we'll be needed."

When we rounded the corner, however, we found Springheel Jack was not the focus of attention of the Metropolitan Police. We couldn't even see Dee, though I had no doubt he was watching from behind some rooftop chimney. Nor were we needed—indeed, I thought, no efforts on our part would be welcome. The coroner's van stood in front of a rooming house that bore the address we had for the second added man. As we watched, an attendant opened the van's rear doors and two constables exited the building carrying a stretcher—on which rested a sheet-draped corpse.

# CHAPTER TWENTY-FIVE

"It's possible," I said to Hoong while we pressed ourselves into the shadows across the street, "that that's not our man. The fact a man's dead at this address might be a mere coincidence."

Hoong said nothing, but the look he gave me told me he was as little convinced of the likelihood of that as I was. The prospect of it being true diminished even more when we saw that the last member of the police force to leave the building, the smallest finger of his left hand wearing a splinted bandage, was Captain William Bard.

Or to try to leave. As Bard stood in the open doorway a caped, black-clad figure reached out from behind him and, quick as an eye-blink, yanked him inside and shut the door.

"Why—" I said.

"Quite," said Hoong.

We waited to see what would happen next. After some minutes the door opened again and Captain Bard, his face ashen, stepped out and rapidly approached a pair of constables. He spoke and gesticulated; one constable entered the building and the other dashed around the block to its rear yard; but very soon both returned empty-handed. Bard's pallor was replaced by an angry flush. He climbed into his car, spoke curtly to the constable at the wheel, and was driven off.

Hoong and I loitered across the street, waiting for Dee to show himself and instruct us on our next steps. In short order, Dee, dressed once again in civilian clothing and satchel in hand, walked around the corner and headed our way. Passing us without a glance, he indicated by a small hand gesture that we should follow. We did so, staying back and finally catching him up in a nearby park where he'd stopped as if to admire the irises. Which, standing brightly in the afternoon sun, were indeed admirable.

"Dee!" I said, as Hoong and I came up beside him. "What's happened?"

"What's happened? What's happened? I've become a useless fool, that's what's happened!" Dee gave a disagreeable laugh. Fresh beads of perspiration bloomed on his pale brow. "Perhaps we should just sit and drink tea, and wait until only one man remains. He'll collect the tontine assets and we'll collect him! Doesn't it seem to you gentlemen that that would be a more rewarding way to proceed than the path we've been following?" Dee's expression was as unpleasant as his laugh.

"Dee"—Hoong repeated my words calmly—"what's happened?"

"The man," said Dee, "is dead. He died this morning. We thought him a suspect but he was a corpse!"

"How did he die?" I asked.

"The same way as the others, of course! He was the victim of a butterfly sword. Naturally he was, because his killer was the same. A man I've not been able to identify, much less bring to justice! What use am I to anyone, can you answer that? What use?"

Eyeing Dee, Hoong asked, "What did Springheel Jack discuss with Inspector Bard?"

"They had a lovely talk, that they did. A captain of the Metropolitan Police terrified of a storybook villain! Really, it's laughable."

"Jack did break his finger," I pointed out.

"No, Lao." Dee thrust his sweating face close to mine. "*I* broke his finger. I dressed in the costume of a childhood nightmare and the heroic Inspector Bard didn't look beyond it. It was my fear of exactly this sort of deficiency in the Metropolitan Police that made me determined to investigate Ma's death myself, but I seem to be no better at that work than the heroic Inspector Bard."

"Did the heroic Inspector Bard say anything of interest to Springheel Jack beyond confirmation of the means of death?" Hoong asked. He seemed not at all unnerved by Dee's increasingly short-tempered behavior.

"He did not, but Jack did, to him. Jack explained the workings of the tontine and suggested that the Metropolitan Police would do well to put a watch on the home of Shin Xiao and his family, and to search for Captain Lu Yan and do the same. Jack also mentioned Jiang, who may have returned to his trip-wired dwelling by now. Any one of them may be the next victim and any one of them may be the killer, and I've been face-to-face with them all and did nothing!"

"Dee, the self-disgust you're experiencing is the opium trying to defeat your attempt to—"

"Hoong, if you don't stop being reasonable I'll be forced to thrash you."

"In your condition," Hoong said, "you would not win."

"My condition! I warn you, don't suppose my condition—"

"Mr. Dee, sir." Dee's expostulation was interrupted by a

cheerful new voice. "I'm glad I found yer. I think I've brought yer news of interest."

We all three turned to see the thief, Jimmy Fingers.

"You!" said Dee. "Why are you here?"

"As I said, sir. I've brought news."

"How did you find me?"

"Well, that were partly luck, sir. It's abroad that a China-man were killed near 'ere—"

"Chinese! A Chinese man. And if this is the news you've brought you're sorely behind."

"Oh, no, sir, that's not my news. I were saying how I found yer. When I 'eard about the dead—the dead *Chinese* man, I said, Jimmy, me boy, that's where you'll find yer employer, for a man such as Mr. Dee will be interested in this poor sod."

"And interested I am, and what of it?" Dee snapped.

Jimmy Fingers gave a puzzled frown. "Well, sir, so I came looking—"

"Pay no mind to Dee's tone," I said to the young thief. "He's feeling poorly. Please continue with what you've come to say."

"Oh, yes, sir!" The fellow brightened. "I'm sorry yer unwell, sir," he said to Dee.

"Lao, if you insist on broadcasting news of my health all across London I shall include you in the thrashing I intend for Hoong. Now, Jimmy, get on with it."

With widened eyes, Jimmy Fingers swallowed and said, "Well, sir, I've just come from St. George's, Bloomsbury, from the Christian mission there. They serve up a free workingman's tea that's not 'alf bad, though a fellow's forced to sit through an awful lot of tommyrot about saints and salvation—oh, begging yer pardon, gentlemen, if I've offended!"

"I'm the only Christian among us," I ventured, "and if tea is accompanied by one of the Reverend Robert Evans's sermons, I can't say I disagree. I'd urge you to get to the point as rapidly as possible, however, before Dee widens his circle of upcoming thrashings to include you."

"Oh, no, that won't do! I've already felt one of those and 'ave no yearning for another. What I'm telling yer is this. Just as the Reverend Evans finished and we'd begun our tea, a China—a Chinese man rushed in, fell at the reverend's feet, and begged for sanctuary. 'E babbled on as 'ow people were after 'im for the money, the money, and they'd already killed the others. 'E begged the reverend to let 'im stay right there at the mission. Now, this struck me as something would be of interest to yer, sir, so 'ere I am." His grin returned.

Dee, Hoong, and I looked at one another and as a single man exclaimed, "Jiang!"

"Jimmy, you've done well." Dee fetched a half crown from his waistcoat pocket and handed it to the thief. "If there is any further intelligence on the subject of Chinese men that you find interesting, I'll likely find it interesting as well."

"Yes, sir!" Jimmy tucked away the coin and sprinted, grinning, down the street.

"Now," said Dee, "Lao, you will come with me. Hoong, we must find Captain Lu. That's a task well suited to your knowledge and abilities."

"Are you certain you wouldn't prefer that I accompany you? You're in no better condition now—"

"Damn my condition! Finding Lu is vital and if you come with Lao and myself, who will do it? No, your task is clear."

"Very well. If I succeed, will you then withdraw the threat of a thrashing?" Hoong asked.

"I intend to thrash you on general principles, but not until the urgent business is complete. Please be so good as you head to Limehouse to take my satchel back to your shop. Thank you. Now, Lao, come. I think we have no time to lose."

# CHAPTER TWENTY-SIX

St. George's Church, Bloomsbury, was an imposing Anglican edifice in the classical style. Built two hundred years ago to serve those who referred to themselves at the time—and for all I knew, still did—as "the better classes," it featured a flight of steps leading from the pavement to a high columned porch. A statue of King George the First in Roman dress rode atop the tiered tower, itself influenced by Pliny the Elder's description of the Mausoleum of Halicarnassus. It was this kind of absurdity that made me, although a Christian, so reluctant to participate in the rituals of my adopted religion. But the Reverend Robert Evans had, after all, been instrumental in my coming to London; this, I had felt, was a debt to be repaid early in my stay by the sacrifice of half a dozen Sunday mornings. Therefore, although Dee and I on our previous visit had been only to the study in the vicarage, I already knew the church interior to be an affair of dark wood pews lined up squarely between tall stone columns on hard marble floors, looked down upon by stern stained glass windows. The predominant impression the church gave to those sitting in services was that the joyful buoyancy of ascending to heaven was only to be earned through the tough-minded stamina of tight-jawed effort.

Dee and I, in the throes of effort of another kind—and with Dee appearing abnormally winded, and perspiring—once again bypassed all that somber holiness, this time to make for the Christian mission. This institution sat to the rear of the church's side yard behind the aged stones of the small graveyard. It occupied a humble building that had once been a stable for the vicar's horses. On one side it nestled against the church. At its rear it backed against a high wall, which also wrapped the graveyard on three sides, leaving that resting place to be approached only from the street. The mission's loft contained half a dozen beds for the temporarily indigent (or temporary beds for the permanently indigent, as Reverend Evans did not believe in coddling those who could not find, in fairly short order, a way to better their own circumstances). On the ground floor were the kitchen; a storeroom for clothing, blankets, and other such donated goods; and the dining area. All were furnished, in contradistinction to the church interior, in a plain workaday manner. The building itself, also contrasting with the church, was in a state of shabbiness. It was clear the Halicarnassian steeple was given preference over the former stables in the disposition of the church's building funds.

We made our way through the graveyard to the door of the mission building. A lift of Dee's hand as we approached cautioned me to silence. While I thought this instruction gratuitous, in Dee's current state a reproof would likely be ill-received. Dee laid his hand upon the knob and turned it slowly, making no sound. He opened the door in similar fashion. I was satisfied we'd gained entry in such a way that unless a man were directly facing the door, he would not be aware of us.

Unfortunately, Jiang Gwan Li sat in a straight-backed chair directly facing the door.

On the one hand, we had found him.

On the other, the element of surprise was his. With a blood-curdling scream he rushed straight at us. At the last second, as Dee reached to seize him, he jumped aside with a madman's grace and ran past me, out of Dee's grasp. Dee, spinning to chase after him, pivoted a quarter turn too far and stumbled into me. With a curse he straightened himself again and ran out the door. I followed, to see Jiang leaping some graves, skirting others, hurtling through the graveyard until he reached the pavement. I thought he'd race down it to freedom, but instead, howling like a specter, he turned right, dashed up the steps, and charged into the church proper, shrieking, "Sanctuary! Sanctuary!"

I took note, as Dee and I ran after Jiang, of the fact that every face on the street was turned to the odd spectacle of one Chinese man bleating for sanctuary while being pursued by two others. When I heard a constable's whistle I was struck by the thought that Dee and I might soon be off to jail again, while Jiang went free. I redoubled my speed. If we could capture and hold Jiang, our virtuous roles in this adventure could be asserted. We could send for Inspector Bard, if need be, who would no doubt affirm our explanation. Indeed, since the situation involved Chinese men, it was possible Bard had already been alerted. Although the prospect of seeing the inspector did not delight me, it would no doubt give Dee great pleasure to place the man who was now our chief suspect in these crimes into the hands of the Metropolitan Police.

I tore after Dee, galloping up the church steps. He yanked open the heavy doors and I was right behind him. I had to stop and blink in the shadows of the church. Dee, who apparently had the eyes of a cat, made straight for the altar. My vision adjusted and I saw what he must have seen: in the dim, incense-scented stillness, the altar cloth was swaying.

Dee waved me to the altar's left side while he moved slowly to the other, speaking calmly. "Jiang Gwan Li. You remember me—Dee Ren Jie. We were friends in France. This other man is Lao She. He's my friend, and also yours."

Silence from the altar. Now I was near it, I could see the toe of a cloth shoe protruding from the folds in the fabric.

"Jiang," Dee continued, "we have no wish to harm you. We understand your alarm. It's our hope that you can help us identify the person who is after you and your companions."

Again, no response. Dee and I both glanced back in alarm as a light from behind signaled the opening of the church door. A constable stood silhouetted against the brightness of the doorway. Dee waved him back but he entered and closed the door behind himself. Dee's wave must have had some effect, however, for he came no closer. I thought at the same time I heard a faint creak from off to the right, as of a door hinge, and Dee swung his head that way also, but nothing more ensued. Nor did the foot under the altar cloth stir.

Dee crouched before the altar. "Jiang, I'm going to lift the cloth. I won't come nearer. I want you to see my face and recall who I am and that I am no danger to you." He reached for the rich velvet skirt that wrapped the altar and raised it as he had proposed. The dim light revealed a strange vision: Jiang Gwan Li, wide-eyed and ashen, pressed against the cabinetwork as though he feared being devoured by a ghost. "Jiang," said Dee, "do you remember me? Will you come out?"

After a long moment of silent staring, Jiang inched forward. He stopped, inched, stopped again, and then slowly crept out from underneath the altar and rose to his feet.

"Now, Jiang," Dee began, but from behind Dee came a bellow as a masked man burst from the shadows of the vestry door. He wore a loose black tunic and trousers, and a workingman's large leather gloves. Continuing his unearthly roar he ran toward us, a sword held high. Dee crouched, pushing his shoulder into the knee of the sword-wielding stranger. The man fell over Dee of his own forward motion.

Jiang scurried up the aisle like a mouse being chased by a cat. "Stop him!" Dee shouted, involved in his own struggle with the masked swordsman.

I stuck out my foot to trip Jiang as he raced past me. I succeeded, but he knocked me over also and we both tumbled to the floor, rolling like thrown dice. Jiang jumped up, looked left and right, and dove under a pew.

The air was pierced by a constable's whistle. "Stand still! Stand still! All of you, stop!" The constable ran toward us, blowing his whistle and waving his truncheon. "Stop in the king's name, you rat bastards, or I'll brain you!"

I spotted Jiang popping up from the pews and running up a side aisle. I took off after him, attempting simultaneously to evade the constable, who had clearly decided we were all miscreants to be halted in the progress of whatever it was we were doing.

Jiang zigzagged back between the pews as I reached the aisle. I followed. Jiang jumped onto a pew, stepped up onto its back, and from there leapt to the back of the next one. I took a breath and followed him in doing that, too. Like cats we leapt from pew-back to pew-back, until the constable decided also to try this means of travel. In the way of most constables he was large; in the way of many he was also clumsy. His first leap resulted in a resounding crash as the pew he landed on teetered and fell over onto the one behind it. Unfortunately that was the one I was standing upon. Knocked from my perch, I flew through the air. Not being Dee, I did not land on my feet.

I looked up to see Dee charging up the aisle. "Dee!" I shouted, barely in time to alert him to the danger I'd seen—the masked swordsman had seized a silver candelabra from the altar and hurled it at Dee's head.

Dee ducked and rolled and was up again before the candelabra clanged to the floor. That brief delay, however, had allowed the constable to catch up with Jiang, who had apparently also fallen when the constable's leap turned the pews to dominoes. Jiang had just stood again when the constable caught him and held him, truncheon on his neck. Jiang flailed, struggling to get free.

Dee approached. "Constable, ease your hold. Jiang—"

But as Jiang's eyes met Dee's an unearthly howl echoed in the holy space. The masked swordsman came racing up the aisle. The constable let go his hold and turned to face him, but the swordsman pushed aside the constable and ran Jiang through.

I was aghast. Dee spun to apprehend the swordsman, but the mortally wounded Jiang fell to the floor between them. Dee leapt over him, and then was forced to duck when the swordsman's weapon—the short-bladed dao—came flying at him. The swordsman, pushing over altar furniture and candlesticks in his wake, disappeared through the vestry door.

I jumped up to go after him. Dee stepped to follow but from the floor came his name, very faintly. "Go!" Dee said to me, and knelt to Jiang.

Running into the vestry, I saw nothing and no one. As I hastened toward the door to the churchyard the Reverend Robert Evans emerged from his study. "What's happened? Such noises I heard!"

Without an answer I burst out the door. The churchyard, but for gravestones, shade trees, and the singing of birds, was empty.

I ran back into the church. "He's gone! He's gone!" I shouted to the constable. "Gather other men! Go after him!"

Reverend Evans was on my heels. "What's happened? I—" He stood horror-struck, taking in the scene before him. "Is that man dead?"

On that last word Jiang, his blood flowing freely onto the marble floor, feebly lifted one arm.

"Not yet," snarled Dee, leaning over the dying man. "Jiang," he said. "Jiang, is there anything you can tell us that will help us avenge you?"

I was unable to see whether Jiang made a response, for at that moment the church door flew open once again. Captain Bard and a pair of constables came hurtling down the aisle. "What happened? Where's the attacker?" Bard shouted. "Did you let him get away?"

Dee leapt to his feet. "Did *we* let him get away? We'd have had him but for your bungling constable. I have a mind—"

I grabbed Dee as he lunged toward Bard. "No!" I said into his ear. "This is not the way!" He shook me off and glared at the inspector, but made no further effort to attack him.

Bard stopped as though frozen, and stared. Finally he spoke. "Dee Ren Jie? Here in London?" Bard smiled, not a pleasant sight. "And in the middle of a case of dead Chinamen?"

Dee's eyes burned but he made no response.

"Well, now. This is a surprise." Bard looked Dee up and down, then unhurriedly shifted his attention to me. "Who are you?"

"Lao She," I said with raised chin. "I'm a lecturer at the University."

"Are you?" Bard's tone wasn't so much disbelieving as dismissive. I might in fact be a lecturer, it seemed to say, but as I was Chinese, no lecture I delivered could be of value. Returning his gaze to Dee, he shook his head, allowing himself another small smile. "Dee Ren Jie. Well, well. Now. You will both stay here while I investigate this death. Sit down, gentlemen, this will take some time. Then we'll all return to the station together and have a chance for a good long natter." To his constable in sharp tones he said, "Watch them. If they try to run, use your truncheon."

Bard then knelt beside Jiang, who now had the pallid face and staring eyes of a corpse. Dee and I remained where we were, and the constable, though keeping a stern glower fixed upon us, made no attempt to enforce Bard's directive that we sit.

"Dee," I said quietly, "did Jiang say anything to you before he expired?"

Dee shifted his glare to me. "Yes. Yes, he did."

"And what was that?"

"He said," Dee answered, straightening his clothing, which had gone quite askew, "that it was all the fault of the pictures."

# CHAPTER TWENTY-SEVEN

"The pictures?" I whispered. "It's the fault of the pictures? What could that possibly mean?"

"I don't know." Dee leveled a long look at Reverend Evans, who had dropped down heavily onto a pew. The clergyman stared wide-eyed at what had just happened on his hallowed floor. "But I do know this," said Dee, advancing on the reverend. "You, Reverend Evans, were aware that Jiang Gwan Li was here."

Reverend Evans turned his face to Dee. "I—I'm sorry, what did you say?"

"Someone alerted the killer to Jiang's location. Who could that have been"—Dee's voice got louder—"if not you?"

"But," stuttered the reverend, "but all who were at tea in the mission saw this man run in."

"None knew who he was but you."

"I? I didn't know! Who he is? This poor man?" Evans waved a vague hand at Jiang. "He—he was asking for sanctuary. It's my Christian duty—"

"Your Christian duty!" Dee roared, and threw himself at the reverend.

"Dee! Stop!" I seized Dee's shoulders and pulled him away. It was more a testimony to Dee's debilitated state than to my brawn that I was able to do so. "Stop this at once! You're not behaving as a rational man!"

"Rationality hasn't proved itself a valuable quality in this case yet!" he retorted. "And as for you, Lao, your true colors show in circumstances such as this. Again you take the side of the Britisher against your countryman."

"My countryman is conducting himself ignominiously. What possible reason could Reverend Evans have for alerting the killer to Jiang's location?"

"Somehow it's money. It's always money, those times it's not a personal hatred." Again he glared at the cleric.

"If you're considering attacking that man again I'd advise against it." That voice came from Inspector Bard, who'd stood and was pointing at Dee with his bandaged hand. "I have no reason to think you didn't commit this murder yourself."

Dee pierced Bard with a scowl. "What you have, Captain Bard, as ever, is no reason at all."

Dee leapt lightly onto a pew back. From there he sprang up. Flying high through the air, he reached forward to one of the chandeliers whose chains disappeared into the darkness of St. George's high ceiling. I held my breath as the fingers of his left hand slipped past it, but his right hand was able to grasp on. The lamp, with Dee pendant, made an ominous creaking as it swung to and fro.

"Come down! Dee!" Bard roared. "Reverend! Where is the mechanism? Constable, cut the cable!"

Following Bard's orders, a constable ran up the stairs to the choir loft to search out the ropes used for lowering the chandeliers. Another constable, truncheon out, waited underneath for Dee to drop, with or without the chandelier.

Dee, however, had other plans. He pumped his legs, swinging

them in front and dropping them behind, then in front again. The arc of the chandelier's sway grew higher and wider. After a third such pump, Dee let go the chandelier and flew to the entablature above the columns at the entrance.

He tottered.

"Dee!" I cried. I was sure I was about to see him fall.

But no. He steadied himself, slid his feet along the narrow ledge, and, once he reached the oculus window with its stained glass image of the dragon (St. George himself being on the opposite wall), he swiveled it open and slipped out.

"After him!" Bard howled.

Two constables chased up the aisle after Dee, though it was clear, to me at any rate, that they had no hope of catching him. They raced out the door, Bard following.

With the constables' numbers diminished and Bard gone, I could also have effected an escape. However, the inspector knew my name, and my residence in London was no secret. The wiser course seemed to be to stay and claim ignorance.

I searched out and discovered my hat, then seated myself on a pew out of the hearing of Reverend Evans. That gentleman appeared to be still in shock, but I thought it best to avoid the possibility of his correcting any response I might give to Inspector Bard's interrogation. I waited with calm patience until Bard returned and came stalking over.

To the inspector's shouted demands that I tell him where Dee had gone, where Dee was living, and what Dee was doing in London, I replied that: (1) I had no idea; (2) to my knowledge his current residence was in Switzerland; and (3) again, I had no idea. While my responses to all these questions were truthful, my answers to the second and third were a touch disingenuous, for I chose to interpret them more literally than perhaps intended. Yes, Dee was sharing my rooms just at present, but he could hardly be said to be living there; and since at that moment I had, in truth, no idea where Dee had gone in London, I had also no idea what he was doing in London.

"I've only just met the man," I said. I realized that avowal might imply I'd made Dee's acquaintance within the hour, not the week, but I reasoned it was up to Captain Bard to request clarification.

He did not, but demanded, "What were the two of you doing in St. George's?"

"Dee is a countryman. He'd requested I show him some sights of London."

"And you *happened* to choose this church, where a Chinaman *happened* to get himself murdered before your eyes?"

"I'm a member of this congregation. I consider this church well worth a visit. It has, after all, a statue of King George the First atop the steeple. Though I promise you, Inspector, had I known a murder was about to occur here I would have organized our day differently." By which I meant developed a plan to stop it, but let the inspector believe what he might. I went on, "May I give my witness statement? I have responsibilities at the University. Here is my card. You may of course contact me if there's anything further you require."

Bard didn't seem happy, but he could have no grievance with my cooperation. He called over one of the remaining constables, to whom I carefully delineated the events of the chase and the killing.

"And you didn't see where the swordsman went?" the constable inquired, his voice holding more weary hope than eager expectation.

"Up the aisle and out of the church. Beyond that, no. An officer followed but came back empty-handed."

The constable dutifully kept his eye on me as he reported to Inspector Bard that my statement was complete. Bard, though clearly reluctant to let me depart, had no reason to demand otherwise. I went to sit beside the Reverend Evans before I left. "Sir," I said quietly, "are you quite all right?"

"Yes, Lao," he said automatically, and then, "no. No, I am not. This sort of thing . . . No, it won't do at all."

"No, of course not," I said. "Sir, one request?"

He looked at me blankly.

I said, "Judge Dee will be able to get to the bottom of this situation faster than the Metropolitan Police. This will only happen is he's left free to do it, however. A certain amount of enmity exists between Judge Dee and Inspector Bard."

Evans turned his gaze to Bard, who was kneeling with the recently arrived coroner beside Jiang's body. "Does it?"

"It does," I said. "I'd account it a great favor if you'd not speak of our visit here earlier. Knowing Dee and I came here together will be of no use to the Metropolitan Police and will hinder Dee in his work." I didn't mention to him that it would also hinder me in my hopes of staying out of difficulties, as I'd told the reverend then, but had not told the inspector now, that Dee was sharing my rooms at the Wendells'.

"I see," Evans said vaguely. "I'm not to mention seeing you earlier. I see."

"Yes," I said. "Thank you." Whether the Reverend Evans fully understood my request, or intended to comply, I couldn't tell. However, at that moment Bard, looking up, noticed me. He gave me a suspicious frown, I who had been so impatient to leave. "Take care of yourself, sir," I said to Evans, and then, adjusting my hat, stood and strode up the church aisle like a man with somewhere to go.

# CHAPTER TWENTY-EIGHT

What I myself did in the succeeding hours you'll learn in due time. I make a brief appearance in this account, but right now Dee's progress, as reported to me when next I saw him, is what I invite you to follow.

DEE DID NOT descend from the dragon window to the church porch, but concealed himself behind a column capital until the constables had attained the pavement. Only then did he emerge. He swung onto the church roof, clambered up and over it, and leapt from the other side onto the roof of the mission. By this time the constables, perplexed, were stopped on the pavement peering about. Dee flattened his body against the slates, securing himself from sliding off by gripping the roof ridge, and plucked a loose fragment of slate from the roof (the mission building, as I've mentioned, was in bad repair). He aimed it toward one of the headstones. It hit its mark. The constables, hearing it, were off. Dee watched as their arrival at that marker came to nothing but, as he'd intended, they concluded that their quarry had gone in that direction. They dashed past the grave and back out into the street. After a moment one ran left and the other, right.

Dee eased himself from the roof, crept from tombstone to tombstone, and, reaching the graveyard gate, went neither left nor right, but ran straight across the road. He raced into an alley, over a fence—startling a chambermaid hanging out the wash—and out the opposite alley to the next street, along which he continued to make great haste.

Was Dee's speed as he rushed along the pavement an effort to elude the constables in the event they realized their error and returned? Lamentably, it was not. The physical discomfort of his attempt to abandon opium—the itching of the skin, aching of the muscles, sweating of the forehead, and cramping of the gut—was, now that Hoong's elixir and the thrill of action had worn off, causing him great distress. Add to that his fury and disgust at what he perceived as his own failure, not only to solve Ma's murder, but to prevent the same fate from befalling others of his former compatriots; his anger at what he accounted, variously, the incompetence of the Metropolitan Police, the hypocrisy of the Anglican Church, and the self-satisfied obliviousness of the entire British population; and he felt only one path remained open to him.

He flew to Limehouse to find an opium den.

The only such place of which he was aware was that run by Chin Peng Da, but he did not go there, for even in his diminished state he realized his presence would not be welcome. Instead, reaching the area, he was compelled to search through the narrow lanes for another establishment. He didn't know precisely where to look, but the sad truth is that many Limehouse denizens recognized full well the air of a man in need of that which Dee required. He was directed in short order to a set of cellar rooms. He turned over some coins, settled on a couch, ordered a pipe, and when it was gone, sent for another.

DARK HAD FULLY fallen when Dee lifted himself off the opium couch and made his way across London. And this is where I briefly reenter this tale.

I took dinner at the Wendells', as usual. I'd been shaken by the events of the day and found myself preoccupied with questions about where Dee was and what he was doing—whether he had, in fact, escaped the grasp of the Metropolitan Police, or might even now be locked in Inspector Bard's cell and in need of rescue once again—as well as the larger question: If Jiang was not the murderer, but the most recent murderee, then who was killing these men? I made an attempt to conceal my worries from the ladies, who fortunately were engrossed in a discussion of an incident at the hat shop in which a pretty young woman made light of the advances of her handsome young companion—until he purchased for her a hat she'd admired. Her attitude altered and they left the shop arm in arm.

After dinner, we took coffee in the parlor. The ladies' interest then turned to how I had spent my day. *If only you knew*, I thought, but recounted an invented day I might have spent at a different time with a different countryman, seeing London.

As I was coming to the end of my story, the scraping of a key and the rattling of the knob at the front door announced that Dee had arrived at the house but was for some reason unable to let himself in.

In a flash of intuition I discerned that reason.

Hoping I was wrong, I jumped to my feet and went to open the door. Mary rose from her chair and followed.

I was not wrong. On the doorstep stood Dee, his hat missing, jacket open, tie loosened, and hair chaotic.

"Ah, Lao, good man," he said, slurring his words. He peered at me with unfocused eyes. "I couldn't . . . my key, you see . . . I'll just go up now." As he attempted to stumble past, I heard Mary's gasp from behind me.

"Dee," I said. "You cannot enter. My God, man, you reek of the opium den."

Dee sniffed his jacket arm and chuckled. "So I do. I suppose this suit will have to be cleaned. Now please step aside."

"I will not."

"Come, Lao, this is the wrong time for foolish games. I need to lie down."

"No games are being played here. You cannot enter this house. Go elsewhere until your head is clear. You are a disgrace!"

I closed the door in his surprised face and shot the bolt.

When I turned to Mary she was ashen. "What has happened to Mr. Dee?"

I had already used the word, and Mary had no doubt heard me. I could see no path other than the truth. "Dee, I fear"—I took Mary's elbow and guided her back to her seat in the parlor—"has partaken of opium."

Mary looked stricken and her mother, appalled.

"Opium!" exclaimed Mrs. Wendell, her eyes big and round as coins.

"Oh, dear," said Mary softly, sitting, dropping her gaze to her hands in her lap. "I'd not have thought that of him. No, I never would."

"Nor I!" the mother said. "He seemed such a respectable man. A judge, after all." She frowned and looked sharply at me. "But it leads me to another question. Mr. Lao, when you came here you promised us opium was not a vice in which you indulged."

"Nor is it, I assure you," I answered. "That Dee has fallen victim to its lure is dreadful but it has nothing to do with my own case. As you saw, I turned him away."

She was not placated. "Did you know about this habit of his when you requested he be permitted to share your rooms?"

"I did not, I give you my solemn word. And I hope you know I am a man on whose word you may depend."

Mrs. Wendell's mouth set tightly, but Mary's eyes lifted to meet mine. She gave me a wan smile and my heart sang. "Yes, Mr. Lao," she said. "Indeed, I'm quite confident of that."

# CHAPTER TWENTY-NINE

And Dee?

Having been turned away at the Wendells', what became of Dee?

Dee drifted through the London streets.

At times he was not at all sure where he was. At other times he knew the place precisely, though how he'd got to it he could not have said. When a pair of toughs stepped out from a mews he laughed to find himself in the hutong lanes of Peking. He fancied they called him "Bannerman" in a disparaging tone. Though of course it was I, not Dee, who was Manchu, he stoutly took the part of my beleaguered ancestors and replied in English that he was sorry not to address them in their native tongue but they were so ugly he couldn't tell whether they were German or French. Although the nature of the slight could only have confused them, they recognized it for an insult and attacked. Fortunately they were not trained fighters, for if they had been, Dee, in his state, would likely not have been able to drive them off. Drive them off, however, he ultimately did.

He was surprised and dismayed, as he staggered away from

that encounter, to discover he'd returned to the battlefields of France. Wounded men cried for assistance, shells exploded, and warning sirens screamed, but try as he might, he couldn't locate the battle. He ran this way and that way, but the combat was always behind him.

He felt enormous relief to suddenly be transported back to London, but Ma Ze Ren loomed out of the fog, repeating three times, "My poor wife is a widow, my poor wife," before becoming Guo Song, who offered Dee an opium pipe. As Dee reached for it, Guo was replaced by the British nurse who'd first introduced Dee to opium. She smiled and vanished, taking the pipe with her.

Some time later, in some other place, Dee tripped over the body of Jiang Gwan Li, which was lying on the pavement. He turned to go the other way but Jiang's body was there again. Jiang appeared every way Dee turned, always in the attitude in which he had died. "How are you able to move so fast?" Dee in exasperation finally challenged the corpse. Jiang rose into the air, laughing, and said, "It's the fault of the pictures."

"Dee Ren Jie!" roared a voice. Dee craned his neck to search the murk above his head. Inspector Bard, back in his British officer's uniform, stood twenty feet tall, raising his riding crop to strike a cowering Chinese laborer. Dee flew up into the sky to stay his arm. Before he reached him, Bard shouted, "Why have you come to London? I thought I was rid of you! But this time you won't stop me," and disappeared.

Dee, falling from the sky, dropped onto the grass at the edge of a park. A face, that of a British woman, leaned down near his. The widow Ma, he thought, and tried to speak her name, but could make no sound. Her horrified countenance pulled back sharply and she ran across the street into the mouth of a giant beast.

He heard again, "Dee Ren Jie!" but not this time from

Inspector Bard. This voice was Commissioner Lin's, and Dee began to tremble. Lin, once again on his judge's tall chair, pointed a stern finger at Dee. "You have ignored my orders."

As with the widow Ma, Dee tried to speak but was unable.

"The opium has left you useless," Commissioner Lin asserted. "Judge Dee, I am ashamed for you. To be so intoxicated that you cannot see what is right before your eyes!"

Dee began a feeble protest, but Commissioner Lin, like all the others he had seen this night, vanished into the fog.

And Dee, lying on the grass, passed out.

# CHAPTER THIRTY

For a second time Dee awoke with the dawn to find himself stiff, cold, and in a strange place. He felt disagreeable sensations he knew to be the start of a descent from a dangerous overindulgence in opium. He knew, too, that the only way to lessen the agonies to come was to get up, move, and continue moving.

He stumbled to his feet. Staggering from park to pavement, he peered about and found the area familiar. He was in Mayfair; if he was not wrong, the home of Colonel Livingstone Moore, buyer of the contents of Ma's shop, stood just across the street. Dee had no interest in Colonel Moore at the moment, and even less in being seen by the colonel in the state he was in. He was glad, however, to have his bearings.

A few streets along, near the site of a building being constructed, a wobbling Dee found a workingman's tea cart. He took a cup, asking for three spoons of sugar from the young proprietor who winked and said, "Busy night, then?"

Dee didn't reply, but purchased a second cup of the same. Feeling himself somewhat braced, Dee returned the chipped china to the young man for immersion in his tepid rinse-water and walked on.

And for a second time, he arrived at Sergeant Hoong's shop in a piteous state.

"Dee!" Hoong looked up from his account book. Immediately he came around the counter to bolt the door and turn the sign to "Closed." "Not again?"

"Again, Hoong. Please, none of your arguments against this vice. I've made them all myself on my way here. I beg of you a cup of tea and my Springheel Jack satchel." Dee lowered himself onto a stool.

"You cannot be thinking of going out in costume in the state you're in."

"I can think of nothing else. I must get to the bottom of what has happened, Hoong, or I shall never be able to account for myself to my ancestors. Or to Commissioner Lin."

"Ah, yes, Commissioner Lin. Lao tells me that you and Commissioner Lin have spoken."

"Twice, Hoong! He berates me for my opium use. He indicts me for being too deeply under the drug's influence to see what's right before me. If I don't solve this case I will have reason to fear encountering Commissioner Lin in the afterlife. And my father." Dee looked up at Hoong. "And yours."

"The appearance of Commissioner Lin in your dreams," Hoong said, spooning herbs into a teapot and pouring hot water in to steep, "is your own mind telling you what you already know and refuse to act upon."

"No doubt. Or perhaps it's Commissioner Lin. In any case, I must continue my work."

"Drink that first."

"Is this the same foul brew you forced upon me yesterday?"

"Are you in the same condition as you were then?"

"My God, Hoong, your rationality is close to unbearable."

Hoong made no answer, but stood waiting for Dee to drain his cup. Hoong refilled it, Dee drained it again, and thus they continued until the pot was empty.

Dee, though no more inclined to embrace Hoong's potion than the first time he'd tasted it, had to acknowledge that once it was within him his aches and his bleariness began to subside. After a few minutes he stood, pleased to find himself capable of that action. "Now," he said, slapping his sides, "if you are quite satisfied that my faculties have been restored, I would be indebted for the return of my satchel."

"I am satisfied of no such thing." Hoong nevertheless fetched Dee's costume bag from beneath the counter.

"Well, then, I shall have to leave you unconvinced. Spring-heel Jack has business to attend to." Dee vanished into the rear of the shop and returned clothed in the villain's black garb. "Now, Sergeant Hoong, tell me this: have you made any progress in locating Captain Lu?"

"I'm sorry to report that I have not."

"In that case, my direction is clear. Since Captain Lu is one of only two remaining tontine members, it is rational—you see, Hoong, I can be rational, too—rational to assume the other, Shin Xiao, the absent-minded, lazy merchant's son with the exasperated Indian wife, is either the killer, or soon to be a victim." Unbolting the door, Dee peered into the street to assure himself it was empty. He pulled on his mask and ran to the building opposite, where he took hold of a drainpipe, swung up onto the roof, and was away.

From rooftop to streetlamp to alley and back to rooftop, despite aching head and tired limbs, Dee made his way to the home of Shin Xiao. If Shin was the killer, he would soon head for Captain Lu's home to eliminate the last tontine member besides himself. How Shin would succeed in finding Lu where Hoong had failed—and how Shin had learned the identities of the other tontine members—were questions Dee's mind, not yet totally cleared of the opium haze, could not answer, but this was a time for action, not contemplation.

Also, Dee reluctantly but resolutely admitted to himself, it was possible the killer was Captain Lu. In that case it was Lu who would soon be arriving at the home of Shin.

Dee reached a rooftop across the street from Shin's home, where a constable was positioned at the gate. Grimly gratified to see Inspector Bard had taken Springheel Jack's warning to heart, Dee stood on the roof ridge, cape billowing behind him, until he realized the constable might see him and attempt to give chase. Such an action would draw both the constable and Dee himself away from their watch on Shin's home.

Dee crouched down and settled in. He determined to let his mind be untethered, to flow this way and that through the facts of the case like a stream in a jagged landscape until some previously unnoticed feature of interest presented itself. The time spent in watching over Shin's home might, he hoped, in this way become productive, rather than a maddening and possibly fruitless wait for—the killer!

Dee sprang to his feet. The masked man in the loose tunic and workingman's gloves—the man from the church, who had murdered Jiang—had appeared on the roof of the house next to Shin's. Dee swung himself to the drainpipe and down. When he reached the ground, the killer had vanished. Dee raced across the street, shouting at the startled constable to summon help. As the constable's whistle screeched, Dee threw open the front door.

# CHAPTER THIRTY-ONE

Dee burst in upon a scene as horrific as he had feared. Shin Xiao, still looking perplexed, lay dead in a pool of blood on the hallway floor. His open eyes stared at nothing, while his wife's stared in shock and terror at a masked man whose gloved right hand held a bloody military bayonet.

Dee leapt over the body to put himself between the killer and the panicked woman. "Run!" he shouted to her. "Gather your children and run!" The woman looked at him, in his own mask and caped attire, and screamed. Then she turned and dashed into the kitchen at the back of the house.

Dee, spinning to face the swordsman, was hit with a thunderous dizzy spell. He staggered into a side table. Picture frames and porcelain cups went flying to shatter on the floor. The swordsman, seeing his chance, slashed at Dee. Feverishly, Dee twisted to evade three wild swings of the blade. The swordsman stepped in and thrust straight. Dee turned to his left. The sword barely missed him.

Suddenly Dee was back on the battlefield, bombs bursting everywhere, the smell of mustard gas thick, men dead and dying, lying in the mud. Over one of those bodies Dee tripped and fell. Landing on his knees, he looked up.

The swordsman raised his blade for a final thrust.

Dee shook his head. This was not the battlefield; it was Shin Xiao's hallway. The body was Shin's. The floor was not mud and blood, it was parquet. Covered by a runner.

Taking a mighty breath, Dee picked up the edges of the runner and yanked. His powerful pull sent the swordsman flipping backward, sword flying in the air. The bayonet landed two inches deep in the mahogany paneling, and the swordsman crashed to the floor with a thud.

Dee sprang to his feet. He was still unable to fully focus, but hid that fact from his opponent with clenched fists and a loud roar. The swordsman rolled over, yanked his bayonet from the wall, and, apparently assessing his chances, sped out the front door.

After pausing for a single centering breath, Dee seized an umbrella from the stand by the door and tore out after the swordsman. Dee, at his best, was capable of gliding through a crowd like a breeze through branches. But the fight had cost him more than it normally would. Racing along the pavement, he bumped shoulders with a businessman and nearly knocked over a newsboy. A nanny pushing a pram appeared in his speeding path, too suddenly for Dee to do anything but somersault into the air, hoping to vault high enough to avoid a collision. Avoid it he did, if only by inches. As he landed on his feet he saw the swordsman turn the corner onto St. George's Drive.

Dee reached the same spot moments behind the man. Not seeing him, Dee halted, narrowing his eyes to scan the area. On a bus pulling out from its stop up ahead he caught a flash of movement: the swordsman, leaping on board.

As the bus started to lumber along the bumpy road, Dee

put on a burst of speed. He vaulted from the pavement onto the bonnet of a Hispano-Suiza whose driver dropped his jaw when he saw Dee leap from in front of his eyes to the back of the bus. Dee almost missed his grip on a pole at the foot of the steps, but managed to swing himself aboard. Regaining his balance, he pushed through the wide-eyed passengers in the rear and onto the bus's lower deck.

The masked swordsman sat hunched beside a window near the front, completely still, as though he hoped by not moving to make himself invisible. His bayonet was sheathed; Dee was glad to see that, as it meant passengers would be in less danger when he apprehended the man.

Though the swordsman was nowhere near invisible, his fellow riders were ignoring him, likely considering him just one of London's many eccentrics. But the sudden appearance of a second costumed, masked man was apparently too much for some. A commotion began as passengers made haste to pull away from Dee.

Dee swept a stern gaze through the bus, motioning with his hands for everyone to stay calm. He pointed to himself, and to the swordsman. In recounting this story, Dee credited the quick subsidence of the disorder to the sensible British bus ridership, who understood instantly that his actions would be to their benefit. I have felt that stern gaze myself, however, and seen the commanding bearing which Dee adopts when it suits him. Costume and mask notwithstanding, I have no doubt that it was these things, and not any inherent English rationality, that caused the bus riders to fall quiet.

Dee began a stealthy approach up the aisle. He was four rows behind the swordsman when the ticket taker, having completed his duties with regard to the upper deck, trotted down the front staircase with a jaunty, "Tickets, please."

Passengers with tickets handed them over, to be punched

and returned. Those without purchased the needful from the book the ticket taker had at the ready. The masked swordsman acted as though he hadn't heard.

"Ticket, sir." The ticket taker appraised the swordsman with an odd look, but soldiered on. "If you haven't got one, I've one right here." He held out the book.

Up the swordsman leapt. He drew his sword and sliced the ticket book in half. Paper snowed down upon the shocked passengers.

"Madman on the bus!" shouted the ticket taker, but in moments the madman was no longer on the bus, for he'd thrown the window wide and swung out. Howling with laughter, and clinging one-handed to the window opening, he sheathed his sword. Like a human spider he worked his way toward the front.

Dee vaulted over a man cowering in the aisle and jumped onto the steps to the upper deck. He sped up, hoping to dislodge the swordsman from above and drop him to the street, but when he reached the upper deck, the swordsman had pulled himself over the rail and was standing in the sun, laughing as the bus rattled along.

Between Dee, at the front, and the masked swordsman, in the rear, sat a number of passengers. An old man snored; a mother held a baby in her arms; and in the aisle, two redheaded boys dueled with wooden swords under the indulgent gaze of their nanny.

Dee and the swordsman locked eyes. Before either could make a move toward the other, the bus bounced over a bump. One of the young boys, losing his balance, fell against the swordsman. The swordsman swept the child aside with a fierce backhanded swat.

The nanny gasped.

The other boy, furious at this insult to his brother, kicked the swordsman in the shins. The swordsman was reaching for the smaller child when Dee's umbrella came down on his wrist.

"You have no quarrel with these children. Your fight is with me."

The swordsman straightened up and once again laughed. He drew his sword and thrust toward Dee. The two children, squashed into a protective embrace by their nanny, watched enthralled as this pair of masked adults—one with a billowing cape!—fenced back and forth along the aisle of the bus, one using a bayonet and one armed with only an umbrella.

The swordsman swung wildly, hacking at Dee. Dee parried and ducked, coiling his cape in his free hand and flicking it at the bayonet. The swordsman jumped back out of the cape's reach. The nanny clutched her charges closer and the mother shrank back with her baby, who started to cry. A slash from the sword sliced off the top of the old man's hat. The man started, blinked, and went back to snoring. In the half second the swordsman was distracted by this hit, Dee stabbed his umbrella into the man's side.

The swordsman howled. Dee parried his next thrust and stabbed him again. The swordsman looked wildly around. He snatched the baby from its mother's arms.

The woman screamed, "My child!"

The swordsman clutched the baby close to his chest.

"Villain!" said Dee, freezing where he was. "Are you such a coward that you'll hide behind an infant?"

Arm wrapped tightly around the howling baby and the bayonet in his other hand raised, the swordsman backed slowly up the aisle. Dee, not daring to approach, felt the bus begin to slow as it neared a stop. The swordsman leaned to his right, scrutinizing the crowd on the pavement. In a sudden movement he threw the baby into the air, as if it were a missile aimed above Dee's head.

The mother shrieked. Dee flung down his umbrella and sprang upward. He seized the child. The momentum of the baby's flight pulled Dee backward. Dee somersaulted, landing on an unoccupied seat.

The bigger of the two red-haired boys broke from his nanny and ran to Dee, holding out his arms. "The baby!" he yelled. "Give me the baby and trounce him, sir!"

Dee placed the baby in the boy's arms with a swift nod of thanks. Drawing a needed breath, he turned to the swordsman. The swordsman, seeing Dee unencumbered, backed away, sheathing his blade. He grasped the railing and swung himself over. He attempted to slide into the bus through the lower-deck window, but shrieks arose and hands reached out to push him back. He found himself dangling above the motorcars below.

Dee, using the same lightness skill he'd employed at Jiang's rooming house, danced from seat to seat, making his way in moments to the swordsman. He peered down as his enemy swayed over the traffic. The swordsman's eyes grew desperate. Dee extended his hand. The swordsman clutched it.

At that moment a lorry cutting across the road caused the bus to brake sharply. Dee, already leaning forward, was thrown off-balance. He'd likely have been able to recover, even allowing for his weakened state, but for the fact that the swordsman, realizing his opportunity, yanked on Dee's hand. Dee tumbled over the railing, the swordsman thrusting him away as he fell.

Only instinct born of years of training enabled Dee to right himself in the air, land on his feet, and roll, thus dissipating the energy of the fall. Slapping the ground to end the roll, he attempted to regain his feet. But his customary ability to rapidly recover had deserted him in the face of his withdrawal from opium. The breath knocked from his lungs, Dee lay on the pavement feeling the world spin. When it righted itself, he saw the bus disappearing around a corner. Whether the swordsman was still aboard he did not know.

Moreover, within seconds Dee found himself looking up into the faces of half a dozen constables who'd raced to surround him. He snarled; as one they drew back. This standoff continued for some minutes as Dee attempted to re-gather his strength. Another snarl and a few waves of his caped arms proved sufficient to prevent further encroachment by these representatives of the Metropolitan Police, who seemed content to lay siege to his square of pavement without actually invading it.

Just at the point when Dee felt ready to rise and depart, however, an invader did present himself. Inspector Bard broke through the constable circle and gasped when he saw who was contained within it. "Why are you standing here?" he shouted to his subordinates. "Take him, lads!"

"Sir," said one constable, "that's . . . it's Springheel Jack, sir."

"Of course it isn't! This man is a dangerous maniac hoping to frighten the populace with his fantastic garb. He's already committed a number of serious crimes. Now use your truncheons! Take him!"

As the constables raised their cudgels, Dee jumped to his feet. "Oh, but yer wrong, me copper. I'm Spring'eel Jack and that's a fact." He leaned into Bard's face and watched him shrink away. "Yer lads are wiser than yerself, I'll say that. Mayhap yer in need of another lesson." With that he seized Bard's unbandaged hand and bent back the smallest finger. As the man went ashen Dee released him with a laugh, finger intact. "Now go about yer duties and find the fellow who's killing men on yer patch, Inspector Bard, or Spring'eel Jack will be back to see yer again!"

Dee swept a quick circular kick that made contact with

each constable, not hard, but enough to make the men jump away. Bard he tweaked in the nose and slapped on the top of the head. Then Dee sprang up onto a fence, where he turned again and flapped his cape, emitting a loud cackle. As the men of the Metropolitan Police flinched, he leapt down on the fence's other side and fled.

DEE MANAGED HIS escape from the pursuing constables handily, again utilizing roofs, lampposts, fences, and alleyways. It was only when he walked through the door of Sergeant Hoong's shop that his exhaustion overtook him. When the bell over the shop door rang, Hoong looked up from his perusal of a months-old Chinese newspaper. He rose, bolted the door, and once again turned the sign, which if it had been a live creature would by now have been quite dizzy, to "Closed."

"Dee," he said, as Dee sank onto a stool, "if you persist in appearing here in various pitiable conditions I'll never do business again."

"I apologize. If I could beg of you one more pot of that unpleasant but revivifying tea I'll be on my way."

"I think not." Hoong folded his arms.

Dee's eyebrows rose. "Sergeant Hoong? Am I no longer welcome here?"

"Judge Dee, you are welcome here, in any condition and at any time. That tea, however, has imperfect powers of, as you say, revivification. You've pushed it—and yourself—to its limits. I shall make you a different brew, which you will drink. You will then go into the back room and sleep." From drawers, glass jars, and brass canisters Hoong took pinches of herbs, leaves, and flowers, then dropped them into a teapot.

"I have no time to sleep, Hoong. Another man has been murdered." Dee made no effort to rise, however, but narrated his tale as the tea steeped.

"If this is true," said Hoong, "and the tontine is at the center of it all, then Captain Lu, sadly, must be the killer. We can warn the bank that there are irregularities and instruct them to alert the police and delay the captain when he arrives to claim the tontine. I shall do that while you sleep. Don't protest, it will do you no good. This is not a sleep for the ages, Dee. The effects of the potion last an hour or two at best. But it's necessary. You can do no good for anyone in your condition."

"My condition again!" said Dee, but again stayed where he was. Finally he said, "If Lu doesn't appear at the bank and needs to be found?"

"Then we will find him. After you sleep. You certainly can't find anyone as you are now. I'm not entirely sure you're capable of finding the teacup I have just put before you. If you can manage that, then drink."

# CHAPTER THIRTY-TWO

And now we have reached the point where I myself reappear in the story. I'll make a more lengthy return later, but I would not be giving an honest report of this time without an account of my own actions. Although this account is brief and those actions appear little related to the investigation, they were not without fruit, as you shall see.

Despite my friend's shocking transgression in arriving at the Wendell home in a state of opium idiocy, I went to bed that night in a lighthearted mood. Dee's gallantry and charm had been revealed for a thin shell, now cracked to expose the flawed man beneath; whereas, by turning him away, I had demonstrated my own steadfastness and determination to do right, and had seen this noted by the person whose good opinion mattered most to me. I was buoyed again at the breakfast table the following morning when Mary, buttering her toast, said, "Mr. Lao, your defense of the propriety of this house last night was appreciated."

"Indeed it was," declared her mother, coming in from the kitchen with an egg caddy. "An opium-addled man in my house! How could he have thought!"

"I'm sorry," Mary continued, "that you were forced to choose between your friend and your hosts."

"That was not the choice as I saw it," I said.

"Of course not." Mrs. Wendell smoothed her skirt under her as she sat. "It was a matter of physical safety. We might all have been murdered in our beds if that man had gained admission."

"Oh, no, no," I hastened to reply. "Judge Dee would never harm either of you. Or myself," I added, though of that I was less sure.

Mrs. Wendell harrumphed and Mary smiled sadly.

"No," I said, "none of us was in danger from Judge Dee at any time. However, I see no way for one to be unalterably opposed to the use of this drug, as I am, and simultaneously tolerant of the user."

"Are we not taught to hate the sin but love the sinner?" Mary asked.

"Indeed we are. But I could not allow Dee, having indulged to the point of near-irrationality as he did yesterday, to proceed without thought through the door of a respectable household and thence to bed. Such an act on my part would have offered the sinner not love, but forbearance for the sin. I cannot stop him from doing as he likes. What he does, however, is not without its consequences. I believe demonstrating these consequences to be the more loving approach."

"Why, Mr. Lao," said Mary. "Your reasoning is both subtle, and perfectly Christian. If only you would attend church with me! I believe I could promise you good news."

Oh, how my heart soared to hear that! I also, however, chastised myself as I beheaded my egg. Was it possible Mary had refused to allow herself to return my affections simply because she was unconvinced of my dedication to our shared faith? Could my lack of enthusiasm for churchgoing have been misconstrued as a lack of sincerity when I professed Christianity? Could she have been thinking of me all this time as—my face burned—a "rice Christian"?

"Mr. Lao?" said Mrs. Wendell. "Are you well? You've gone quite red."

"I'm very well, thank you, Mrs. Wendell. I do feel slightly warm—perhaps the change in the weather? In any case, I have duties at the university, so I must be off. I thank you as always for a delightful breakfast."

I beat a hasty retreat from the Wendell home to cover my awkwardness, but I walked to the university with a spring in my step. If the distance between Mary and myself could be bridged by the simple expedient of my attendance at St. George's, Bloomsbury, for Sunday services, why then, I would become a most faithful member of the flock! Perhaps I'd find something of interest in Reverend Evans's sermons, after all; and simply to have Mary at my side would make that somber church bright with light.

Well, Mary wouldn't be at my side. She would be in the choir loft, under the direction of the fervent Washington Jones, joining her heavenly voice with the others to lift words of praise to our Maker. I did the same silently now as I walked. I thanked Him for this glorious spring morning and for renewing my hope for happiness with Mary.

On impulse I turned from my course onto a street nearby. A short way in stood a jeweler's shop whose display window I had often admired. A small token of my sincere affection might not, at this juncture, be taken amiss.

I stopped briefly to peruse the window, in which lay a display of men's ascot pins, as well as the newer type of collar pins and even tie clasps. I had mastered the collar pin, and the four-in-hand and Windsor knots, but the tie clasp had not yet made its way into my wardrobe. I reflected that as I was presenting myself here in England as a representative of Modern China, perhaps I ought to dress in the most modern style. I recalled that Dee, when he had first appeared at the Wendell home, had worn a tie clasp. I looked the pieces over, trying to imagine myself wearing one to fix my necktie to my shirt. Some were rather handsome, including a small group bearing various family crests. I would never, of course, presume to wear one of those; still, they seemed well-made and I admired them. One crest looked familiar, though I could not remember where I'd seen it. Perhaps one of my students was from that august family? I found the same crest again in a set of cufflinks and shirt studs of the type worn with formal dress. When I looked more closely, the crest was borne by an ascot pin, also, and a pocket-watch fob. A near-complete set of men's jewelry, then, missing only a signet ring. A family fallen on hard times, with no male heir and no hope of one, and thus no use for men's ornaments? This was a melancholy thought, and I was in no mood for melancholy on this fine spring morning. I shook myself out of my reverie and entered the shop.

"Good morning," I said to the young man behind the glass counter. "I'd like to see your brooches, if you please."

The young man's countenance as he reached into the counter and withdrew a velvet tray was so dyspeptic that I almost asked him if he felt ill, but my attention was drawn to the tray itself. It bore only poorly made, glittering baubles.

"No, I'm sorry," I said, "these won't do. I require a selection of quality goods."

"Sir," the clerk replied with a pained smile, "it's our experience that items such as these are generally of interest to gentlemen of your . . . kind."

"Of my kind?" I bristled. "Precisely what do you mean to imply, young man?"

At this juncture the boutonniere-wearing manager appeared by the clerk's side. "May I help you?" he asked.

"You certainly may," I replied. "I've asked to see a selection of your better brooches and this young man will show me only gewgaws." I waved my hand over the tray.

"Sir, I'm sure—" The manager stopped speaking as the clerk whispered in his ear. They continued back and forth in low tones. Finally the manager turned a wide smile to me while the clerk removed the baubles and replaced that tray with one holding jewelry of superior stones and workmanship.

"I'm sorry, sir," the manager said. "It appears there was a misunderstanding. Mr. Laughton mistook you for a Chinese."

"Mistook me—"

"Yes. As I say, I'm very sorry. Your excellent command of English and your fine bearing should have alerted the young fellow that your homeland is obviously not China, but Japan. I ask for your indulgence. Mr. Laughton is new to our shop and hasn't yet acquired the discernment we hope he will in time develop. Please, have a look at these." He gestured at the newly placed tray.

I looked from the manager to the mortified young man, who was now wearing a small, apologetic smile. "Sirs," I said, drawing myself up. "I understand. And now *you* must understand that I am, in fact, Chinese. And that I will not be setting foot in this shop again." I spun and left, deliberately failing to wish them a good day.

# CHAPTER THIRTY-THREE

I passed the remainder of the morning at my desk at the university in a state of gloom. To be welcome in a shop only once I had been declared Japanese—no, such an insult was intolerable! Could it be that Dee was right? That no Britisher was capable even of respect for Chinese persons, let alone the sort of affection that I had the audacity to hope for from Mary? I was loathe to admit the possibility. Yet if I were being honest, my experiences since coming to London would indicate that, as regards very many English people, that might indeed be the case.

And Dee? Where was Dee? I'd turned him out into the night in the belief that I was ultimately helping him. Or had I? Had I really just thought to impress Mary, and her mother? Had I, as Mary put it, in fact chosen between my friend and my hosts—and chosen poorly?

I tried to continue my work on my students' lessons, but by midday I was in quite a state. I needed to speak with Mary and assure myself I was not operating outside the bounds of possibility in harboring hopes for happiness with her. After all, she had promised me good news, had she not?

I also needed—more urgently, I had to admit—to find Dee and

be assured he'd come to no harm. To turn away a man in such a state that he barely knew his own name! *Really, Lao,* I was forced to ask myself, *could this be called an act of friendship?*

I knew where to find Mary. At this hour she'd be fulfilling her duties at the hat shop. Thus though easy to find, she'd be in no position to speak with me on any serious subject.

I had no idea, on the other hand, where to find Dee. Searching for him might prove a fool's errand—and if found, he might be disinclined to speak with me at all.

However, I could remain inactive no longer. I left my office and set off for Sergeant Hoong's shop.

DEE, AT THE moment I was exiting the gates of the university, was waking in the back of Sergeant Hoong's shop feeling like a new man. He stretched, he sat up, he swung his legs off the bed and stood. Finding his clothes on a table where he vaguely remembered folding them two hours before, he dressed and walked through to the shop itself. "Well, Hoong," he said, and stopped. Hoong was sharing a pot of tea with the thief Jimmy Fingers.

"Dee," said Hoong. "Are you recovered?"

"I am so much improved, Sergeant Hoong, that hunger has taken over my every sense. I feel as if I haven't eaten for days."

"You may well not have. Most men I see in your condition have been neglecting their appetite for food."

"Yer in a condition, sir?" said the young thief, standing. "I'm sorry to 'ear that."

"Mr. Fingers is here at my invitation," Hoong told Dee. "As I've been unable to locate Captain Lu in either Limehouse or the area around Pennyfields and Ming Street, it must be the case that he resides in a district of few Chinese. If so, Mr. Fingers may be of aid in the search."

"Well done, Hoong! I supposed I needn't ask whether you've alerted the bank where the tontine is held?"

"And yet you are asking. I have. I was informed that as a result of a commotion there caused by the man's nephew, the manager was already familiar with the name of Captain Lu."

"Ah, yes. Lao's finest hour. Priggish he may be, but the man has a good deal of potential, Hoong." (Note: information on this part of the conversation was supplied to me by Sergeant Hoong.) "So Lu has not appeared to claim the funds?"

"Not yet. The Metropolitan Police and, thanks to a well-placed pound note, I here at the shop will both be advised when he does."

"Your resourcefulness is noted, Sergeant. I'm hoping, however, that since he appears to be in no hurry—and why should he be, as there's no one else left to collect—we can outflank him before that. Jimmy, I'll give you your brief, but only once we've eaten. I assume you'd welcome a meal? *As for meself, if I don't eat somethin' soon, I might 'ave to eat yer!*"

With that Dee leered and swept his arms wide as though to pounce on the thief. Jimmy Fingers jumped back.

"Why, sir," he said, seeing Dee and Hoong both smiling, "that were very good. Very good indeed. I'd 'ave thought I was talkin' to one of the lads, so I would."

"It was your tutelage, Jimmy, that gave me that skill. Hoong, will you join us and permit me to buy you a meal to repay you for all you've done for me?"

"A meal," Hoong said, "would not even begin to square our accounts. With you gone, however, I'll be able to return to serving my customers, should I still have any. Please enjoy your meal and don't feel you must hurry back."

Hoong ushered Dee and the thief out the door and turned his sign to "Open."

"Jimmy, my lad," said Dee as they walked through the cobblestone streets, "have you ever had a Chinese meal?"

"Can't say as I 'ave, sir. But if yer invitin' me to join yer, I wouldn't say no."

"I am, Jimmy, I am. And here we are. This is one of the finest Chinese restaurants in London, which means it's one of the finest restaurants in the city altogether."

"If you say so, sir."

"I do." Dee and the thief entered Wu's Garden, the place to which I'd introduced him.

They were shown to a table and Dee perused the handwritten menu strips on the wall. When the waiter came with teapot, cups, and chopsticks, Dee placed his order.

"I suppose I'll 'ave to wait and see wot we're meant to be eating, then?" Jimmy said, when no translation was forthcoming.

"You will, and while we wait, tell me: Do you know how to use chopsticks?"

Jimmy did not, but as might be expected of a young man of his demonstrated dexterity, he mastered the art in short order. By the time the spring rolls arrived he was eager to try his new skill.

"And wot might these be, sir?"

"Very good is what they are, Jimmy. And you may use your fingers to lift one."

"Well, me fingers is me best feature, sir!" Following Dee's lead, Jimmy took hold of a spring roll and swiped it through the dish of mustard.

Dee kept a careful gaze on the thief as he bit in. Jimmy's eyes widened. He grabbed up his tea and swigged the whole cup, and then he laughed. "Why, sir," he said, "that's marvelous, that is! Tasty and no mistake." He scooped up more mustard with the remainder of his roll, gobbled the thing down, and reached for another.

Dee and Jimmy Fingers contentedly devoured the spring rolls with copious amounts of hot mustard and, following those, a plate of steamed pork buns. The turnip cake and pan-fried noodles had arrived together, and Jimmy was demonstrating his deftness with the tableware when Dee said, "Jimmy, you're an able student, and I'm pleased to see how well you take to the cuisine of my home. Good afternoon, Lao. Would you care to join us?"

When Dee spoke those words I was still a meter behind him. He had not turned in his chair; nor had I uttered a word since I'd entered the restaurant and surveyed the scene, hoping to find Dee here as Hoong had suggested I might. Spotting him with the young thief, I'd begun threading my way across the crowded dining floor.

"Dee," I said, closing on their table and standing between them, "good afternoon to you, too, and can you see behind your head?"

He looked up with a smile. Jimmy Fingers had started to stand but I waved him back to his seat. Dee said, "I heard your footsteps approaching. From their sound I thought it was you, and Jimmy's look of recognition confirmed it. I may be taking liberties, Jimmy, but I don't think you know many Chinese men in London aside from Sergeant Hoong, Mr. Lao, and myself? Hoong, I think, having only recently rid himself of me, would not come unless he had news. If he had he'd rush in, not walk at a casual pace. Thus, Lao, your presence was verified. Please, sit down."

The waiter had by then brought a chair, and so, once again amazed at the speed of Dee's thoughts, I sat. "Dee," I began. "Last night—"

"Have a turnip cake, Lao. They're very good. Nothing happened last night that bears discussing. Except the apology I owe you for any discomfiture I caused you with Mrs. and Miss Wendell."

"But I—"

"Yes. Now we must move on to today's work." As we were now three at table, and both Dee and Jimmy Fingers seemed to have prodigious appetites, Dee ordered a dish of clay-pot rice with sausage. We shared salty turnip cake and silky noodles while Dee explained to me and the young thief the current situation involving Captain Lu.

"Oh, my," I said. "I'm very sorry, Dee. I know the captain is your friend. This must be a great disappointment to you."

The new dish arrived on the table. Spooning it to our bowls, Dee said, "It is no greater a disappointment than life must be to Lu, to allow himself to go down this road. But we must do our duty."

"But Dee," I said, thinking back, "it was Captain Lu himself who brought to your attention the existence of the tontine. He sought you out when he learned you were in London. Why do that, if he is the killer? Why not just continue his villainous work, collect the tontine funds, and remain in the shadows, hoping you would never find the motivation behind the murders?"

"Because he knew I would. We spent two years in France together, Lu and myself. He knows my methods and that I do not give up. He might have been able to finish his killing and gather the funds before I discovered the reason, or he might not. By coming to me he hoped to exempt himself from suspicion, thus freeing him to finish the implementation of his plan."

"This fellow yer discussing," said Jimmy Fingers. "'E sounds a right clever gent."

"He certainly is," said Dee. "I believe he's lying low, waiting for his chance to claim the funds."

"But the bank's been warned," Jimmy said. "If 'e's that clever 'e must know it would be. And didn't Sergeant 'Oong tell us 'e bribed a clerk to send word when 'e comes?"

"Yes. But Lu may well have also bribed a clerk, to allow him to collect in secret. Possibly even the same man. Therefore we must search out Lu for ourselves." Dee put down his chopsticks. "Since Lu is not to be found in Limehouse or in Pennyfields, he must be in an area where a Chinese man would be noticed. Jimmy, I suspect you have a great many contacts throughout London."

"I do that, sir!" said Jimmy with pride.

"I'd like you to throw wide whatever nets you can. Have word brought to you of any Chinese man living in modest circumstances—not in poverty, but not high society, either. No stevedores and no diplomats, do you understand? Quiet men with quiet lives, outside the neighborhoods where one might expect to find them. Let it be known there's a pound note in it for whoever brings information on the right man. Without, of course, the quarry knowing he's being hunted. You can make Sergeant Hoong's shop your headquarters, though you must be sure not to interfere with his commerce."

"I'm yer boy, sir." Looking for all the world like a Guangdong farmer at his midday meal, Jimmy expertly shoveled the remaining rice from his bowl into his maw. Then he jumped up.

Dee laughed. "Jimmy, if you find Captain Lu, I'll cook you a meal myself."

Jimmy grinned, turned smartly on his heel, and dashed from Wu's Garden.

# CHAPTER THIRTY-FOUR

"I think," said Dee, "to end this meal, perhaps a small bowl of walnut soup. It's very good for the brain, you know. I don't know about you, Lao, but given the sluggishness of my understanding of this case, I feel my brain could use some assistance." He waved the waiter over and ordered two bowls.

I replenished our teacups and asked, "What next steps are you intending to take, Dee? You cannot be planning to just wait until Captain Lu is found."

"All I can think," Dee said, "is for us to participate in the search." He regarded me. "Unless, given the trouble I've brought you, you've decided to wash your hands of—"

"Dee!"

He nodded. "Very well. And thank you." He sipped at his tea. "My expectation, Lao, when I came to London, was that I would carry out my work alone. I had not thought to find men upon whose skills and steadfastness I could depend. Getting swept up in the arrest of the agitators was, I felt, an unfortunate, possibly dangerous, inconvenience. Yet that event reunited me with Hoong and introduced me to you. In retrospect, how fortunate I was."

I felt myself redden as I had at the Wendells' breakfast table. Luckily our walnut soup arrived, sparing me the necessity of speech. I would have been hard put to declare Dee capable of such sentiments, and never would I have expected to hear him express them.

The skills to which Dee alluded were clearly more in Hoong's column than in mine, though I fancied I was not useless in the physical world. But in the steadfastness category I would set my record against Hoong's without a moment's pause. Silently I vowed, hearing this expression of gratitude from Dee, to redouble my efforts in that direction.

After a few spoons of sweet soup, Dee spoke. "Once we've exhausted this brain-enriching liquid, I suggest we divide up and scour separate areas of London for Captain Lu. We can meet in perhaps two hours at Sergeant Hoong's shop. That ought to allow enough time for his opinion of me to rise again. If Captain Lu has escaped our net and tried to claim the tontine funds, we'll learn about it then. Gentlemen!" Having, I supposed, heard footsteps approaching as he'd heard mine, Dee turned in his chair. I looked up to see Ezra Pound and Viscount Whytecliff. Dee said, "It's good to see you again."

"And you, Mr. Dee," said Pound. "Mr. Lao." He nodded to me, and Whytecliff smiled upon us both. Pound continued, "I'm pleased to know you enjoy the food at Wu's Garden. I find it acceptable myself, as do most of the Chinese of my acquaintance."

"Oh, come now, Pound." The viscount's family ring shone in the light as he smoothed his tie under its plain gold clasp. Pound himself wore a blue silk ascot held in place by a ruby pin, an item of dress that before the war would not have been remarked upon but today could only be considered a bit of deliberate foppery. Whytecliff continued, "The Chinese of your acquaintance include every Chinese in London worth knowing."

Pound smiled. "I can't deny it. I make it a point to acquaint myself with the modern-day representatives of such an ancient culture."

"Do you?" Dee said thoughtfully. "Perhaps I can prevail upon you to help us, then." From his jacket pocket he took two sheets of paper. He glanced over them, and then with a tiny smile I think no one saw but myself, he slipped one away and handed Pound the other. It was the list of names of the men who'd come over from France—the copy he'd written in English.

Pound took the paper, glanced down the list, and curled his lip. "Mr. Dee. As Whytecliff said, I have made the acquaintance of every Chinese in London *worth knowing*. Two of these names mean nothing to me. Quod erat demonstrandum." With Whytecliff peering over his shoulder he thrust his finger at the list, stabbing the names of Ma Ze Ren and Jiang Gwan Li. "These other two are familiar, but certainly not worth knowing."

"Ma Ze Ren," said Whytecliff, looking puzzled. "Isn't he the shopkeeper who was murdered last week? Did you know him, Mr. Dee?"

"I did. Why do you say, Mr. Pound, that he was not worth knowing?"

"Because both these men debased themselves and their— your!—ancient culture by taking roles in those execrable moving pictures."

"Pictures?" Dee asked. "Ma and Jiang took roles in moving pictures?"

Jiang's dying words came to me with a jolt. I almost reminded Dee of them, but he shot me a look before my mouth was even opened.

"Appalling ones," Pound said. "Pictures that promote the absurd notion of the Yellow Peril. As if any Chinese could pose a threat to a white man. Or even a white woman, which is what these pictures largely concern. Yours is not a fighting race, after all. The proposition that a healthy British shopgirl could not drub a Chinese attacker"—here he feinted an upper-cut at the viscount, and smiled—"well, it's preposterous."

Not a fighting race! I began a protest but Dee kicked me under the table. I lifted my teacup and looked away, to recover myself. Dee was clearly interested in this subject. "Tell us more about these pictures," he requested.

"Chinese are recruited to act the villain in heinous moving pictures that only serve to disseminate fear—the fear that the web of the evil Chin-ee will ensnare the pure-hearted English lad and draw his virginal lass to her ruin. They make similar pictures in America, I understand. These pictures insult both your people and ours." Pound tossed the paper back on the table. "I cannot imagine what could possibly make a Chinese man lower himself to take part in such endeavors."

"Pound," said the viscount reasonably, "hunger can drive a man to many things."

"Hunger? Ma Ze Ren owned a thriving shop, did he not? You visited it many times, Whytecliff, and acquired some fine *objets*. To my understanding the shop produced quite a good living, thank you very much. The only hunger that could have driven him to this degradation is the hunger for money—and that hunger, as we all know, is the root of all evil!"

"Your Bible tells us that, certainly," said Dee. I was impressed that, as a nonbeliever, he had got the reference, but Dee was a man of many surprises. "I suppose you don't know where the film studio is located that makes these shameful moving pictures?"

"Mr. Dee! You're not thinking—oh, of course, you're not! You're going to give them what for! Well, I'd certainly like to see that."

"Pound," said Whytecliff, sounding alarmed, "we're expected at—"

"Oh, Whytecliff, I wasn't being literal! I'm sure Mr. Dee will give us a full account the next time we meet. Good day, gentlemen." Pound settled his hat on his mountain of hair.

"Mr. Pound? The location?" said Dee.

"Oh! Sorry, old man. The studio calls itself Princely Pictures. A misnomer if ever there was one. They're down by the docks on New Gravel Lane."

"Thank you."

"My pleasure. And now, *bonne journée.*"

As soon as the two gentlemen were out of earshot I said, "Dee! Jiang's words—'It's the fault of the pictures!' Do you—"

"Yes, indeed, I do. I think I'll pay Princely Pictures a visit." He signaled the waiter for the bill.

"I'll come with you."

"No, I think you'll be more useful joining the search for Captain Lu. This may be a false trail. Even if it's true Ma and Jiang performed in these Yellow Peril pictures, that may mean nothing in relation to the killings. You know London well. Choose a likely area and ask around."

"Very well." I frowned.

"Do you dislike that plan?"

"No, no. The plan is sound. Only something is troubling me. The two who just left, Mr. Pound and Viscount Whytecliff . . . I don't know. I can't say what it is."

"You're not telling me you're disconcerted by the pompous peacockery of the writerly classes?"

I laughed. "No, that's not it. I see that daily among the literature students at the university, who have far less to show for themselves than Ezra Pound." I shook my head. "But it isn't coming to me."

"When that happens," Dee said, "I often find action to be the remedy. Let us go out into the streets, Lao, and act!"

# CHAPTER THIRTY-FIVE

M y own adventures once Dee and I parted are not worth relating, for there were none. The area I selected for my hunt was the very one in which I resided: the streets around the British Museum. The neighborhood was not posh but was highly respectable. I reasoned the thief, Jimmy Fingers, was not as likely to have contacts here as in other less savory places. But respectability aside, it was also true that sadly, since the war, a number of homes in the area were occupied by widows, as was the case throughout England. Some, no longer having the income of their husbands to rely on, had taken in boarders— my own situation with Mrs. and Miss Wendell. Captain Lu might be boarding at a decent home within blocks of my residence and I'd be none the wiser.

If he was, though, I saw no sign of him. Nor of Mary, who occasionally dashed through the neighborhood on errands for the hat shop. The possibility of encountering Mary had played no part in my choice of district to canvass, of course. Still, my mood, already much cheered by Dee's friendly reception, would have lightened further to see her.

Neither did the action I was taking, as Dee had suggested

it might, jar loose from my head the answer to the maddening question of what I had heard or seen of importance in Wu's Garden that I could not now bring to mind.

While my interviews with shopkeepers and homeowners were coming to naught, however, Dee's investigation yielded far more interesting fruit. It is to him, then, that we will now turn.

DEE'S RAPID STRIDES took him to the battered warehouse building on New Gravel Lane that housed the filming studio, Princely Pictures. As he entered, a harried young woman looked up from her Remington typewriter. Before he could speak she said, "Second door on the left."

"I'm sorry," said Dee, "you must—"

"Second on the left. He'll see you as soon as he's free."

"Who will?"

"Mr. Bolton. He does all the Chinese pictures. He's who you want to see for a part."

Not correcting her misapprehension of his mission, Dee thanked the young lady, who had already returned to her rapid finger-tapping. He turned down the indicated hallway and entered the second door on the left. If Mr. Bolton was responsible for "doing" all the Chinese pictures, then he very much wanted to speak with Mr. Bolton.

The room was empty aside from a table and some straight-backed chairs. Dee took a seat and waited. True to the young lady's word, within minutes the door opened and in gusted a red-haired man whose tie was loose and his jacket open.

"Yes, yes!" he said, looking Dee up and down as Dee stood. "You'll do nicely, if you can act. Can you act? Do you read English, or will you need instruction in Chinese? Come, the camera's set up, you can show me your stuff."

"You're Mr. Bolton?"

"Of course. Ted Bolton. Director. Filming starts next week. *Falling Flowers.* That's what you're here about, right? A part? There's the gambler—no, I don't think you're right—but the second herbalist, we haven't filled that yet, or the opium den door guard—I saw him as younger but you do look broad and strong—"

"Mr. Bolton, my name is Dee Ren Jie and I'm not here about a part in a picture."

Bolton stopped. "You're not? What do you want, then?"

"I'm investigating the death of my friend Ma Ze Ren."

"You are? You're investigating? You're not with the police, surely?"

"No, I'm not. Ma's widow has asked me to look into the circumstances of his death." This was, of course, not true; but as Dee told me later when relating this interview, the mention of a widow often softens men's hearts. He went on, "I've recently learned Ma Ze Ren acted in your pictures. Can you tell me how that came to be?"

Bolton shook his head. "Shame, what happened to him. He was good, you know. Caught on fast, Ma did. No long rehearsals and wasted film with him. And one of my most convincing Chinese Devils. Oh, no offense, Mr.—Dee, you said? I don't think of your people that way myself, no, no, no. But it's the picture-going public, you see. It's what the public wants. The Oriental Menace! The Yellow Peril! You're sure you wouldn't like to try for a part? A Chinaman can make a pretty penny in this business."

"I'm quite sure. However, I'd like to see some of Ma Ze Ren's work. If it's not too much trouble."

"The pictures he acted in, you mean? Well, there's the new one, almost finished. Good job everything's shot. Last we'll have from Ma, a great loss. Come on then. You'll be among the first to have a look at our new villain! A heinous Chinese mastermind to rival Moriarty. You know who that is, eh? Sherlock Holmes's greatest enemy! A criminal genius. Well, so is our new Oriental Menace, and exotic to boot. The public will lap it up, you can be sure. Here we are."

This speech was delivered as Bolton led Dee farther along the hall. They entered another small room, this one windowless and equipped with a cabinet, a projector, a screen, and some chairs, on one of which lay a bound set of papers. Bolton opened the cabinet and withdrew a film reel in its metal canister. "Have a seat. I'll just thread this up."

Dee sat and lifted the sheaf of papers. He saw on the top page the typewritten words "Strangers on the Western Front" and Ma Ze Ren's name. "What's this?"

"Oh, that's Ma's. It's a scenario. That's what we make films from. Tells the director what the story's about, that sort of thing. Then, of course, it's the director who really makes it into something. You should see the scenario for this one." He indicated the reel in his hand. "Nothing to it, bare as bones. Some man named Arthur Ward, shouldn't even be allowed to call himself a writer. I use more words shaving in the morning."

"No doubt. But about Ma's scenario?"

"Not bad. Touching. Ma was in France during the war, he told me. In the trenches. Seems there were a lot of Chinamen there. News to me. He wanted to make a movie about it. That's one of the reasons he worked here. Get on the inside, you know. He asked me to read that and I did. Really not bad. Can't make it, of course."

"Why not?"

"No money in it! The public don't want to watch Joe Chinaman going about his business, even if his business is war, and it certainly don't want to see Chinese heroes. I mean, can you imagine? People want villains! The Oriental Menace, that's the ticket! And that's what we give them. Here, you watch this. Let me know afterwards what you think. I'll be through there, in the filming studio. If you change your mind about a part, I'd be happy to give you a try."

Bolton showed Dee how to turn the lights off and the projector on, and then he left.

Before starting the moving picture, Dee read through Ma's filming scenario. It was the story of a naïve Chinese shop boy recruited to France for adventure, for income, for glory. Dee recognized certain of the characters the shop boy met and several of the events that occurred: some endearing, some fearsome, some funny, some sad. Ma had related his years in France, including the boy's—Ma's own—wounding by shrapnel, without sugarcoating but also without self-pity. The boy's marvel at the ways of the wide world shared the page with war in all its horror.

The scenario was, as Bolton had understatedly put it, touching.

And Dee saw clearly why a British film company would turn it down. "Films such as these," he told me later, "must be made in China, by our own people. The humanity and heroism of men like Ma are not even credited by the British—or indeed, any Europeans; and certainly not by the Americans. What, then, would drive London or New York or Hollywood to make a film about it? No, Lao, this is one of those situations where China must arise and grasp hold of our own story, and our own future with it!"

This stirring pronouncement was yet to come, however. Now, Dee laid the scenario aside, threw the various switches, and sat back to watch Ma Ze Ren on the flickering silver screen.

The new film was called *The Insidious Herbalist*. Ma Ze Ren had a starring role as the herbalist's depraved assistant, also called Ma. It was he, wearing a filthy robe, a long queue, and an unctuous smile, who attempted to lure an innocent young English woman (wide-eyed with trust and clothed in a spotless white dress) to join him in the opium den; he who, when she demurred, threw her like a sack over his shoulder and bore her off there, her screams and futile pounding of pale hands on his back availing her nothing; he who, when the drug forced upon her had her in its power, delivered her to the evil herbalist to further degrade; he who went about London on the herbalist's evil business. (The insidious herbalist himself, Dee noted, was portrayed not by a Chinese actor but by a European with taped eyelids, a long drooping mustache, and Mandarin fingernails.)

As the film went on Ma met with lascars and Moham-medans—also presented in bitter caricature—in dark rooms to make dark plans; he robbed a clergyman at knifepoint and assaulted a duke. Toward the end he engaged in a fistfight with the young woman's courageous beau, who, having scoured London tirelessly for his beloved, had arrived to rescue her. Ma was defeated and the woman (and her virtue) saved, but the evil herbalist slipped away into the shadows, to rise again whenever Princely Pictures thought the time opportune.

Observing Dee sit through this film, one would have thought him unperturbed. He watched motionless from begin-ning to end. When the images on the screen stopped, he sat for another few moments. Then he stood, lifted the film reel from the projector, and placed it in its steel canister. This he laid on the chair with Ma's scenario. Leaving the room he made his way to the filming studio and entered though the double doors. The camera was rolling. The red-haired direc-tor stood with bullhorn in hand as a young man and young woman embraced and sighed in the throes of romantic love. Dee waited until the scene was finished and Bolton called "Cut." Then he approached.

"Mr. Bolton."

"Dee! What did you think of my new Yellow Menace?"

"He is indeed horrifying. Before I leave I have one more question, if I may."

"You're sure you don't want to try for a part? Now that you've seen what we can do? I do need someone to replace Ma."

"Yes, I'm quite sure. But tell me, how was it Ma Ze Ren came to you?"

Bolton wrinkled his forehead. "Young swell called Dover. Pinkie ring, posh clothes. You know the type. Goes about recruiting Chinamen for us—for the other studios, too, but we always get first crack at his men because we pay best."

"You mean you pay the Chinese men best?"

"Oh, my, no, all the studios pay them the same. They work for peanuts, these Chinamen! Except Ma. I wanted to keep him, so I'd give him a few shillings more. No, I mean the recruiters. All the studios pay them. If we didn't we'd have to go looking for Chinamen on our own. I don't have time for that—so much to do to make a moving picture, and all of it the director's job! This Dover, I can't say where he gets them. He doesn't seem the type to frequent the sort of places where Chinamen hang about. Apart from opium dens, and I don't suppose there's much good fishing of men to be done where everyone's in a stupor, eh?" Bolton winked. "But find them he does, and they're all eager to work. I say, Dee." A thought seemed to strike Bolton then. "If you're too reticent for the camera, how would you like to recruit for us? You must be acquainted with a good number of Chinamen. I mean, your lot all know each other, right? How does that sound?"

"It sounds," said Dee slowly, "an interesting idea. But I'd like to get a sense of how this Dover goes about it. Is there a way I could find him, to speak to him?"

"Of course, yes. Don't know where he keeps himself but

he does have a telephone. I'll just find his number." Bolton rustled through a tattered memorandum book from his breast pocket. He tore a corner from a page of his filming scenario and scribbled on it with a blunt pencil. Brightly, he said, "You could form a team. You and Dover working together—oh, the Chinamen I'd have!" He peered anxiously at Dee. "You do know how to use a telephone, then?"

"I do. Thank you." Dee took the scrap of paper.

"Looking forward to our association! I'll just see you out, shall I?"

"No need. You're a busy man. I'll find my way." Dee left through the double doors again and walked down the hallway. When he reached the room in which he'd watched *The Insidious Herbalist*, he entered, retrieved Ma's scenario and the can containing the film, and tucked them both under his jacket. Tipping his hat to the young woman at her typewriter, who barely glanced his way, he left the studio.

He did not return the way he'd come; rather, he continued along the waterfront to a pier jutting into the river. Striding to the pier's end, Dee lifted the film canister and with a great circular motion hurled it far out into the Thames. It landed with a satisfying splash. He watched it sink.

"The Thames is a dirty river," Dee said to me later, recounting his actions, "and in adding *The Insidious Herbalist* to the detritus in it, I increased the level of filth manyfold."

# CHAPTER THIRTY-SIX

My own afternoon was spent in a fruitless search for a Chinese needle in a London haystack. Twice I was told of a Chinese man boarding with a widow in the neighborhood of the British Museum; both times it turned out to be myself to whom my informant was referring. I knew many of the area shopkeepers, and inquired of them, but none could say he'd lately seen a Chinese face in his shop that was not my own. If Lu was living nearby, I concluded, he must be so well disguised that his own mother would take him for a different race.

Additionally, as I carried on with my unproductive investigation, I continued to be troubled by the notion that something had already happened, the significance of which I'd missed. I'd first felt this sense at Wu's Garden, and it would not leave me, though the puzzle would not complete itself, either. Ultimately, however, this preoccupation proved useful. Minutely turning over in my mind the conversation with Dee and then with Pound and Whytecliff, I came across, not the explanation for my unease, but a different anomaly.

Pound had said, in chiding Whytecliff, that the shop gave Ma a good living. Whytecliff, who according to Pound knew the shop well, did not contradict him. And, thinking back, that had been the opinion of Ma's shop assistant, Li Zi Rong. Yet the young widow Ma had told us that Ma's great hopes for the shop had not yet been realized. She'd also said he worked long hours in the shop, where she herself rarely ventured because it upset the customers to see her there; while Li, contrariwise, had said Ma spent most of his day elsewhere.

What did this mean? Where was that elsewhere?

I abandoned my researches and, not being Dee, hailed a taxicab to carry me off to Limehouse.

THE FORMER SHOP of Ma Ze Ren appeared abandoned, but when I knocked at the door a face appeared behind the glass. Li Zi Rong began to wave away the importuner, but seeing it was I, he unlocked the door and opened it.

"Lao She! I'm pleased to see you again. Is there something I can help you with? May I offer you tea? I'm finishing up the final tasks here before I return the keys to the landlord."

Through the open door I saw the shop's dusty interior floating in a melancholic gloom of empty shelves and bare floors. I didn't step inside, but said, "I'm pleased to see you also, Li. I won't bother you for tea, but I do have a question to ask the widow Ma. Have you her address in Norfolk?"

"I'm afraid I haven't. She intended to stop at first with cousins while she determined where to settle, but to my knowledge she hadn't quite concluded which of her apparently numerous relatives would be her hosts."

"Was there no destination on her trunks?"

"They were sent on to await collection at the rail station."

"I see. That's disappointing."

"I suppose," said Li, "that as the buyer of the shop's goods, Colonel Moore might know a way to contact the lady. In a situation of business one often finds additional papers that need signing and things of that nature. He'll likely have wanted to be able to reach her."

"A fine idea, Li. I'll go see the colonel. And if I may ask you—did I understand you correctly to say that the shop provided Ma Ze Ren with a good living, and also to say he spent little time here?"

"Yes, both are correct."

"I see. Can you tell me where his time was spent?"

Li glanced at the pavement and then back up at me. "I don't like to speak ill of the dead."

My breath caught. "Surely Ma didn't frequent opium houses?"

"Oh, no, no! Ma Ze Ren had no appetite for opium, or even alcohol. No, Lao, his weakness was gambling."

AS I MADE my way by bus to the Mayfair home of Colonel Livingstone Moore, I considered Li Zi Rong's information. Possibly, I reflected, this was an extraneous journey. Ma's absences from the shop and his reports to his bride that his dreams for the shop had yet to be realized could both be explained by the same sad truth: he passed his days—and spent his earnings—in a futile effort to find his fortune in the fall of cards, the click of mah-jongg tiles, or the spots on a pair of dice. Gambling was a vice of the Chinese people much older than the more recent habit of taking opium. At first glance the two seemed very much in opposition. The latter caused stupor in men, while the former drove them to frenzy. The reality, however, was that both were ways for devotees to turn their backs on their actual circumstances and the resolute labor required to improve them, in favor of a much better world that existed only in their fevered minds.

Not that either iniquity was restricted to my countrymen. No less a personage than the Viscount Whytecliff was a slave, albeit a willing one, to games of chance, if Ezra Pound was to be believed. It was a tragic irony that the "newest game sweeping London" that had Whytecliff so in its thrall—the fast-moving Mei-jongg with its beautiful cards of Chinese scenery—was the same at which, according to what Li had just told me, Ma Ze Ren had lost his money as quickly as he made it.

I alighted from the bus in Mayfair and walked the short distance to the Berkeley Square home of Colonel Livingstone Moore. The late-afternoon sun turned the pale stone of the façade a rich honey color and limned the hippogriff above the door. In the park across the street the lawn and the trees coming into leaf displayed innumerable shades of green. I lifted the ring from the bronze lion's mouth and knocked. In short order the imperturbable butler led me into the colonel's den.

"Why, Mr.—Lao, is it? Lao She, righty-ho! You're the scholar," the red-faced colonel huffed. "I remember. Came to see my collection with that other gent. Back for more, eh? Nothing new, I'm afraid. Still, some of my beauties are worth a second look. Go right ahead, take your time."

My gaze swept the room. The colonel was correct; I saw only what I'd seen before. "Really, I've come on a different errand," I said. "But about your collection—I don't understand. Are you not the buyer of the contents of Ma Ze Ren's shop? The shop is empty. Where are the antiquities?"

The colonel's eyes widened. "Oh. Well. As to that, well, I, yes—I've had them put in storage! Just for a bit. Just until, until I make space. The right places, you see. Must find the right places for beauties like those. Important, yes indeed, must be displayed correctly, indeed they must. In storage, yes, that's the answer."

I didn't require Dee's fine investigative instincts to perceive that the man was lying. But why? Before I could question him further he said, "But you didn't come here to see my antiquities after all, isn't that right? What can I do for you, then?"

"I was hoping you could help me locate the young widow Ma. I had some business with her husband that was left unfinished."

"No, no, I'm sorry, I can't help you. I have no idea where the lady—"

At that moment the parlor door opened and the lady herself stepped into the room.

"Colonel—" Seeing me, she stopped. "Oh," she said. "Oh, I'm sorry, I didn't know—I'll come back—" She began to back out the door.

"You'll do no such thing, Mrs. Ma," I said forcefully. "I came here to learn your address in Norfolk, but I see that despite what you told Li, Dee, and myself, you have not gone to Norfolk! The colonel was just saying he didn't know where to find you, and yet here you are in this very house. I demand to know what the two of you are playing at!"

I doubt they would have told me anything without further persuasion, the nature of which I was trying to envisage. In the event, I was not called upon to provide any compelling reason for the widow Ma or Colonel Livingstone Moore to explain themselves, for a blow landed on the back of my head and everything went black.

# CHAPTER THIRTY-SEVEN

While I was getting myself into a spot of trouble at the home of Colonel Livingstone Moore, Dee was elsewhere. My consciousness also being, for the time being, elsewhere, it is Dee we shall now follow until just before that moment when his path crossed mine again.

DEE WATCHED THE film canister sink into the brown water of the Thames. Then he turned and walked off the pier. His first task was to find a telephone kiosk. The area around the filming studio offered no such amenity, but as Dee was headed to the West End in any case, he made his way in that direction. "I had," he told me later, "two theories I wanted to test." (Here I would like to add, with gratitude, that his testing turned out to be opportune, as both his theories turned out to be correct.) He soon came to more civilized streets, and finding one of those handsome white boxes, Dee entered, dropped two pennies in the slot, lifted the earpiece from its cradle, and dialed the number he'd been given.

First came the pips, and then a man's voice. "Knightsbridge 4323."

Testing his first theory, Dee affected a French accent and

said, "Bonjour. It is Count Jouard who calls. I should like to speak to the Viscount Whytecliff, *s'il vous plaît*."

"Oh, I'm sorry, sir, he's gone out."

"Oh, *quel dommage*. I've rung to invite the viscount to a garden party at my estate. Some of my . . . nieces . . . from Paris will be there. I think the viscount will quite enjoy himself at such a soiree."

"Oh, I'm sure you're right, sir. Perhaps you'd like to leave the details with me? I'll make sure to tell the viscount immediately upon his return."

"No, no, an invitation left in a telephone message? *Très vulgaire, mon ami*. I shall send an invitation card. The viscount, he resides at seventeen Halkin Place, *n'est-ce pas?*" Dee plucked this Knightsbridge address out of the air.

"Oh, I'm sorry, sir, that's not right at all. I'll give you the correct one, shall I?" And with that the viscount's man recounted the viscount's true address to the false count.

"BUT DEE," I asked him later. "What first led you to the theory that the viscount was this recruiter?"

"He was described as a swell with a pinkie ring. Whytecliff fit that description, and we knew he was acquainted with Ma. When I heard that the recruiter used the name Dover—"

"The white cliffs of Dover!" I exclaimed.

"Exactly." Dee smiled drily. "One might have hoped for more imagination from a poet, but as it turned out, such hopes would have been dashed."

That explanation came later, as I say. Having expressed his thanks and left the phone kiosk, Dee proceeded to test his second theory.

THE VISCOUNT'S LONDON flat was located in Blackthorn House, a limestone-and-brick mansion built a few years before the war. It would be easy to mistake the large structure for the city home of some duke or earl, a member of the landed gentry who desired a residence in town reflective of the grandeur of his country estate. Indeed, Blackthorn House had been built to engender just such an assumption. In reality the building, of four stories, housed fourteen flats, plus, in its garrets, servants' quarters. Thus could young swells provide themselves with a Knightsbridge address at far less cost than the expense of maintaining an entire household—including the house—in London.

The fact that Whytecliff kept a flat at Blackthorn House rather than a grander manse suggested to Dee the correctness of his theory. To further test it, he required access to the young man's abode. He entered through the large iron-and-glass door and, reinstituting the bearing of a businessman and the tones of a toff, he inquired of a starched gentleman behind a marble counter whether the Viscount Whytecliff was at home.

"No, sir, the viscount has gone out."

"Oh, bad luck," said Dee, though he meant the opposite. "Perhaps his man is in?"

"I'm sure I don't know, sir. I could telephone up if you'd like."

"If you'd be so good. Only, he'll have left a carpet for my inspection, you see. A small but extraordinarily valuable item. The viscount does have an eye! This carpet, you see, requires repair, and as my shop—well, modesty forbids, but the viscount places his trust in us and we strive to give satisfaction."

"Whom shall I say, sir?"

"Chang. Lee Chang."

The starched gentleman lifted the handset from the telephone on the marble counter. He dialed, spoke starched words, and, his conversation complete, instructed Dee that the viscount's gentleman's gentleman would receive him on the second floor.

Dee entered the elevator. The operator, eyeing Dee with suspicion, closed the cage and the machine slowly drew them up through the space at the center of the wide staircase. Dee gave the man a shilling upon arrival, to improve his opinion of the Chinese race. Stepping out into a large, well-appointed hallway surrounded by four doors, Dee found another starched gentleman waiting at the only door open.

"Mr. Chang?" Unsurprisingly, the gentleman's voice was the one Dee had heard through the earpiece in the telephone kiosk.

"Yes." Dee offered a deep, deferential bow and came up with an unctuous smile. "I've come to inspect the viscount's newly acquired Ningxia carpet, to give a price on repairs."

"I'm sorry," the gentleman's gentleman sniffed. "The viscount left me no instructions to that effect."

Dee noted, again without surprise, how the man's attitude toward Lee Chang was at variance with his approach to Count Jouard. "Oh. Oh, how unfortunate," said Dee. "He was most anxious I inspect it. It will be one of his new acquisitions. From a recently closed shop in Limehouse, I understand."

"I see. The contents of that shop have been delivered, but most items are still crated until the viscount has the opportunity to select their placement. You can see some for yourself." The man stepped back, to allow Dee not entry, but the privilege of the view. "But to this point we have not unpacked any carpets."

"I see," said Dee, who had, in that one glimpse, indeed seen enough. "Well, I suppose the viscount will get in touch again. Thank you." He turned and took his rapid leave down the carpeted stairs, ignoring the "Shall I—" of the gentleman's gentleman. He tipped his hat as he strode through the entrance hall, drawing a raised eyebrow from the starched gentleman at the marble counter.

The purchase of the contents of Ma's shop—for a cheap price—had been accomplished not by Colonel Livingstone Moore, but by the Viscount Whytecliff. This had been Dee's theory, borne out when he saw some of the familiar antiquities already shelved at the viscount's home. Whytecliff, Dee suspected, had fallen on hard times, possibly as a result of his attendance on cards and dice. The sale of Ma's treasures could go a fair distance in settling Whytecliff's debts. Until that was accomplished, Whytecliff, for pocket cash, had the recompense he earned providing Chinese men to Princely Pictures.

These facts put Ma's death in an entirely new light, for they implied Ma's killing and the murders of the other men might stem from different motives. If that were true, more than one killer could well be involved.

Since the Viscount Whytecliff was not to be found, it was Colonel Moore who would have to be questioned on this subject. Therefore it was to the colonel's Mayfair home that Dee hurried.

# CHAPTER THIRTY-EIGHT

It was in that same Mayfair home that my consciousness returned to me, though our reunion was unsteady.

With a blacksmith pounding hammer on anvil inside my head, I opened my eyes. I saw before me four people, talking earnestly among themselves. At their feet sat two large gray cats twitching their tails. I soon realized they were all identical in pairs; they must, in fact, be two people and one cat, and my own vision must be double, possibly related to the throbbing in my skull. Pleased with myself for this logical reasoning, I next faced the puzzle of who they might be. The large gentleman was simple: he was Colonel Livingstone Moore, whose sitting room I remembered being shown into. The lady . . . Why, she was the young widow Ma! Yes, yes—she had arrived after me, and had been as surprised to see me as I her. I had something to ask her. What it was I couldn't recall, but perhaps if I approached her? I attempted to rise from the chair in which I sat and found myself unable to move. Though that is not quite true: I could move somewhat, but I couldn't stand.

I looked at my wrists and found each bound to a chair arm with a silken cord. How extraordinary. What could this mean?

Had I suffered some sort of fit, in which I'd fallen and hit my head? Had my host restrained me in an attempt to forestall further harm?

I was on the verge of calling the attention of Colonel Moore and the widow Ma to the fact that I'd awakened and would enjoy an explanation of my circumstances when I heard the lady say urgently, "We can't kill him! I won't have it!"

"You won't have it? Do you see another choice?" That question came not from the two Colonel Moores, but from another two people who walked into my line of sight. Again, I realized immediately they were both one, and that one was the Viscount Whytecliff. Whytecliff, here? With the colonel, and Mrs. Ma? And whom were they discussing killing, or not killing? My confusion was rapidly growing.

"I want no part of this!" cried the widow. "It's been wrong from the beginning."

The viscount replied, "Don't be absurd. It was all for you. Did you seriously think I was going to allow a Chinaman to raise my child?"

"I never should have let you near me."

"But you did. You wanted me as much as I wanted you." The two viscounts and the two widows merged before me.

"No!" said she, pushing him away. "I had . . . needs, and I was weak. My husband was a good man."

"Your husband," said Whytecliff with a sneer, "was hardly a man at all. If he had been—"

"Stop this, you two!" That bark came from Colonel Moore. "What's done is done. Don't care about your lovers' spat, not at all. Question is, what's now to be done with this man"—he nodded at me—"and the other? The smart one."

*What's now to be done with this man?* My blood suddenly ran cold. The man they were discussing killing or not killing—could he be me?

"I say," I said, "would someone please untie me and explain yourselves?"

"Oh!" expostulated the viscount, spinning to face me. "Oh, excellent! He's heard us. Lovely. Now he knows more than ever. And I suppose you'd just let him walk out?"

"I won't have you kill him," the lady said.

"There's no other way!"

"Fools! Both of you." That was the colonel again. "Of course there's another way. Lady's right, Whytecliff. Can't kill him. He's a scholar. Well-known in places. Chinamen dying all around us, no one taking much notice, but this one, find him in an alley, some would raise their eyebrows. No, no. Can't have it."

"I certainly hope not!" I asserted, praying I sounded more courageous than I felt. "Untie me at once."

"Very soon," said the colonel. He walked to the other side of the room, out of my sight, and I heard the sounds of a drawer being opened and shut. Other sounds came that I couldn't identify. When the colonel reappeared, he was holding a hypodermic syringe. "Here, Whytecliff. You'll do the business."

"What's that?" the viscount asked.

"Why, it's opium, man! We'll fill him with it and turn him out. A Celestial found wandering the streets in an opium stupor—who'll believe a word he says? People on Berkeley Square plotting against him, a viscount murdering a Chinese merchant, a widow in the family way—no, no, you see, intellectual or no, now he'll be just an opium fiend, like the rest of them! No one will pay him any mind. Be fortunate not to end in Brixton. Now do it."

My blood, already cold, turned to ice. No. No! Death itself would be preferable to this! To be seen as one more Chinese man with character too weak to resist the vile scourge? To offer another confirmation of the distorted picture far too many Occidentals had of the Chinese race? I was speechless with horror.

The viscount smiled cruelly and took the syringe from the colonel's hand. I fancied I saw a look of concern, even sympathy, on the features of the young widow, but she made no move to interfere as the viscount slid up my shirtsleeve and plunged the needle into the vein on my imprisoned wrist.

At first I felt nothing but the stab of the syringe. Within moments, however, all my fear drained away. Flooding through me in its place came a greater sense of peace and relaxation than I had ever known. All my worries dissolved in the repose of calm and concord. Well-being was everywhere, distress banished to some place so far I could hardly recall the sensation.

I looked with wonder at the three faces peering down at me. Such kind people, these, to have offered me this gift.

O opium! If this was your effect, how wrong I'd been to disparage you, to vilify your users, to disdain your adherents. What fool could fail to see your glory? I was ashamed.

Dee! I must apologize to Dee. I must find him and beg forgiveness for my failure to understand. I would go right now; but though I tried to stand, I could not. I looked at my arms, my legs. Nothing was now restraining me except a heaviness in my limbs. On the carpet I saw two snakes, one on each side of my chair, as beautiful as silken cords. The flowers in the carpet were themselves interesting, moving gently in a soft warm breeze. I was tired. Very well. Perhaps I'd rest now, and go later. I'd find Dee when I could.

Dee! But here he was! How marvelous! My friend, rushing into the room through the thrown-open door as though aware of how much I wished to see him. He stared around, at me, at the others. I smiled and attempted to speak to him, but my tongue declined to function. I saw Colonel Moore step

Dee's way. The colonel held a fireplace poker. How odd; the day was too warm for a fire. He lifted it above his head and swung it down. Dee flashed to the side, yanked the poker from the colonel's hand, and snapped the edge of his palm into the man's fleshy neck. With a great thump the colonel dropped onto his knees. A moment later he fell face-forward in the carpet. He stirred, settled, and began to snore.

From my chair I observed this activity with delight, as though watching a theatrical play. Dee peered at me with an expression of concern and incomprehension. He had not much time to consider my situation, however, for Viscount Whytecliff proceeded toward him, fists raised.

# CHAPTER THIRTY-NINE

Now we shall briefly again exchange my view of the situation for Dee's, reversing the clock twenty minutes or so until I reenter the scene of the action. For at this point much action developed.

DEE TRAVERSED BERKELEY Square on his way to Colonel Moore's home. He paused before crossing the street and looked around him. This area of the park seemed familiar. Trying to recall why, he stood at the edge of the lawn, gazing at the colonel's dwelling on the other side of the road. His eyes strayed to the pediment above the door where the hippogriff bared its claws.

A memory came flooding back. In his mind he was lying on the grass, right here in this spot. A woman's face, the face of the widow Ma, leaned close to his; then, with a horrified expression, pulled sharply back and ran across the street into the mouth of a giant beast.

The hippogriff—that was the beast! Dee had been, he knew full well, in the depths of an opium delusion when he saw this sight, but he now realized that although much of what had happened that night had been illusory, some had not. The young widow had in fact seen him as he lay here. The horror on her countenance had not been fear for his condition, as he'd imagined—O the vanity of man!—but dread that he'd recognized her, she who was supposed to be well on her way to Norfolk.

He understood, also, that Commissioner Lin, whether a spectral materialization or, as Hoong would have it, the result of Dee's own mind attempting to emphasize that which he already knew, had been speaking literally when he said Dee was too immersed in the depths of an opium dream to see what was right before his eyes.

Dee hurried across the street, cursing himself for not having had the wit to tell truth from dream before this. Had he made that distinction he might have arrived at his current thinking much sooner. At the viscount's flat, when he'd discovered the real destination of the contents of Ma's shop, Dee had thought the widow to be the victim of a scheme perpetrated upon her by Colonel Moore and the viscount. But her continued presence in London and her familiarity with the colonel's home led his thoughts in rather a different direction.

Thus, arriving a few moments later on the colonel's doorstep—though still innocent of any knowledge of the events transpiring within involving myself—Dee nevertheless knocked with urgency at the bronze lion's ring. When the butler, Perkins—also unaware of the situation in the sitting room—admitted Dee to the house and ushered him to that room, both stopped frozen at the scene revealed when the door was opened.

Dee recovered instantly. "Summon the police!" he ordered the butler.

"But sir—"

"The police!" Dee roared in a voice that came from the battlefield.

The butler fled down the hall to the telephone.

Dee swept into the room. Nearest to him was Colonel Moore. The colonel snatched up a fireplace poker. Dee waited for him to swing it up overhead. When the poker began its descent Dee sprang aside. The colonel stumbled, unable to stop his own forward momentum added to by the weight of the poker. The angle of his head left his neck exposed, and into this Dee slammed a blow that dropped the large man to the floor.

"Oh, well fought!" said Whytecliff, his voice a blade of sarcasm. "Now you've disposed of the comedy act, let the curtain go up for the main attraction!"

Dee whipped his attention to Whytecliff. In classic British boxing fashion Whytecliff came at Dee with a left jab, right cross. Dee parried the attack right and left and spun around, giving a small foot sweep and tapping Whytecliff with a left tiger tail kick. Evading the sweep and brushing off the kick, the viscount sneered, "You're quick on your feet for a Chinaman."

I tried to raise my voice in objection to this unsporting slur, but my voice preferred not to be raised.

The viscount moved in again, feigning with a left shot and coming over with a right hook. Dee parried and ducked underneath. Swiftly, Whytecliff responded with a tight left uppercut that Dee evaded by shifting his weight. This was shaping up to be a marvelous bout! Dee raised his right foot and brushed Whytecliff's left fist away with his right hand. He pounced and delivered a tiger claw palm strike to Whytecliff's temple. The viscount staggered. Dee followed with a right thrusting punch, but Whytecliff deflected it. He came under with a left and a hard overhand right that grazed Dee's chin.

Dee stumbled back and shook his head. He spoke to Whytecliff. "It was you who killed Ma. Out of jealousy and greed in equal measure."

"Greed, certainly," said the viscount, smiling. "And a

horror of the thought that my child could be raised by a China-man. But I had no reason to be jealous."

"Ma was married to your lover."

"Well, of course, and that's why she became my lover. Ma was unable—"

"I know. I was in France with him. He suffered that wound working to help England win the war."

"By digging trenches."

"For British boys to fight in. And repairing their trucks, and building their barracks buildings, and loading their weapons."

"For which he was well paid. And that, by the way, makes him a mercenary. As a patriotic Englishman I have no use for mercenaries."

"What you call patriotism is hollow and, to any true patriot of any country on Earth, offensive." Dee sprang upon the viscount.

Bobbing and weaving, Whytecliff avoided Dee's strikes. He leapt lightly back and positioned himself behind my chair! Was I now to join the combat? But what was my move?

I had no time to consider this question; the answer was decided for me. Whytecliff leaned across and fired off a rapid attack of punches. Dee deflected them all. Whytecliff, no doubt, thought Dee would not attack with my person in the way of his blows.

He was correct.

Dee threw me to the floor.

From my new position on the carpet I saw Dee spring up and throw a right high crescent kick at Whytecliff's head. The viscount ducked. But the crescent kick had been a ploy! Dee shot out a thrusting kick that threw the ducking Whytecliff back several feet. *Oh*, thought I, *well done, Dee!*

Whytecliff staggered but didn't fall. He moved in again with a left-right combination. Dee stepped back to absorb the energy. Deflecting the first blow, he brushed away the second with a left tiger claw. He shot out a right tiger strike at Whytecliff's head, but Whytecliff ducked, shifting to come around with his right hand. Dee parried and slammed into Whytecliff with a left-right tiger claw strike, which crashed into his jaw and tore streaks through his face.

The two broke apart.

In this lull, I heard the voice of the gray cat, who peered down into my eyes as I lay upon the carpet. "They speak of the patriots of Earth," it said. "Patriotism has many meanings in many different places, you know." It pointed upward with its tail.

Looking past the cat, I saw that the ceiling of the room had vanished. Staring down from above were many cats, much larger, circling with the stars behind them. "We are from Mars," they said. "We've come to observe the people of Earth."

"How charming," I told them. "You're most welcome."

"Very courteous of you. Please come one day to Cat Country on Mars, where you can observe us."

"I will be delighted to do so."

At that moment my attention was drawn back to the room where I lay, for my friend had spoken.

"And the others?" said Dee. I was taken aback to hear him breathing hard. "Did you kill them also?"

Whytecliff, hands on knees, also panting heavily, sneered at Dee. "Why would I have? What would I stand to gain? Ma's death delivered to me my child—and, I suppose, burdened me with his mother, but then, she's a delightful little thing, isn't she? Of course I can't marry her. But I'm a gentleman. I'll acknowledge the child and it will need a nanny, which ought to suit all around."

The young widow Ma, whom I could just make out hovering

in the blurred air at the end of the room, covered her mouth with her hand.

"You also, by Ma's death, gained the contents of his shop," Dee continued, "which you intend to sell to extricate yourself from your financial difficulties."

"Some, indeed," Whytecliff agreed. "Some I'll give to my friend Moore here"—he gestured at the snoring lump beside me on the floor—"for acting the Shylock in our transaction, as my own funds were . . . depleted."

"By gambling. Where, in some tawdry den, you met Ma."

"I think," whispered the gray cat to me, "that Dee is attempting to throw the viscount off his stride with these taunts."

"Oh, do you?" I replied, also low. "Can we say his strategy is succeeding?"

"No." Hissing as Whytecliff stepped closer, the cat leapt to the far side of me for safety.

"Oh, come now. Tawdry?" said Whytecliff, in answer to Dee's remark. "Second Sons is quite a respectable establishment, for a gaming hall. In fact the most venerable in London. They have been in operation for over one hundred years—"

"Only proving this vice has a long history in your culture."

"And a longer one in yours. Though historic, the place has kept up with the times. Second Sons were the first gambling house in London to feature Mei-jongg. Ma was one of the game's earliest devotees. Poor Ma. He was as dedicated a punter as I, with far fewer means."

"It was the exhaustion of his means," Dee said, "which you no doubt encouraged, that allowed you to persuade him to appear in those repulsive moving pictures. The films even your friend Pound can't bear."

"Oh, Pound. He's rather full of himself, don't you agree? But you worked out that it was I. Such a clever Chinaman. Dover, Whytecliff—first class, don't you think?"

"No. Lazy, rather."

Whytecliff sighed. "I suppose I'm fortunate, then, that I don't care a sniff for your opinion. And you needn't think, by the way, that Ma took much persuading. I've rarely met a man so eager to make his fortune without actually working. With, I suppose, the possible exception of myself. It really is a shame I was forced to kill him. His eye for antiquities was quite remarkable. The finest pieces from his shop, of course, I'll neither sell nor hand over to Moore here. The colonel's a blowhard with no discernment whatsoever. He'll believe me when I detail for him the value of what he's getting."

"You'd cheat your own partner in this crime, then?"

"Of course! You can't have expected to find honor among British thieves any more than among your own?" The viscount laughed. "No, the best pieces I intend to keep. The Chinese aesthetic, after all, is the finest in the world. As is your cuisine. It's unfortunate that, having idiotically toppled the emperor and universally fallen prey to the lure of opium"—with a grin he gestured at me, lying on the carpet—"your people have become far too degraded to be worthy of what centuries of your betters produced."

Again, I desired to make a protest, but again found myself unable to raise my voice, or even a finger.

The viscount made a sudden lunge at Dee and the battle resumed.

Whytecliff moved in with a barrage of punches. Dee shifted one way and another, dodging them all, until he found his opening. He snapped a shadowless kick to Whytecliff's leg, simultaneously swatting him with a tiger claw to the face. He followed that with a swift left-hand tear.

Momentarily stunned, the viscount froze. Dee slipped in, slamming Whytecliff with his shoulder, ramming into his body and applying a tiger claw strike to the groin. He whirled, unleashing a flying elbow strike to the jaw, but I was surprised to see him miss his mark. Whytecliff straightened, grinning. Dee, I realized, was sweating profusely.

My cat-friend had noticed the same thing. "The problem, as I see it," it said, "is that Dee is still suffering the effects of his attempt to quit that opium with which the viscount mocked him. He is not at his best."

"You may be correct," I said. "What shall we do?"

"In my opinion you cannot let the insults the viscount has laid upon your people go unanswered. For my part, I shall take refuge at the top of the étagère."

The cat sprang onto that piece of furniture and curled its tail around its crouching body. All was up to me, then. I lifted myself until I sat upright. This caused my head to spin. The room soon righted itself, but I saw, to my amazement, that Dee and Whytecliff had been replaced. No doubt tiring of the fray, they had given way to their seconds. The battle was now being waged by a five-toed Chinese dragon, such as would be found on the emperor's standard, pitted against the lion of the British coat of arms.

Using the overturned chair as an aid I propelled myself into a vertical position. The lion, I saw, was on the point of overpowering the dragon, which looked rather ill. I turned to the cat. Uncurling its tail, it pointed to a vase on the shelf below where it sat. I remembered that very vase from the tour the colonel had given Dee and myself of his "beauties." Ming, he had said, but of course it wasn't. I'd noticed immediately that the piece lacked the subtlety of even the most ornate Ming porcelains. Clearly it was Qing in the Ming style, no doubt produced for export and certainly made no earlier than fifty years ago.

"A fine idea," I told the cat. "Thank you for the suggestion." I took the vase from the shelf, crossed the room, and smashed it to pieces on the skull of the lion of England.

# CHAPTER FORTY

Crowning the British lion with a counterfeit Ming treasure expended what vigor I'd been able to arouse in myself. With a wink at my cat-friend, which licked its paw to indicate its approval of my actions, I sank happily back onto the carpet and closed my eyes. Therefore we will now take up the story once more through the open eyes of Dee.

THE CARPET BEING littered with insensible men, Dee examined each for signs of life. When he was satisfied they all still breathed, he approached the only person conscious, the widow Ma. She sat huddled on a chair in a far corner of the room, and she sobbed.

"I'm so ashamed," she said, lifting her tearful face to Dee.

"Were you a party to Ma's murder?" Dee demanded in severe tones.

"No, no! Roger—Viscount Whytecliff—he flew into a rage when I told him I was carrying his child. But not at me! It was about Ze Ren. He said Ze Ren had no right to the child. That it would be beyond deplorable were he even to lay a hand on any child in the Whytecliff line. He said terrible things about your people." She dried fresh tears. "Ze Ren didn't even know. I hadn't told him. And then one day I came home from my marketing to find police in the shop, and Ze Ren dead on the floor. I knew immediately what had happened. After the police left I went to Blackthorn House and confronted Roger. He never denied it."

"But you didn't tell the authorities?"

"I was at a complete loss what to do. Roger said if I went to the police he'd tell them he'd done it at my bidding and then I'd go to prison, too. My baby would be born there and taken from me! He said . . . he said if I sold him the contents of the shop for a cheap price, through the colonel so it wouldn't appear suspicious—"

"And also because the viscount has quite depleted his resources."

"I didn't know that then. He said if I did it, he'd marry me." Once again she commenced sobbing.

"Although apparently another thing he does not have," Dee said, "in addition to resources, is any intention of going through with your marriage."

"Yes, I heard him say that to you." She seemed despondent. "Can you see? I thought I had three choices. I could be a poor widow with a child, dependent on my relations in Norfolk; or I could be the Viscountess Whytecliff, mother of an Honorable. Or I could attempt to alert the authorities to Roger's crime, and end my days in Holloway! Oh, Mr. Dee, what was I to do?"

Dee was not required to answer this plea, for at that moment came a furious pounding at the front door. The butler, Perkins (who, as we found later, had been watching the battle wide-eyed from the entryway), conducted four constables and two inspectors into the sitting room. In this case it was not an instance of double vision, but rather, of double dominion. Each inspector, of whom there were, in fact, two, had brought his own constables. One of the inspectors, a tall, thin man, was unknown to Dee. The other was Captain Bard.

"Well!" said Bard, hands on hips. "What have we here?"

"Inspector," Dee said calmly. "Are you not a bit beyond your province?"

"This is Inspector Fox's patch," Bard acknowledged. "His office is in Scotland Yard." In Bard's tone Dee could hear the envy the inspector made no effort to hide. "But as the situation involved Chinese, I was also sent for. Seize him, lads."

"Let's not be hasty," admonished Fox. Bard clenched his teeth and didn't reply, suggesting to Dee that Fox was of the higher rank. "I'd like to hear everyone's story first. Lads, if you'll check the gentlemen on the floor for their state of health, and sir"—Fox turned to the butler—"if you'll telephone for an ambulance, which I fancy we'll require, perhaps we can begin with the lady."

The Lay of the Battle of Berkeley Square as sung by the widow Ma did not differ in any salient points from the version provided by Perkins. Each witness was questioned individually in the dining room by both inspectors while the constables remained with the balance of the party, conscious and unconscious. The widow and the butler both corrected Bard's false presumption of Dee's guilt and painted him instead as the hero of the tale. The widow additionally explained the viscount's role, and the colonel's, in my own distress. As I was, at the time these interviews took place, attempting to reestablish contact with the cats of Mars, I was not privy to Dee's reaction to the news of my first, albeit involuntary, use of opium. I imagine he indulged in a small smile, though when I later interrogated him on the subject he denied it emphatically. In any case, when the ambulance arrived, Colonel Moore and Viscount Whytecliff were loaded into it, but I was not.

"If the lady's account of the sequence of events is accurate," Dee said to the two inspectors, "my friend will awaken soon. If Mr. Perkins will provide him with a blanket"—the butler nodded his assent and went to fetch that article—"I have a point or two to discuss with you gentlemen. When Lao is ready I will see him to his lodgings."

"You'll ask him to come round to Scotland Yard at his earliest convenience, sir?" replied Inspector Fox. "We'll need his statement."

"Fox! I must protest," Bard said. "You'll let both these men go? What surety have you that either of them will ever be seen again?"

"This one"—pointing to me where I lay—"is by all accounts a well-known academic without a blemish on his name. The other"—gesturing at Dee—"is, as we have been told by two witnesses, the rescuer of his friend and the means by which we've identified a murderer. On what grounds would you have me detain them?"

"I know that one," Bard grumbled, meaning Dee. "He can't be trusted."

"A declaration, even from an inspector of the Metropolitan Police, that a man can't be trusted is not sufficient to justify his arrest. There are times when every policeman finds that inconvenient, but there you are. You'll see your friend comes to Scotland Yard, sir?" he repeated to Dee, with a slight emphasis on the "sir."

"Yes, of course," said Dee. "I trust tomorrow morning will do? I doubt he'll be fit any sooner than that. Fine, you have my word. Now, on another point," he continued as if Bard weren't fuming, "Mrs. Ma and I have both told you that the Viscount Whytecliff admits to the murder of Ma Ze Ren. I am willing to believe him, and to believe the lady when she protests she had nothing to do with it."

"She's still an accomplice after the commission of a crime," Bard said.

Fox rubbed his chiseled chin. "Perhaps," he said, "in light of the lady's . . . delicate condition, we might recommend leniency to the Crown. That would be the Christian thing to do, eh, Bard?"

While Bard muttered under his breath something to the effect that Christians don't wed Chinamen and then have liaisons with the minor aristocracy, Dee said to Fox, "That would be admirable, Inspector. Now, however, I'd like to draw your attention to another matter. The viscount denies involvement in the killings of the other men who took part in the tontine."

"Tontine?" said Fox. "Killings? What men would these be?"

"Inspector Bard?" Dee said politely.

Bard blew out a breath and outlined for his colleague the tontine and the men who had died. He finished by saying, "But as to Viscount Whytecliff's denials—well, of course he'll say he had nothing to do with those deaths!"

"Why?" Dee asked. "He's admitted to one murder. He can't be hanged six times. Why not confess, indeed, boast, which seems to be his nature, if he committed and got away with them all?"

"An excellent point," said Inspector Fox. "Although, if the viscount didn't commit those other crimes, who did? Have you a theory?"

"I don't," Dee said.

I was still non-sentient or I'd have reminded Dee of our suspicions of Captain Lu. Dee said nothing further on the subject.

"Well," said Fox, "in this case I'm inclined to agree with Inspector Bard." At this Bard snorted. "It's a natural thing to deny a crime. Perhaps we'll find him confessing later. Or perhaps, instead, we'll find him rethinking his earlier confession and retracting that. This is a situation we shall have to consider as things move forward. If, that is, you will permit me to assist in your investigation, Bard."

From the look on the countenance of Inspector Bard as the two men took their leave, this request was nothing more than a face-saving pleasantry that Bard did not, after all, find pleasant.

# CHAPTER FORTY-ONE

In the event, it was not Dee who saw me home; or more precisely, Dee saw me only partway home. By the time I'd returned to myself enough to make the journey, Sergeant Hoong had been summoned. The butler, Perkins, led him into the colonel's sitting room where I, to my foggy but pleased surprise, was in a chair and actually sitting. Perkins brought us all tea, and Dee said to him, "Thank you. I'm sorry for all this trouble. I'm afraid you'll soon be without a situation."

"Yes, sir. Even if for some reason the police fail to lay charges against Colonel Moore, he is clearly not the man of honor I took him to be and therefore I cannot continue in his employ. Also"—he looked about the room—"the colonel has extremely poor taste in antiquities. I shall give notice through his solicitor immediately."

"Where will you go?"

"Oh, you needn't fear for me, sir. A man of my experience is always in demand. Scorpion and I will land on our feet."

"Scorpion?"

"Yes, sir. Come, Scorpion."

The gray cat, tail held high, followed the butler out. I was sure I saw it wink at me as it passed.

Once the tea was inside me and I felt I could stand—though not without the strong arm of Hoong on which to lean—Dee and Hoong hailed a taxicab and we drove to the home of Mrs. and Miss Wendell. As we neared I became concerned for my level of dishevelment.

"I don't like to appear unkempt before the ladies," I said to my companions.

"We're putting forth the story that you were the victim of a collision with a careless driver," said Dee. "The ladies will feel nothing but sympathy for you."

"Ah. Thank you." I took a deep breath. "Also, Dee, I feel I must apologize. When I berated you for your opium use I had no sense of the drug's effects. The magical way it clears off, as the sun does the morning fog, the worries and cares that burden a man's heart—"

"Please don't go on," Hoong said. "You'll remind Dee of the many reasons to continue the use of this drug."

"I have no wish to do that. But surely there are as many reasons to cease its use to set against them."

"There are only two, but both can be guaranteed. One is the loss of faculties. The other is the loss of life."

"Gentlemen." Dee chuckled. "You may both go on, or stop, or do whatever you like. The reproaches of Commissioner Lin are enough for me. I've put paid to this habit."

"Reproaches?" Hoong leaned across me to inquire. "You have spoken to the commissioner more than once?"

"I've barely spoken to him. He, however, has spoken to me on two occasions, yes. I'm beginning to suspect our association will be an ongoing one. Ah, here we are. Hoong, I leave Lao in your care, as I'm no longer welcome at the Wendell home. I'll take the taxicab and meet you back at your shop."

"Where no doubt you'll take up residence. Very well. I'll stay here until Lao is asleep again. No, Lao, do not protest. Perhaps, Dee, should I have a stray customer or two, you'll see your way to fulfilling their needs to the best of your abilities?"

"My abilities as a shopkeeper are minimal and those as an herbalist have never been tried. Still, I shall do my best."

"I'm in your debt. Come, Lao."

Hoong bundled me out of the car and into the Wendell home where, as predicted, the ladies made a fuss over my injured self.

"I'm perfectly all right," I assured them, my heart touched by the concern extended to me. (I admit, especially that shown by Mary.) "Or at least, I shall be by morning. If Sergeant Hoong might be allowed to accompany me upstairs—"

"Oh, Sergeant Hoong," said Mary, "you're a military man, then?"

"I was at one time," Hoong replied. "I'm now a merchant here in London, happily leading a quiet and uneventful life." I fancied I heard a certain irony in his tone, but if it was there his face did not reflect it. He continued, "I hope I'll be permitted to stay until Lao She has bathed and retired? Also, if you'd be so good as to supply a kettle of hot water, I've brought some herbs for his health."

Mrs. Wendell frowned. "Not opium or any such, I trust?"

"Certainly not."

"Very well," the lady said, though she still sounded doubtful. "You may draw Mr. Lao a bath and I will put on the kettle."

Hoong helped me to my rooms, stood by as I bathed (I needed no aid sinking into the hot water, but I did require persuasion to rise from it), and, once I was in my bed, forced upon me a brew that gave me to understand first-hand the legitimacy of Dee's earlier complaints. I'd have complained of it, too, but for the fact that as he removed the cup from my hand I lay back and fell into a dreamless sleep.

# CHAPTER FORTY-TWO

I awoke in the morning with that sense one has at times of having moved not at all during the night. Stretching my limbs, I found I felt refreshed and buoyant. I dressed and was about to hurry downstairs for breakfast, as I was famished, when I found a note on my dressing table. *Call Scotland Yard,* it read. *Make an appointment to see Inspector Fox, but don't go there immediately. Come to my shop. Hoong.*

Inspector Fox? Who was he, and why should I see him? Or not see him? I tried to recall the events of the day before. My mind filled with hazy images: a hypodermic needle, the colonel, the widow Ma, a gray cat. Other cats in the firmament, and the Lion of England—I shook myself. Aside from an ache in the back of my skull this action produced nothing. Perhaps Hoong was right in instructing me to join him at the shop before I faced an inspector at Scotland Yard.

But first, breakfast.

On my way to that repast I made a stop at the telephone in the front hall and followed Hoong's instructions, setting an appointment with Inspector Fox for later in the day.

"Mr. Lao!" Mary chirruped as I entered the dining room. "How are you feeling?"

"Much better, thank you. You're looking lovely, if I may be allowed to say so." She wore a pale blue flannel suit over a white blouse with a petite bow at the throat.

"Oh, my. Thank you."

She beamed, I commenced buttering toast to hide my sudden discomfiture, Mrs. Wendell poured tea, and breakfast began.

We each ate our fill, which in my case was rather more than I usually took. This circumstance did not go unremarked upon and provided me with an opportunity to praise Mrs. Wendell's porridge. (British women, I had found, enjoyed having their cookery complimented. In this they differed from our Chinese ladies, to whom praise was a great embarrassment.) Mrs. Wendell stood and began to clear dishes from the table. From courtesy I rose as she did.

Mary stood also. "I must leave. I'm stopping by the church to see Washington—Mr. Jones—on the way to the shop. Mr. Lao"—she stepped into the hall to put on her hat, which today was a soft blue cloche with a jaunty green band—"I trust you still intend to come worship with us Sunday?"

"Indeed I do."

"I'm glad." She smiled, and then, turning from the mirror, said, "Do you know, I was intending to speak to you after Sunday services, but come, step into the parlor with me for a moment and let's talk now."

Talk? The parlor? Mary and myself?

Into the parlor we stepped.

"Last evening," she began, "after you'd fallen asleep, your friend Mr. Hoong took tea with us and told us the details of your accident. It sounded dreadful! A drunken rag man! Your poor head hitting the pavement like that—and all those bruises—!"

The tremble in her voice sent a thrill through me, but it also made me fear emotion would soon overcome her. I hastened to say, "Oh, but I'm quite all right now, as you see."

"Yes, I know, and that's just my point! Mr. Lao, you could have been killed. But you weren't. God was watching over you. I said I had good news. This is its proof! God loves you!"

She stood before me, eyes glowing.

"I . . . but . . . what is your good news?"

"The Gospel! The good news! What better news could there be? Mr. Lao, since you said you'd come to church on Sunday I've felt it. God wants you to know how much he cherishes you. It's written in Luke 15:24, 'for this my son was lost, and is found.' You Chinese called your emperor the Son of Heaven, but he was overthrown. But the Son of God can never be overthrown! And to him, you Orientals are the Prodigal Sons. God loves you, Mr. Lao, and rejoices in your return to him!"

So completely was I at a loss upon hearing this that I could not speak. I felt suddenly weak in the knees, no doubt a residual effect of yesterday's experiences. Putting my hand out as an aid I lowered myself into a chair. My aim was inaccurate, however, and I knocked into a small table. Brightly painted cardboard squares went flying in all directions.

"Oh!" I said. "I'm so sorry!"

"No, Mr. Lao, don't get up, you must rest. I'll do it." Mary scampered about retrieving the squares. "In any case we'd finished playing. My mother lost two shillings to me! Do you know this game? Mei-jongg. It's the newest craze sweeping London! The cards have such beautiful pictures of China. This set was a gift to my mother from my sweetheart. You know him—the music master at church, Washington Jones. You'll see him again on Sunday. I do hope you get to know one another well. I know you'll be great friends." She lowered her voice to speak confidentially. "Just between us, Mr.

Lao, I believe he's on the verge of proposing marriage. If he does, I intend to accept."

"AND THEN," I said bitterly, "she showed me a card depicting the hutongs of Peking! She said she found the atmosphere of the lanes both picturesque and menacing. Menacing! My own birthplace is in Yellowthread Lane." I was sitting on a stool in Sergeant Hoong's shop, drinking tea and detailing for Hoong and Dee my shattered dreams.

Hoong poured more tea. "I sympathize, Lao. From what I observed Miss Mary Wendell is charming indeed."

Dee said, "I'm also very sorry."

"You? I think not. You doubted my chance of happiness with Mary from the start."

"Many times in my life, Lao, I've been proven right and have regretted the circumstances that made me so."

"And the gambling!" I went on. "To find the ladies wagering between themselves on 'the game that's sweeping London.' The very game of which we first heard from the abominable Viscount Whytecliff."

"That game, and that viscount," Dee said, "are more abominable than you know."

He proceeded to recount for Hoong and myself the story of his visit to Princely Pictures. He finished, "Thus it seems Ma's losses at Mei-jongg were responsible for his degradation on the silver screen."

"Horrible," I said. "Just horrible. Viscount Whytecliff has a good deal to answer for. And Dee!" I exclaimed as something returned to me. "I should have seen! Because I did see, you see."

"I imagine you saw quite a lot yesterday," Dee said.

"No! I mean, yes, I certainly did, but this was before any of that. The viscount's jewelry! I saw it. Gold, with his family seal. In a jewelry shop. The entire set. Worth quite a lot, I'm sure. Some American will buy it up and parade around implying he's related to the British aristocracy. I knew the crest was familiar, but I couldn't recall where I'd seen it. On Whytecliff's signet ring, of course. Had I realized it was his I'd have known he was hard up for money much sooner."

"That would have been useful," Dee said, "but I don't suppose it would have changed the outcome very much."

"The man is a complete cad." I shook my head. "And his admission that he killed Ma Ze Ren—that's all but evidence that he's also responsible for the other killings, isn't that so?"

"Actually, I think not," said Dee.

"No? But then who? Oh!" I said. "I do apologize. My mind is still moving slowly. Before the excitement of yesterday we were seeking Captain Lu for this very reason."

Before Dee could reply, an insistent knocking came at the locked door. Hoong waved away the supplicant, but he didn't leave, only tattooed harder. Rising, Hoong walked across the shop and peered out through the glass. He grunted and threw the bolt, admitting Jimmy Fingers.

# CHAPTER FORTY-THREE

" **G**ents!" said the young thief, striding into Hoong's shop. "A good morning to yer! I trust everyone's well. Mr. 'Oong, that wouldn't be the brew I had 'ere yesterday?"

"Yes, Jimmy, it's one and the same. Please sit down and join us."

"Oh, grand! Mr. 'Oong's tea," Jimmy Fingers said, sitting, "is tasty and that's a fact. Obliged." He accepted a cup from Hoong. "Mr. Lao, yer looking a mite peaked. Nothing wrong, I 'ope?"

"I'm quite well, thank you," I said, not wanting to burden young Jimmy with either my romantic troubles, or the tale of my unintended opium indulgence.

"Glad to 'ear it. Now"—he beamed around the room—"I'm come bearing good news."

"You've found Captain Lu?" Dee asked.

"Can't be sure it's yer man," Jimmy Fingers answered. "But it's said a Chinese fellow, of an age and bearing as described to me by yerself, sir, is living in a flat in George Court, not far off the Strand. Been there some years. Keeps 'imself to 'imself, 'e does. None of the lads knows aught about 'im. Not even 'is name. But," he finished with a grin, "it's said that 'e's a military man."

WE ALL FOUR swallowed our tea and left the shop as one.

"You needn't come if you don't feel up to it, Lao," Dee said, but I put a stop to that line of country.

"I've been chased, beaten, knocked unconscious, and filled with opium in pursuit of this killer," I said. "I will not be left behind now."

"Very well. And you, Jimmy? Your work is done."

"Oh, but sir, if I may? I'm 'oping to see a fight again. An honor it would be, to watch you once more."

"I think a fight unlikely," Dee said. "But come along, then."

No doubt against his own preference for foot travel but with my well-being in mind, Dee led us to Commercial Road where we hailed a taxicab to George's Court.

The address given us by the young thief belonged to a small block of flats. Within, after a quiet consultation with, and a handing-over of silver to, the indifferent manager, we were given Captain Lu's flat number and permission to access the stairs to take us there. Upon reaching the correct floor and locating the correct door, Dee knocked.

"Enter," was heard in return.

I was about to counsel caution, but Dee turned the knob and walked straight in. Facing the door from an armchair sat Captain Lu, pistol in hand.

"Dee!" I cried.

Dee didn't flinch and Lu just smiled. Laying the gun on the table beside him, he said, "Oh, it's you, Dee. And Lao and Hoong, if I'm correct. And who's the British gentleman still in the hall, hiding behind the door?" Lu spoke in English, probably for the benefit of the hiding British gentleman.

Dee replied in the same tongue. "Hello, Captain. That's

Jimmy Fingers, an associate of mine. Come out, Jimmy, and meet Captain Lu."

Jimmy emerged from his place of concealment, his countenance skeptical. He doffed his cap but said, "Sir, I thought we was looking for a murderer. 'Ave I led you to the wrong gent?"

"No, Jimmy. He's the right man, but he's not a murderer. Are you, Captain?"

"I'm not," said Lu. "When you knocked I thought you might be, however."

"Thus the pistol, and the unlocked door."

"Yes. I had decided, if the man was foolish enough to come here, I might as well finish him off. Gentlemen, please sit. I regret I have but two additional chairs. Hoong, if you'll pour a drink for yourself and your friends? I have some excellent moutai in the cupboard."

Dee took a chair from the small table and brought it to face Lu. Hoong crossed the room to the cupboard, from which he withdrew a bottle and delicate porcelain winecups. With perplexed glances at one another, Jimmy and I remained standing.

"Well, Dee," said the captain. "Have you identified the killer?"

"I believe I have."

"But Dee," I said, "if you say the killer is not Captain Lu, does this mean you now think the Viscount Whytecliff is in fact responsible for the murders?"

"A viscount!" said Jimmy. "A nob, running around London stabbing China—Chinese men? This is too rich. Wait till I tell the lads!"

"Yes, well, all that will come later. I believe the captain has something to say. As he's unwell, I suggest we hear him out."

"You know, then," Captain Lu said.

"I could not help observing, Captain, that you are not the same robust soldier from the fields of France."

"Yes," said Lu. "Soon after I came to England I was told by a doctor I had not long to live. I went immediately to a Chinese herbalist, of course, and thus managed to outlive the doctor's projection by half a decade."

"You also immediately joined the tontine," Dee said. "As you have no need of riches, and were considerably older than the other men, that was another indication to me that you were ill."

"I joined for the men. I thought I had no chance of coming into the money. I was sick and all the men were younger than I. Including, I was assured by the bank manager, the two whose identities I didn't know. The manager was baffled by the fact that I joined at all, and more so when I increased my contribution."

"So that was you."

"It was. I must say, it was perhaps petty of me, but I rather enjoyed not enlightening him. Have you noticed, Dee, that all bank managers, both at home and abroad, are cut from the same pompous cloth?" Lu smiled. "What family I have in China are few enough, and distantly related. They're also wealthy. They have no need of anything from me. No, these men were my family, forged on the battlefield. I joined the tontine for them."

"But now all the men are gone."

"A tragedy. I assumed I'd be the first, but I'm the last. Hoong, if you'll give your compatriots their moutai? Thank you." Hoong handed round the wine cups. "But none for me, I'm afraid," said Lu. "Moutai is a delight forever beyond me now. I have my herbal elixir here in this bottle. I'll pour it in a wine cup and as I down it I'll imagine the pleasure you gentlemen are having. I've left a will, Dee. It names you as my heir."

This pronouncement, delivered with no change in tone, was received by Dee with the smallest of nods. I had the odd feeling he had somehow expected it.

"You'll get the tontine funds in their entirety," Lu continued. "It's my hope that you'll use them to send the men's bodies home to China, to their hometowns. Myself included, when it comes to that. Additionally, I'd like you to come to the aid of the wife of that murdered man who had young children."

"Shin Xiao. I'd be honored to do as you ask." Dee spoke with gravity. "With your permission, Captain, I'd also like to assist Ma's widow. She's with child."

"Is she?" Lu's eyebrows rose. "But I thought Ma—"

"The child's not his. But the woman's been hard done by and would, I think, make good use of a fresh start."

"Of course, then." Captain Lu smiled. As Lu lifted his wine cup to us, I saw Jimmy Fingers wipe a trickle from the corner of his eye. "Come now," Lu said. "The men will go home, the widows will be taken care of, and all will be well. Ganbei!" We all lifted our cups, also, and drank.

Baijiu is a difficult liquor to find in London, and that particular style called moutai I hadn't had since I left home. I shut my eyes to savor the pungent aroma and dark taste, and the warmth spreading through my abdomen.

Therefore, until I heard young Jimmy cry out, I didn't know that Captain Lu had slumped back in his chair, dropped his wine cup, and died.

# CHAPTER FORTY-FOUR

I sprang from my chair to go to the captain's aid but Dee waved me back.

"It's no use, Lao," he told me. "He's gone. It's as he wanted. He was determined to live until the murderer was caught, so that the villain would not steal the tontine funds when they were delivered to the last man. That last man was himself, and now the funds will be mine, to do with as he requested. He has put himself beyond the reach of pain."

"So the murderer is indeed Whytecliff?" I said. "I admit, Dee, that I'm mystified. Just earlier you said you thought it was not."

"I'm still of that opinion. But I do know who it is. Come, gentlemen. It's time we finish this."

I shook my head. Apparently I was still thinking slowly, for I had no idea who Dee's target was or where we were going. Hoong bowed to Captain Lu, who looked peaceful in his chair. Young Jimmy also took a final look at the captain, and tipped his cap. We all four proceeded down the stairs and through the lobby, past the manager who, consumed as he was with his *Daily Mirror*, took absolutely no notice of us.

Once again a taxicab bore us across London, this time back to Limehouse. "Dee," I said while we rode, "if you didn't think Captain Lu the killer, why did you ask for the police to be notified if he came to claim the tontine?"

"For his own protection. What I asked, you'll recall, was that the bank manager detain him. And notify Hoong at the same time as the police. I feared a situation in which Lu was in personal possession of the tontine funds. Also," he said, looking at me, "I was not sure, Lao. Although the Captain Lu I knew during the war would never have done such villainous deeds, men do change. Sometimes they choose to. Sometimes they see no choice at all."

Our destination, as it turned out, was Hoong's shop. Hoong unlocked the door and then went off to see the Chinese funeral director about arrangements for Captain Lu. Once the rest of us were inside Dee bolted the door again and went through the shop to the rooms in the back.

"Mr. Lao," said Jimmy Fingers, "'ave you an idea about wot we're meant to do now?"

"I regret to say, Jimmy, that I haven't. I've found in situations such as this, one can only wait for Dee to make clear his intentions. I suggest, therefore"—I turned the gas ring on—"that you and I raise a cup of Sergeant Hoong's fine tea to the memory of Captain Lu."

Jimmy and I were doing that very thing when the door to the back room opened. Jimmy turned his head and then leapt up from his stool. "No! No! It can't be! It's Spring'eel Jack as sure as I'm born! We're dead! We're doomed! Mr. Dee! 'Elp! Mr. Dee!"

The caped, masked figure emitted a howling laugh. Jimmy stumbled backward. I laughed also, but recovered myself enough to say, "Dee, you're being heartless. The poor young man has had quite enough of a shock today."

The figure bowed and removed its mask, to show Dee's smiling face. "I apologize," he said. "Although, Jimmy, if you desire to remain in my employ, you had best be prepared for the occasional surprise."

Jimmy wiped his forehead, retrieved his cap from the floor, and said, "Sir, you've been one surprise after another since the moment we met."

"Are we going out immediately, Dee?" I asked.

"No, we'll wait for Hoong. And for this note to make its way to its destination." Dee handed Jimmy a folded piece of paper. "Jimmy, if you'll find a likely young lad to take this? Give him this shilling, and say he'll get another when the business is accomplished."

Jimmy grinned, replaced his cap, and was off.

"Dee?" I said. "Am I also to be surprised?"

"I'm afraid so. I'll need the three of you as impartial witnesses in case my note falls short of its target."

"I see. Well, then, have a cup of tea."

Dee and I drank tea in silence. Dee's aspect didn't change, but I fancied he was feeling sadness, for Captain Lu, and for the other men whom he'd known and whose lives had been cut short.

In due time Hoong returned, and soon after, Jimmy Fingers did the same.

"All taken care of," said the thief, "though I were obliged to ask three lads, as the first two refused to go."

"But you found a boy with sufficient courage, in the end?"

"That I did, sir."

"Dee," I said, "where have you sent this child? Into some den of snakes?"

"You may be right, Lao," said Dee. "The note is meant for Scotland Yard. Now! Let us go!" He sprang from his stool, wrapping the cape of Springheel Jack around himself. "Come, all o' yer. Follow me!"

This instruction was not as easily complied with as it might have been, for no sooner were we out in the street than Dee took to the rooftops. Hoong, Jimmy Fingers, and I were compelled to chase along peering upward as one does when trailing a fighting kite whose string has been severed. The analogy, I thought as I ran, might not be entirely fanciful, for Dee seemed full of resolve and might.

A few streets on, Dee leapt to the ground before us. Though we knew he was above, it was quite startling to have Springheel Jack so suddenly appear. Jimmy jumped and I caught my breath. Only Hoong did not appear disconcerted.

"Gentlemen," said Dee, speaking as Dee, "if you'll please hide in this mews and watch its mouth. Thank you." Then he was gone.

We did as he asked. The mews opened beside a pub, the Copper's Beech, and therefore its mouth contained a number of barrels behind which we were able to conceal ourselves. Passersby and hawkers went this way and that. Then into our view came Captain Bard. "Oh, no," I whispered to Hoong. "He'll either spoil Dee's plan, or, if Dee manages to capture the killer in spite of him, he'll take the credit."

"Or perhaps, something else entirely," said Hoong, as Springheel Jack dropped down from the roof and pulled Bard into the mews.

Hoong, Jimmy, and I ducked low, for Jack was dragging Bard over to the barrels that hid us.

"You! Take your hands off me!" Bard sputtered.

"Captain Bard," said Springheel Jack. "On yer way to 'ave yer afternoon pint, then?" He let go his hold.

Bard, released, adjusted the lapels of his topcoat. "Whoever you really are, if you've a tale of another dead Chinaman you'll have to tell it to someone else. I'm on my way to celebrate, for we've solved the case and caught the man who killed them all. I suppose that must make you happy, as you were so concerned for them. If you've come to thank me, you're very welcome. Now get out of my way."

"Ah, but me copper, it ain't solved but in part. I 'ear on the wind that you've got a viscount in custody. This blackguard were the fellow as killed that shopkeeper, Ma, and that's the truth. But 'e says 'e never killed the other men, and I'm 'ere to tell yer that's the truth too!"

"What do you know about it? Unless the *truth* is, it was you!" Bard looked around, as though for a constable to seize Springheel Jack.

"No, 'tweren't Spring'eel Jack," said Dee. "But I did ask meself a question or two. I said, Jack, 'ow did the killer know 'oo the men was 'oo was in the tontine? Even was 'e one of 'em, from France, 'e wasn't to know more than the names of the others 'e'd come over with. The two added men—'ow would 'e know those? And was 'e one of the added men, how would 'e know anything at all? And then I said, ah, Jack, yer a fine fool, and that's a fact! Because there's a kind of fellow could find these things out, and easy it would be, too."

"What are you babbling about?" Bard demanded. "Get out of my way!" He made to shove Jack, but Jack jumped aside, twisted Bard's arm behind his back, and, holding him, spoke in his ear.

"A policeman!" he said. "Ah, that's the fellow. A policeman can go into the bank same as 'e can anywhere else, if 'e's investigatin' a murder. 'Ow, then, Jack, says I, might this policeman know there were a tontine to begin with? Why, that's easy!" Jack twisted Bard's arm a bit harder. "Because it were 'e, over there in France, as thought up the idea!"

"Ow! Unhand me, you costumed madman!"

"See, me copper, Jack 'as learned that 'twas in France that these men first 'eard of such a thing as a tontine. And from 'oo? From a British officer! And this officer said to 'em, if ye fellas want to come to London after the war, I might be able to arrange it. O' course, yer'll want to set up one o' these tontine things, because London can be a dangerous place. This officer, 'e was as good as 'is word, and when the men got 'ere 'e even dropped in on 'em from time to time—to make sure none of 'em was dead yet! Because that was yer idea from the beginning, weren't it, Inspector Bard? To keep an eye on 'em, because they was yer little retirement policy. No 'urry about collectin' the tontine money. That could work itself out when the time came.

"But then, after some years, poor Mr. Ma got 'imself murdered. And yerself, me copper, yer was getting mighty tired of the dockland streets. And yer sees yer chance. So to the bank yer takes yerself, and says to the manager, 'Show me the tontine books!' The manager knows he shouldn't oughter, but a policeman can demand and threaten and make trouble for them as denies 'im. So the manager thinks, wot would be the 'arm? And there 'tis! Suddenly the names and addresses of all the tontine men are there in front o' yer. And the weapon from the first murder is in yer evidence room! Wot luck is that? And so ye set about killing 'em, because after all they're nobbut Chinamen. When only one's left, yer think to yerself, be patient, me copper, and wait for that one to collect the cash. Then I'll go kill that one, yer says, and wot a rich policeman I'll be! Oh, it were a fine plot, Captain Bard, and Jack commends yer for it. But yer made the odd mistake or two."

"Oh, really?" Bard said calmly, still in Jack's grip. "And what would those be?"

"Well, the bank manager can identify yer."

"I had a right to demand those records!"

"Ah! So yer was there, then?"

"I—what—let me go!"

"No, Jack can't do that, me copper. Because the wife of that fellow Shin can identify yer as well. She heard yer voice loud and clear when yer spoke to 'er 'usband."

"I never said a word! I—" Bard stopped, his eyes wide with horror as he heard himself and realized what he'd done. "Let me go!" He struggled in Jack's grip.

"Ah, Captain Bard, Jack thinks ye've hung yerself with yer own rope. Gentlemen, if ye'll come out now."

Jimmy, Hoong, and I stood from behind the barrels.

"These men 'ave 'eard it all, and they'll testify to the same."

Bard looked at us and cackled. "Two Chinamen and a thief? Testifying against a captain of the Metropolitan Police? Their words will mean nothing."

"I'm afraid you may be right, Bard," said another voice. Inspector Fox and a constable stepped from the shadows. "So it's a good job Mr. Dee sent me a note to be here at this hour. Sadly, our British juries might not be prepared to give equal and fair weight to the testimony of all men. But that of an inspector of Scotland Yard will be heard."

"Dee!" cried Bard. "That scoundrel! That Chinese devil! I should have known he'd be behind this! Where is he?"

"I don't know," said Fox, looking around. "I rather thought he'd be here."

"Find him! Take him up! And take up this villain, too! Springheel Jack indeed—unmask him, Fox!"

With a sharp shove propelling Bard into the arms of Fox's constable, Jack leapt onto a barrel and thence to the roof from which he'd dropped. "There'll be no unmasking of Spring'eel Jack today!" He howled a farewell laugh and vanished over the ridge.

"Should the lads give chase, sir?" asked the constable, lifting his whistle to his lips.

"No," said Fox. "What wrong has the man done? Parading

around the streets in costume is eccentric, I grant you, but it's not a crime. And he's delivered to us a genuine criminal, has he not? No, I think the only man to be taken up here today is Captain Bard. A fellow member of the force—I must say, I'm shocked and disappointed. Constable, get him out of my sight."

As the constable dragged Bard to a waiting police car, Fox turned to us. "Thank you, gentlemen. Your statements will be required, though it's unlikely you'll be called to testify in court. I think between the constable and myself we heard quite enough. Though I must say, it's quite the coincidence, isn't it, that you're here so conveniently?"

"Oh, not a coincidence at all," I replied smoothly. "We received word from Dee, as you did, Inspector. He requested our presence in this mews at this hour."

"Did he, then? And I suppose the same must have been true of that costumed fellow. Do any of you have an idea, by the way, of who that man really is?"

"O' course we do," said Jimmy Fingers.

"Jimmy!" I said, turning toward him, but he ignored me and went on.

"That's Spring'eel Jack, that is!" Jimmy said. "How can yer doubt it, Inspector? 'Oo else could move like that, flyin' along rooftops and such? Why, with me own eyes I've seen—"

"Thank you, Jimmy," said Hoong. "As happy as the inspector would no doubt be to hear your tales of Springheel Jack, I believe he has much to attend to?"

"I do," replied Fox. "And I'd like to get home for tea with the missus. If you gentlemen will undertake to present yourselves at Scotland Yard by midday tomorrow to give your statements, it will save me the trouble of coming to find you."

This last was said with a level stare at Jimmy, who

returned the stare with a smile of such beatific innocence that Hoong, the inspector, and I could not help but laugh.

"We will be there," said Hoong. "All three of us."

"If you happen to run into Dee, bring him with you," the inspector said. He tipped his hat and followed his constable out of the alley.

# CHAPTER FORTY-FIVE

Dee and I sat at dinner with the Russells in their home, where Dee was staying for the remainder of his sojourn in London. He had excused himself from the cramped quarters at the back of Hoong's shop and thrown himself upon the Russells' mercy once Captain Bard was locked up and no further trouble was likely to stain their name.

("Although," Bertrand Russell had said, laughing heartily, "you seem to have forgot I'm a former jailbird myself. I'm not sure you could do anything to damage my reputation, Dee. To the contrary, your actions to root out corruption in the Metropolitan Police would probably enhance it.")

We were finishing the remains of a mutton stew of Mrs. Hennessey's preparation, deliciously enhanced by the herbs from Hoong's shop that Dee had left with her. During the meal Dee had relayed to the Russells our recent adventures.

"The reason Bard was so determined to capture you, Dee," said Dora Russell. "It was only partially the enmity you established in France, am I correct? The other element was his fear that you would, indeed, unmask him."

"Yes," Dee agreed. "The more I learned—that the tontine

had been suggested to the men in France by a British officer, that the killer clearly knew the identities of all the men in it including the added ones—the more I began to suspect Captain Bard. He'd seen me investigate many times in the war, and he knew I wouldn't stop until I found the truth. He hoped to get me out of the way least until he'd collected the funds. Though he'd have been happy to get me out of the way permanently, I suspect."

Dora Russell shuddered. "I'm very glad it didn't come to that. Tell me, this Springheel Jack fellow—"

"I was lucky to find him," said Dee, "and equally lucky that he was willing to undertake the bracing of Captain Bard, as well as other tasks he's performed for me in these past days. I felt it might be useful, at certain points, to knock people a bit off-balance. Springheel Jack seemed just the fellow to do it."

"But who is he, Dee?"

"Why, 'e's Spring'eel Jack, and no mistake!" Dee said, at which everyone laughed, and Dora Russell gave up that line of inquiry.

I myself had also taken up new lodgings. Mrs. Wendell continued to eye me with a touch of distrust, as a friend of the opium-using Dee and a patient of the herbalist Hoong; and for my part I could not bear Mary's glow of pride when our paths crossed, as a woman might glow at a dog that she had taught a trick. In this case the trick was my Christianity; although my conversion had come some years before my move to London, Mary seemed to be taking full credit for it and was, she repetitively reported, "so proud of you, Mr. Lao." I'd forced myself to attend church that Sunday as I had promised. I'd met Washington the suitor, now Washington the fiancé. Having discharged my obligations on that front I had no further interest in hearing the dronings-on of the Reverend Evans. Nor could I endure Mary's excitement at the plans she and Washington were making for their missionary trip to my homeland, where they were going to help call my heathen countrymen to Christ. In order to keep my own relationship with Christ unspoiled by platitudinous sermonizing and starry-eyed patronizing, I had thanked the ladies very much for their hospitality and taken the flat in George Lane formerly occupied by Captain Lu. I wondered how many of my neighbors would notice the Chinese man who inhabited the premises was now a different man.

Dora spoke, returning me to the present and the conversation around the Russells' table. "So, Dee," said she, "you'll be leaving us soon?"

"Yes," Dee said, and I felt an unexpected pang. "I've made arrangements for the bodies of all the men, including Captain Lu, to be returned to their hometowns for burial. I'll accompany them by ship to China, see that they all reach their destinations, and then return to Geneva, to take up my post. However"—he smiled—"I suspect I'll be back in London by autumn."

"Dee!" I cried, in surprise. "That's wonderful! I'll look forward to your return." It had only been a few days since I'd met him, and I was rather the worse for wear. Yet knowing Dee had changed my entire view of the streets of London and even the ways of the world.

"Don't speak too soon, Lao," said Dee with another smile. "If I return, it will be on the instructions of Commissioner Lin."

Russell frowned. "Commissioner Lin? Lin Tse Shu? Dee, the man's been dead for years. He left directives for future actions?"

"No. Commissioner Lin comes to me in dreams."

"Dreams, Dee?" said Dora, eyes sparkling. "I took you for a more rational man than that."

"Good advice is useful no matter where it comes from,

Mrs. Russell. If I receive such advice I'm inclined to respect the wishes of my advisor."

"And the commissioner in your dreams has given you good advice?"

"It was he who persuaded me to abandon the use of opium. That alone would invite my consideration of his further requests."

"And has he made one, Dee?" I asked.

"Apparently an event may occur here in autumn that would require my attention. If it does, I'll return, and if I do, I may need assistance again. Therefore, Lao, I'd advise you to think twice before you say you'll look forward to my return. Meanwhile, what will you do with the peace and quiet with which my absence will provide you?"

"Aside from nursing my bruises and settling in at my new flat? Actually, I believe I'm ready to begin a book."

"About this case?"

"Not as it happened, no. I'm not sure either British or Chinese readers would welcome a novel in which Chinese men are innocent victims, a viscount and a police captain are villains, and the case is solved by a Chinese judge and Springheel Jack."

"And a Chinese novelist."

I blushed. "And a Chinese shopkeeper, and a thief. No, that story is not ready to be told. But poor Ma Ze Ren himself, the loneliness that drove him to marry, and many of the experiences I myself have had here"—including my unfortunate infatuation with Mary, which I thought deserved a book of its own—"could, I think, make a touching novel of the life of a Chinese man in London. I don't yet know how to end the tale, however."

Dee said, "Well, Lao, that sounds like a book I will look forward to reading. And as for your ending, remember: no story ever truly ends."

"Nothing could be more accurate," said Bertrand Russell. "But dinners do. I suggest we take our coffee in the library. If you gentlemen are ready for a bit of fun, we've got a marvelous new game to play. Mei-jongg. Do you know it? It's sweeping London. Come, let's take our chances."

# IT TAKES A
# (CHINESE) VILLAGE

## SJ Rozan and John Shen Yen Nee

# SJ:

In Nov. 2020 I got a call from my agent, Josh Getzler. He'd just spent an hour on the phone with a man named John Shen Yen Nee, who was looking for a couple of writers for collaborative projects. One project sounded perfect for me; would I talk to John? Now, this was six months into the pandemic, quite a while pre-vaccine. I was talking to the walls. A live person with a project? Of course I'd talk to him!

What John said, in a conversation that lasted more than an hour, changed my life. We started a collaboration which has so far resulted in the short story "The Killing of Henry Davenport" in the January *Ellery Queen Mystery Magazine*, and the novel *The Murder of Mr. Ma*, coming in spring 2024. There'll be more of both. The essence of John's idea is here, in John's words (though the conversation, as you can imagine, was wild, circling, and far-reaching).

# JOHN:

Chinese Americans can be faced with a cultural double life. Many learn the history of China through stories, people, myths, and anecdotes. But non-Chinese Americans often only know China as a rival power or as an exotic faraway land.

Encountering the unfamiliar, people can try to frame it in familiar references. In relation to Chinese culture, we hear "so and so is the (insert famous comparison) of China." Naturally, then, the very real seventh-century magistrate Di Ren Jie is known in the West—when he's known at all—as "the Sherlock Holmes of China." Likewise, Chinese author Lao She emerges as "the Charles Dickens of China."

These shorthand labels create immediate comprehension but strip away cultural context and diminish their subjects. The individual is posited as a mere Chinese shadow of a luminary Westerner. There is even an implicit sense of derivation, despite the Chinese figure often predating the comparison by an era or three.

Both Lao She and Judge Dee were real people, who lived 1200 years apart. Each is worth engaging with as more than mirrored Westerners.

Judge Dee is based on Di Ren Jie, who lived from 630–700 CE—the early Tang Dynasty—and served as a magistrate. In the West, Judge Dee was popularized by Robert van Gulik, a Dutch sinologist and diplomat. He translated classic works about Judge Dee from Chinese and expanded the canon of Judge Dee through a series of original novels in the 1940s and 1950s. Fans of the mystery genre are long familiar with van Gulik's two dozen Judge Dee titles. Recently, Hong Kong director Tsui Hark rekindled interest in Judge Dee through his Detective Dee film series.

Lao She was the pen name of Shu Qing Chun, a Manchu Chinese intellectual who navigated wildly turbulent times. Born during the Boxer Rebellion, he died in the Cultural Revolution. He was an active member of the May Fourth movement (not the *Star Wars* meme, but the Chinese anti-imperialist, anti-colonial movement born on May 4, 1919). In 1924, Lao She was teaching in London when he wrote *Mr. Ma and Son*, the story of an immigrant father and son who, at every step, wrestle with an England simultaneously gripped by fascination with Chinese cultural artifacts, and fear of a yellow peril.

Despite living centuries apart, Judge Dee and Lao She arrived in Western literature within the same twenty years.

So let's consider for a moment Sherlock Holmes as the Judge Dee of the West, and Dr. Watson as his Lao She, and turn our attention to the "originals."

# SJ:

I mean, wowee, right? Was there any possible way I could resist this? Or any reason to?

John's thought was to co-write a novel—the start of a series—set in London in 1924. He'd provide plot and cultural context. I'd do the actual writing. Dee and Lao would investigate, eat, dash around London, meet all kinds of Britishers, and do a lot of kung fu fighting. (Holmes and Watson, though they appear in "Henry Davenport," have no part in *The Murder of Mr. Ma*.) I loved the thing. But—London, 1924? Luckily I knew my van Gulik, but Lao She, whom I'd heard of but never read, and in whose voice, as the chronicler, the book was to be written? Plus, John's plot involved the Chinese Labour Corps in France during WWI. The what? And

Bertrand Russell. And Ezra Pound. And opium. For me to get up to speed required huge amounts of research.

Good thing I love research.

And good thing my collaborator knew just what I needed. A flood of books poured in, sent by John. History, novels, biography. A few of Lao She's books, not easy to find in translation these days. I read like crazy.

I also told a couple of people what I was doing and they had help to offer. My cousin Dick, with his encyclopedic film knowledge, made me a list of London-set sound and silent British films of the twenties and thirties. I streamed them all. Laurie King sent a box of maps and photo books. Another friend suggested reproductions of old Sears catalogs for furniture and clothes, so I ordered some. And all on my own I discovered coloring books. Rabbit holes presented themselves right and left, and I went down all of them. I watched season three of *Peaky Blinders*, and all seasons of *Frankie Drake* and *The House of Eliott*, and the *Downton Abbey* movie, for the cars and clothes.

We also needed a kung fu consultant. Many readers know how I hate to write action scenes and how long each one takes me; but even someone who loves it would have a hard time with an art as specialized as kung fu. I was complaining about this shortcoming of mine at a party to a friend, and another friend said he didn't mean to interrupt but he'd studied kung fu and he thought maybe his master, Sifu Paul Koh, would be interested in the project. So I got in touch with Sifu Koh and boy, was he! He teaches here in NYC Chinatown, and he got what we were trying to do right away. He choreographed some wonderful fights.

If we hadn't been in the middle of a pandemic I'd have zipped off to London. But you know, it might be better that I didn't. What's left from 1924 is something here, another thing there, and a few more in other places—buildings and streets embedded in a changed landscape. The Depression, the Blitz, post-war redevelopment, the more recent real estate scramble . . .

The 1924 London of Dee and Lao is a London of the mind.

My mind, and John Shen Yen Nee's.

And the minds of everyone in the village.

Thank you, all.


This essay first appeared online on the *Ellery Queen's Mystery Magazine* blog, *Something Is Going to Happen*.

# ACKNOWLEDGMENTS

## John:

THIS BOOK WAS ten years in the making. It's impossible to list everyone who has helped me in my journey as a storyteller so if I have left anyone out, I apologize in advance. First and foremost, I want to thank my dear friend Alex Segura to whom this book is dedicated. Without his support and guidance, *The Murder of Mr. Ma* simply would not exist. I am deeply grateful to my agent Josh Getzler who paired me with SJ Rozan who is my SFAM (Sister from Another Mother) and partner in crime on the Dee and Lao crime series. Kay McCauley, Alex DeCampi, and Clydene Nee encouraged me to focus on this series. Rick Sanchez and Jake Thomas helped break the story. My old boss, Paul Levitz, gave me a master class in storytelling during our many nights commuting from Manhattan together. Thanks to my children: Jags, Kristian and Lizzie. And to Hilary and Pilot. Finally, I am thankful for the many creators with whom I have had the opportunity to work. There are too many to mention here. I thank you all.

## SJ:

AS JOHN MY BFAM said, so many people were essential to the making of this book. I join him in thanking my agent Josh Getzler, who knows an idea that'll grab me when he sees one, and Jon Cobb at HGLiterary. Thanks also to Taz Urnov, Juliet Grames, Bronwen Hruska, and the entire team at Soho for their enthusiasm and professionalism. I will be forever grateful to Laurie King, Barb Shoup, Carla Coupe, Merideth Wright, Cheryl Tan, Chris Chiang, and Patricia Chao and the aliens. And finally, thank you to Henry Rinehart for the serendipitous overhearing and the connection to:

Our matchless, tireless, generous, up-for-anything Kung Fu fight choreographers

Master Paul Koh
and his assistant, Kristen Rosenfeld,
of Bo Law Kung Fu in NYC.

It always takes a village, whatever the book, and this is one of the most fun villages I've ever spent time in. Thank you, all!